THE DARLING KILLER

THE DARLING KILLER

E. M. JONES

LAMPPOST PUBLISHING

Copyright © 2024 by E. M. Jones

All rights reserved. No part of this publication may be reproduced, distributed, or transmitted in any form or by any means, including photocopying, recording, or other electronic or mechanical methods, without the prior written permission of the publisher, except as permitted by U.S. copyright law. For permission requests, contact Lamppost Publishing LLC.

Published 2024

Hardcover ISBN: 979-8-9910106-0-3

Paperback ISBN: 979-8-9910106-1-0

E-ISBN: 979-8-9910106-2-7

Logo design by Kim Taylor Creative

Cover design by Stuart Bache

The story, all names, characters, and incidents portrayed in this production are fictitious. No identification with actual persons (living or deceased), places, buildings, and products is intended or should be inferred.

For Caitlin, for everything

Chapter 1

I remember.

Greta Shaw opened her eyes just in time to slam on the brakes. She drifted through her gravel driveway, stopping within inches of hitting the garage.

She parked her car and opened the door without thinking.

The wind yanked the door from her grip and swung open, letting the torrential rain pour inside. She snatched her purse and shuffled out, almost falling over, fighting against the wind to close her door.

White lightning split the dark sky above her and thunder immediately followed, shaking the ground beneath her. Straight ahead, her house weathered the storm. Every light was on, as if Clive had made a lighthouse to guide her home. Had there ever been a darker night than this?

Greta rushed forward, trying not to slip on the front walkway. "I remember," she whispered in the cascading rain. "Clive! I remember!"

She heard it coming up behind her: a sound like a freight train in a tunnel. It came roaring over the hills, leaving trees splintered and broken.

Greta spun around as the tall trees at the end of her driveway shook like pitiful saplings. The whole forest moved as one, bending under the hurricane winds. It came toward her, a wind so strong it looked like a blast wave.

She gripped her keys, her fingers slipping on the wet metal. She unlocked the front door, the wind bearing down on her, and barely managed to slip inside and slam the door. The house groaned as the wind washed over it. The lights flickered. Something shattered on the screened-in deck.

Greta leaned against the door. "No, no, no, don't go." The memory was already slipping away. After an entire year, she had finally remembered something about her life. It started in a house like hers, on a night like this. *Clive!* Maybe he could piece it together.

"I'm home," she announced and struggled to calm her breathing. Getting worked up was bad for her heart. Rainwater dripped from her clothes, a soft patter in the quiet house. "Honey?"

Clive's rocking chair was empty, but swaying gently, as if he'd just stood up.

"Clive?"

Their house only had floor lamps. The ceiling fans were equipped with lights, but she'd removed the bulbs after the accident. The sun was allowed to tower over her—all other lights had to be eye level or lower. And none of that fluorescent, LED, soft-white stuff either. She lived in a home, not a hospital. Her living room had an elegant wool rug with red and gold patterns, two couches facing each other (a coffee table between them), and a small wood stove perched on the back wall beside a two-person walnut-colored table. Two handmade rocking chairs faced the wood stove. And still, no sign of her husband.

"Clive!"

Something turned in her chest—her heart, protesting. In her head, the memory kept fading like a dream after waking up.

"Clive!"

She checked the bedroom, the master bath, even the closet. She opened the basement door and yelled her husband's name. She looked in the kitchen, the bathroom, the office. Clive wasn't home. Where else would he be?

Greta spun in a circle. *What am I missing? What did I forget?*

She couldn't trust her memories. Her mind played tricks on her all the time, like making her believe Clive was still alive. Of course, he died in the accident a year ago. And she'd been adrift ever since.

She couldn't remember life before the accident due to a rare form of amnesia. The doctor said it would likely come back, but since that dreadful night, her memory had only fallen further into chaos. She knew she was fifty-one, living in a little town in Southern Ohio. She knew Clive had been her partner for life until last year. Before that, she knew nothing.

"No, please. Please be here." She held her stomach, afraid of getting sick, getting too worked up. "Please be here, Clive, why did you leave? I *remembered* something, I told you it would come back!"

She had so many questions about her life. The accident occurred one week after they moved to Darling, Ohio. But she couldn't remember why they had moved, or where they lived before. They never used social media—all they had was a photo album, and she couldn't find it.

"I need you," she said, losing her breath, her chest starting to hurt. "I can't do this, honey. I can't do this alone."

Then her heart stopped. Greta fell against the wall, holding her chest, gently tapping it. As quickly as it had gone, her heart started again.

Tick, tick, tick.

Her *ticking* heart rose above the thundering rain. The mechanical valve inside her worked hard and diligently. She pressed her hand to the thick scar on her chest. *Tick, tick, tick*, it went. It never stopped—not since her second open-heart surgery. When she saw Clive's lifeless body on the cold metal table, she wanted to tear the valve from her chest and plant it in his. Watch his heart come to life, watch his lungs fill with air.

Something clattered on the deck. After realizing Clive was dead, and with her heart pausing again, Greta needed to busy herself before her heart stopped forever. She plucked an umbrella from the coatrack and stood by the double glass doors, staring at the deck. The rain hadn't let up. Neither had the lightning. Midwestern summer storms were their own sort of brilliant. And the *wind*. She'd never felt a wind so violent. It would destroy her potted flowers if she didn't move them. One had broken already.

Greta opened her umbrella and stepped onto the deck, the wood planks slippery beneath her shoes. Two wicker chairs were set around a metal table with a glass top. Against the house, a hot tub hummed beneath a thick brown cover. Her flowers danced in their pots, their petals falling. If she didn't save them now, there would be nothing left to save.

Her house stood on top of a steep hill. From the deck, she could normally see the bike trail at the hill's base and the river just beyond that. Tonight, the storm kept her from seeing anything. In the distance, even the streetlights in downtown Darling were no brighter than faint stars.

As she moved toward the flowerpots, the wind rose with a great bellow, swimming through the trees, grinding them together. Branches snapped like brittle bones. Most trees held, despite their groans. But their roots were tired. The wind pushed harder, and somewhere close, a tree split and fell, and the house lights flickered again.

This storm's going to tear these woods apart, she thought, clinging to her umbrella, trying *not* to fly away like Mary Poppins. Half of Darling would be flooded by dawn, if not sooner.

A gust of wind hit her. She batted hair from her eyes with one hand and lost her grip on the umbrella. It flew against the screen and stayed pinned there. She grabbed a wicker chair for support, but her fingers slipped.

The wind crawled along her skin, creeping between her teeth. It whispered in her ears and played with her hair. It filled her lungs, replacing her air, breathing *for* her. It pushed against her body, comforting her shaking bones, pressing invisible thumbs against her eyes, as if to mash them in their sockets. She wondered if drowning felt like this.

The wind let go and she fell backward, as if she'd been leaning against a wall and the wall just vanished. As she fell, the wind whistled in the eaves, and—

I remember now, she thought, not falling, but flying. Flying through her memories like a loose kite. The memory had returned—the same one that came to her as she was driving home.

I remember.

How could she have ever forgotten about—

Her head bounced off the deck. Sticks and leaves clattered on the roof, as if the storm meant to bury her house alive.

Memories overlapped, playing fast-forward through her brain. She stitched the images together in her mind—a mental quilt—and stepped back, seeing the bigger picture for the first time since the accident.

When she closed her eyes, her mind was a home. It used to be empty and blank, with enough memories to occupy a small corner of the living room. Now, the house was evolving. Memories moved in. Vandalizing. Graffiti on the walls.

Up, up, up, the house grew. Into something else. Something new.

Greta cupped her hands over her mouth as blood oozed from her head, mixing with the rainwater, leaking through the wood planks beneath her.

"I remember," she murmured. *I remember what I did.*

Chapter 2

Julie Baker rushed inside her house and slammed the door. She locked the doorknob, the deadbolt, the chain lock, dropped her purse on the floor, and took three steps back.

Knock, knock, knock.

There was no one at the door, no one following her inside, but still, she heard someone out there, didn't she? The storm raged outside. She heard trashcans spilling over, tree limbs falling, loose shutters banging against siding.

In her living room, three windows faced the driveway—a great picture window in the middle, with a narrow window on either side. A single curtain rod extended across all three windows, with blackout curtains overlapping in the middle. Julie knelt on the couch and parted the curtains, scanning the driveway and front yard for movement.

Nothing.

On the road, cars cut through the rain, their white and yellow headlights like blurry lanterns in the darkness. She closed the curtains and checked the locks, tapping her finger against the doorknob, deadbolt, and chain.

One, two, three.

Tap, tap, tap.

She lived in downtown Darling. It didn't hurt to be cautious. The small town wasn't exactly known for low crime and upstanding citizens. Buying a house downtown, so close to so many people, once frightened her. But living in the country was far worse. When someone broke in and pressed a gun in your mouth, no one would hear you scream.

Plus, living downtown put her close to the library, and she could walk to work if she wanted. Her proximity to work and people made her days easier. She didn't have to be afraid of what lurked in the small grove of trees behind her house.

The nights, however, were the same as always—long, quiet, *dark*.

Julie draped her rain jacket over the couch's arm, found a towel in the kitchen, and used it to mop up the rainwater dripping from her hair while she inspected the windows. Inside her small, three-bedroom home, every window had a blackout curtain and an additional lock. Julie checked the locks every night before bed, tapping them with her finger.

But Aunt Susan had moved in three weeks ago and loved fresh air, especially at night. More than once, Julie had crept inside her guest bedroom and locked the window while her aunt slept. Aunt Susan never said anything the next morning, but Julie wished she'd stop opening the window—it was dangerous—Julie *knew* that, and so did Aunt Susan.

Right now, all the curtains were in place, the windows closed and locked. The living room light was on, but her aunt wasn't in there.

Julie tossed the towel on the kitchen counter when her phone buzzed with new texts. Her coworker, Tori Duvall, kept inviting her over for a wine date.

The kid is in bed

Stephen's boring and falling asleep on the couch, and I could use some laughs

On a scale of 1 to 1,000 how obnoxious was Carly tonight?????

Julie smiled. Tori had probably started the wine date already. Julie texted back, making up excuses about her aunt visiting, and being tired, and how Carly's level of obnoxiousness was immeasurable by any human metric.

Tori responded with kissy face emojis.

You're no fun!!! See you tomorrow morning!!!
If I don't drink too much...

Right, Tori was picking Julie up in the morning because they had the same shift. Julie had never been to Tori's house, never met her child, Sophie. Never met Stephen. Yet Tori kept inviting Julie over, as if Julie hadn't said no a thousand times already. Tori didn't care. Her life mission was getting Julie to leave her homey turtle shell and be cool *for once in her damn life*. Julie suspected it wouldn't work, but she loved Tori for trying. Picking her up in the morning, for a three-minute drive, was the closest Tori would get to seeing Julie outside of work.

Julie imagined what it would be like—wine dates with a best friend, talking about TV shows, work, kids, and significant others.

It would be normal, wouldn't it?

That life was a dream. Even the thought of kids, family vacations, and every other aspect of typical family life made Julie squirm. She was twenty-nine and had managed to survive her twenties the same way she'd survived her teens: by avoiding people. It didn't always work. She tried having close relationships once. But stuff like best friends and boyfriends and work parties all ended the same way.

With the same thoughts.

No one knows who I really am. They don't even know my real name.

People assumed because she was almost thirty and childless that she was either living wildly or busy climbing a corporate ladder. When they got to know her (however much one could get to know Julie Baker), they realized the truth: she wasn't a reckless youth or vying for someone's job. She was a boring old librarian cat lady. Everyone bought the façade. Everyone except Tori, maybe.

Julie filled Oscar's food bowl, realizing he hadn't shown his mean mug yet. He normally waltzed into the living room whenever she came home, his tail high and twitchy.

She called his name and heard a pathetic *meow* from behind Aunt Susan's closed door. Julie knocked on the door and cracked it open. Oscar ran out as if he couldn't get away fast enough. The room smelled of stale sweat, leftover carry out, and old tea.

"I'm sorry," Aunt Susan mumbled, rolling over in the tangled bedsheets. "I was going to let him out. I just wanted to pet him, but he doesn't like me."

"He's a picky little guy. How are you feeling?"

Aunt Susan lifted her head. Her bloodshot, tired eyes didn't meet the skin around them. Her cheeks sagged. Her thick eyebrows crowded a wrinkled forehead. She smiled. "I'm feeling like it's the end of the world."

Three weeks ago, Aunt Susan appeared on her doorstep, in tears, asking for a place to stay. Julie hadn't seen her aunt in over a year, and when she told Julie about her terminal lung cancer, they both cried, despite all the pain and drama and distance between them. After a few days of living together, Julie liked having Aunt Susan around. She enjoyed coming home to a house with warm lights on, a mug of hot tea, and Aunt Susan watching TV on the couch, curled up in blankets. Never warm enough.

But today, she was in bed looking much worse. She used to pick through a daily pill box but had given that up. There was nothing anyone could do except wait with her.

"Do you need anything?" Julie asked. "You tired?"

Aunt Susan nodded. "How was work?"

Oh boy. Julie had a million things to complain about. On one hand, it felt silly, complaining about trivial work matters to a dying woman. On the other hand, Aunt Susan *insisted* these trivial matters distracted her.

"You know that part-time intern I told you about? Carly? She left early today. To meet her boyfriend for his *birthday*. I get she's nineteen or something, but we could've used her help."

Aunt Susan shrugged. "I still celebrate my birthday."

Silence took over. She wouldn't see another birthday.

Julie tried to laugh and failed. "I don't know, something about her just grates on me. She spends all her time talking to Nancy, and Nancy hates it when anyone stands around talking."

Julie moved about the bedroom, collecting leftover tissues, plates of food, and a half-empty mug with cartoon kittens on it. Aunt Susan wasn't as invested in work stories as she had been other nights. Something was different. Julie almost asked if everything was all right, but she didn't want the answer.

She juggled the dirty dishes with one hand and walked over to the window, tapping both locks and adjusting the thick curtain.

"Why do you do that?"

"Do what?"

"Why do you make sure every window is locked before you sleep?" Her aunt's eyes were heavy and full of clouds, each cloud like a memory, blowing in with the storm.

"Just a habit. It helps me feel more comfortable, you know, since I live alone. Or did, before you came. But I still do it just to be safe. I live in *Darling*, after all." As if the town had anything to do with her compulsive habits.

"Have you always done that?"

When Julie was ten, she'd slip out of bed every night and walk through Aunt Susan's house. She'd check the doors, the windows, the curtains, and then fall asleep. When she inevitably woke up again, she repeated the process.

Three or four times a night, she would check the locks. She did that until she moved out and went to college.

"No," Julie lied. "Just started it recently. There's been a few break-ins in Darling and let's be honest, this isn't the nicest area." She smiled. Aunt Susan didn't smile back.

THE DARLING KILLER

Julie put the dirty dishes in the sink and threw away the trash. She turned off the lights, one by one, until the bedroom lamp was a lonely beacon in the darkness.

She changed into her pajamas and returned to the spare bedroom, itching to curl up in bed with a good book. She wasn't fully used to having someone around. Someone to take care of.

"Do you need anything before we start?" Julie asked.

Aunt Susan blinked those cloudy eyes. "No. I just need to hear your voice."

Beside the bed, a metal folding chair waited for her. A storyteller's chair.

Julie loved reading to the kids at the library. Of all their community outreaches, family events, and summer programs, nothing beat captivating a group of children with words. If the story was good, they didn't fidget. They didn't poke each other, walk around, or ask for their tablets. They listened. They hung onto Julie's words, each sentence taking them closer to that inevitable end. The kids never tried to guess the ending. Their favorite part of any story was the middle. When the characters were just living, and not saying hello or goodbye.

Seated comfortably, Julie picked up *David Copperfield* from the nightstand, one of Aunt Susan's favorite books. The night Aunt Susan arrived, she was tucked in bed, wheezing, complaining about the cancer. About how there was nothing the doctors could do to stop it. About how she'd felt okay, up until then. The cancer was closing in, tightening the noose. And she didn't want to suffer alone.

Julie's solution: reading to her. Aunt Susan did the same to Julie when Julie was a child, and when she started reading that first night, Aunt Susan cried. Took her back, she said. Back to the early days.

When they started *David Copperfield*, Julie promised Aunt Susan they'd finish the book before the cancer ran its course. Aunt Susan glanced at the novel's size and smiled.

Now, Julie flipped to her bookmark. Aunt Susan stared at the ceiling, her chest rising and falling, her eyes wandering. Julie cleared her throat, but Aunt Susan had something on her mind. A question, maybe. Julie didn't like questions. She wanted to read and escape and listen to the rain and wind and thunder.

Aunt Susan turned her head, the question already on her lips.

"Why don't you talk about her?" she asked.

Julie swallowed. There were a few reasons why she didn't talk about her mother, and she wasn't about to list them. Not tonight, not anytime soon.

"Julie."

"*What?*"

Aunt Susan didn't flinch. Her face softened. "We need to talk about what happened that night."

Chapter 3

Twelve-year-old Eli Wright sat on the living room carpet in his gray sweatpants and black t-shirt as images of the hurricane filled the TV screen. Water gushed through the streets. Trees toppled like sticks in mud. After surging through the Gulf of Mexico, Hurricane Nathanial had made landfall in Texas, and sent a windstorm spiraling north. Record-breaking winds were soaring across the Midwest, bound to hit Ohio that night. Seventy-five miles per hour. The earth-shattering thunderstorm outside was only the warmup.

"Is the river going to flood our house?" Lucas asked. He lay on his stomach beside Eli, almost close enough to touch, his small arms locked under his chin to keep his head up. His messy black hair stuck out at odd angles, hovering above big brown eyes.

Lucas looked over his shoulder. Through the kitchen, out the double windows above the sink, the Little Miami River moved with reckless power. It clung to Darling's riverbanks, baseball fields, and backyards, as if terrified to float downstream.

The river had never touched their house before. But Eli didn't have the confidence to lie to his brother about everything being all right. The river was rising faster than he had ever seen.

"We'll probably lose power," Alex said, sitting sideways on the recliner so his long legs dangled over the edge. He didn't look up from his phone, and he hadn't changed out of his polo and khakis. He smelled like the gas station.

Mom sat at the kitchen table, lost in her project. An unlit cigarette hung from her lips—a promise to her future self. The open window above the sink let in sprinkles of rain and served as a potential ventilation system, but those days were long gone. She would smoke outside after she finished.

Mom caught Eli staring and beckoned him over. He sat beside her, his stomach in knots.

"I've done the best I can," Mom said, balancing the cigarette between her lips.

She held up Eli's camo jumpsuit, the one he wore every day. Including earlier, when he walked to the library and ran into Chase and Tyler on his way there. They'd been waiting for him, and just like all summer, they filmed him and called him names. He tried to run around them and get inside the library, but they caught him in the parking lot. When they stopped filming, Eli knew things were about to change. Making videos of his panicking didn't satisfy them anymore.

Chase shoved Eli to the ground and ripped his camo jumpsuit. Eli cried right there in front of them. His favorite librarian, Miss Julie Baker, came running out and sent the guys packing. Eli went inside with her and said nothing. He sat on the floor, in the Fiction section, and read books with cool covers to calm himself down. He checked a few books out, and at the counter Julie asked if he was okay. She knew better than anyone just how cruel those boys could be. Eli was ashamed she'd seen him like that, beat up and crying like a little kid.

It was worse when his dad picked him up and saw the torn jumpsuit. Julie explained what happened, and his dad listened intently, not saying much. In the car ride home, Eli tried to sell it as an isolated event, not a summer-long crusade to ruin his life. His parents didn't know about the bullying, and they didn't need to.

Eli inspected his mom's handiwork on the jumpsuit. His mom used a dark green thread to sew the torn shoulder together. The result was a long, green line, like a scar. It reminded him of his elderly, ancient neighbor, Greta, and the heavy scar she carried on her chest. Not that he'd ever *tried* to look down her shirt (gross), but he would see it sometimes by accident. He'd once asked Mom about it, and she said Greta had open-heart surgery. That was why her heart *ticked* like a clock. They put a fancy state-of-the-art valve inside her.

Mom gestured at the jumpsuit. "If you hate it, we can look for a new one." She reached back, taking a lighter from the kitchen counter. One step closer to a smoke break.

"No, I love it." Eli climbed into the jumpsuit's legs and pulled the rest over his body. He zipped up the middle. "You have the hands of a surgeon," he said, stealing a line from one of her routinely watched medical dramas. "It's cool. See? Like a scar." He knew, deep down, he was too old to be wearing a Halloween costume every day. Mostly, he didn't care. But when Chase ripped it earlier and screamed in Eli's ear, his bright red face about ready to burst, Eli realized that Chase *hated* the jumpsuit. And if Eli could be more normal, maybe they would leave him alone.

"I'm glad you like it." Mom paused, eyeing him carefully. She glanced toward the living room at Lucas and Alex, and she blinked a few times before settling back on Eli.

They hadn't had *the talk* yet, but that was about to change. Mom lowered her voice.

"Did you want to fight back?"

Eli's heart did a funny thing. It felt like a human hand reached in there and squeezed it. Like what a doctor probably did to Greta's dying heart. "No," he lied. "I didn't think about fighting."

Mom nodded quickly, blinking fast. "I love you."

Shit, that squeeze again. "Love you too."

"Promise you love the scar?"

"I love it. Thanks, Mom." He patted his new shoulder, wondering if Mom saw right through him.

"You're welcome." Mom ruffled his hair and stood up. He returned to the living room while she faced the open window above the sink. Every now and then she stood by that window, as if reminding herself of someone younger.

Eli sat beside his little brother, trying to forget the way Mom looked at him. Almost like she wished he *had* fought back. Did Dad think the same thing? Were they embarrassed to have a son who got bullied? Who wore a stupid outfit every day? Did Mom not see the turmoil in Eli's eyes? He thought it had to be obvious: of course he wanted to hurt them. All summer, he'd dreamt of revenge. But he didn't like that part of him. It was a hidden side to himself he never wanted to understand.

"Is it better?" Lucas asked, checking out the jumpsuit's new scar.

"Yeah. Mom fixed it."

"Mom also needs you boys to get ready for bed," she called from the sink. "C'mon, turn off the TV and get your jammies on."

"That's *not* fair," Lucas said. "Eli's always in his jammies."

"You're just jealous." Eli turned the TV off. The impending hurricane disappeared but would live on in their imaginations and nightmares.

"Eli's a big kid," Mom said. "When you turn twelve, you can wear whatever you want. Deal?"

"Fine," Lucas said, breaking into a giggle. "I'll sleep naked!"

"Not if we're sharing a room." Eli pushed him, but Lucas grabbed his arms, hopping up and down, screaming. "Naked! Naked! Naked!"

"Hey! In bed!" Mom laughed. "And everyone keep your clothes on!"

Eli ran into their bedroom with Lucas in pursuit. They shared a set of bunkbeds, and of course, Eli had staked his claim on the top bunk. They shared a closet and dresser—the dresser topped with books loosely held up by bookends Dad had made with his own hands: a pair of matching wooden pirate ships.

They were heavy enough to keep the books from falling, and adventurous enough to look perfect beside the books they guarded. Bookmarks, loose coins, and a small Vietnamese flag occupied the dresser along with the books. Action figures and small amounts of cash were kept in the drawers, packed beneath underwear—a place *no one* would search if looking for important things to steal.

Like the kitchen, their bedroom had double windows facing the river. It was hard to see the water, but Eli pictured it creeping through their yard in the middle of the night, lapping at their house like a hungry monster.

Lucas changed into his jammies and dashed under the covers. K-Pop posters covered his wall. Alex introduced them all to K-Pop several years ago. He didn't listen to it much anymore, but Eli and Lucas still stayed up often, waiting for midnight, when new singles came out. They shared an old pair of wired earbuds and skipped through the songs they didn't like until they found the ones they did.

Eli turned on their night light (a tiny hollow pine tree with a yellow lightbulb inside). Then he dug through his pockets. He dumped a few coins on the dresser, along with his receipt from the library and his EpiPen (peanut allergy).

He climbed into the top bunk. Instead of a blanket, he used a sleeping bag. His family teased him about it, but he liked the cocoon feeling.

He sat on the sleeping bag without getting in. The front door opened and closed. His parents' muffled voices seeped through the walls. The drone of a parent conversation was either the most boring or the most stressful sound in the world, depending on his recent behavior.

Dad spoke calmly, explaining something to Mom, maybe telling a story. He was good at telling stories.

Eli didn't want to drag this out. Didn't want to have *talks* with his parents and hear their concerns and ideas for how to move forward. Even remembering what happened almost made him cry. He wasn't about to sit down and explain his point of view. No thanks.

His parents cared about him—no doubt about it. But what happened made him nauseous and angry. He would relive that feeling when Dad came to him for a serious conversation, even if Dad meant well. Eli didn't want to relive it. He wanted to forget, read his new library books, and dream about kicking Chase in the balls. Tyler, too. With steel-toed boots. With spikes on the soles.

Their room brightened with a white flash followed by thunder. The rain picked up again, banging on the windows. Lucas hadn't said a word since entering the bedroom. Eli leaned over his bunkbed and glanced down. His little brother sat on the edge of his mattress, clutching the covers around him. His unblinking eyes refused to let go of the windows. He sighed periodically, as if forgetting to breathe and letting it all out at once.

"Hey Lucas?"

"Hmm?"

The room glowed white again. The windows rattled, and Eli glanced through them. He thought he saw something outside. A shadow. It wasn't his imagination—something moved along the riverbank. Eli climbed down the ladder, stepping over action figures, kicking aside dirty clothes.

"What?" Lucas asked.

Eli's nose touched the cold glass window. The thing by the river staggered and fell over.

"Eli?"

It had long, lanky limbs. Black clothes. A strange hairdo. It propped itself upright before falling over. Once it stabilized, it would climb out of the river and crawl up the bank and into their yard. It would smash the window and slither inside their house. It would eat him and Lucas first—little appetizers before the main course: Mom and Dad. And after feeding, the thing would clean their bones and assemble them back into skeletons; dress the skeletons and prop them up in chairs, as if nothing had happened. As if their family still lived.

"*Eli!*"

Eli faced his brother. Lucas clenched the covers around his head, flashing the same wild eyes he had as a baby when Mom and Dad brought him home, adopting him into their family.

Eli checked the river again. Small, dead trees twisted on the riverbank, their leafy branches thrashing as the water slowly ripped their roots from the earth. That explained the creature—a stupid little tree.

"I thought I saw something," Eli said.

"Saw *what*?"

The little trees twisted in impossible ways, morphing into evil shapes—dancing devils, begging for mercy.

"A monster," he said.

The room went dead quiet. If Lucas didn't breathe soon, he'd pass out.

"But not just any monster," Eli said. "I saw . . . *Greta*."

A bright smile crossed his brother's face. "What's that old witch up to this time?"

Thunder boomed above them, threatening to rip open the sky. Lucas's mouth dropped; he didn't move a muscle.

Eli continued, not a fan of having his back to the open window. What if the tree creature was closer? Who would see it? Who would stop it?

"She's up to no good," Eli said. He shuffled toward Lucas, lifting his hands little by little. "She's fishing for leeches."

"Gross, why?"

Eli moved closer; his hands held higher. "Because she needs their blood. She's in the river with her mouth open like a trap! Trying to catch a leech in her teeth!"

"Ew, she eats leeches!" Lucas pulled the covers over his mortified face, hiding everything but his eyes.

"That's right." Eli leapt back to the window—a black silhouette against the white flashes of light. "Now the ritual is complete! She's turned herself into an evil witch." Every good Greta story included a dramatic transformation into an evil witch. It worked on Lucas like a charm, and it worked on Eli too, just in a different way. Every time Eli told one of these ridiculous stories, he felt like a little kid again, back when monsters were every bit as real as heroes.

"Not a witch," Lucas whispered. "She'll curse me!"

"She'll curse the whole town!" Eli paused, letting the room fill with rain and distant wind. "She takes a broken tree from the river and turns it into a broom!"

"She's airborne. It's over!"

"She's in the sky!" Eli pointed outside. "She's coming for us!"

"What do we *do*?"

"There's only one way to stop a flying witch." Eli learned this random fact last week and had been *dying* to use it in a story.

"How?" Jumping off his bed, Lucas dropped his blanket on the floor, ready to help fight the battle against evil witches.

"We need a Witch Window."

"A *what*?"

Eli surveyed the room. He picked up a foam sword and a blanket, draping it around his shoulders like a cape. "Long ago, in the magical land of Vermont, there were witches *everywhere*."

"What?"

"Yes! Witches all over the place. An infestation of evil witches."

"But what about *good* witches?"

Eli shook his head, running the foam blade across his neck. "The evil witches took care of them."

"Headless," Lucas muttered, pulling his blanket to his shoulders and fashioning a cape. "What did the Vermont people do?"

"The evil witches had brooms." Eli prowled around the room, hunching over like a hobbled old woman. "Walking was too slow for them, so they took to the skies! They came through the windows. From each family, as tradition demanded, the youngest boy had to be taken and sacrificed."

Lucas drew his own foam sword from beneath his bed. "Greta won't get me!"

"Maybe so. But our swords? Useless." Eli dropped his. Lucas followed. "The only way to keep a witch out, as the Vermont people discovered, is to build crooked windows! Witch Windows!"

"Crooked windows?"

"If you have a crooked window," Eli explained, sailing his hand through the air, "the witches can't fly in. And we're safe. And you won't get sacrificed."

Together, they faced their windows, watching the dark skies for the enemy. Their heads slowly rotated back until their eyes met, their faces changing with escalating terror.

Lucas gripped his hair with both hands. "Oh my gosh, we have a normal window! We have to build a Witch Window!"

"Witch Window!" Eli hollered, pulling out more blankets. "Quick help me tie these up!

Eli hung off the corner of his bunkbed, wrapping a blanket around the metal rod perched above the window that no longer held curtains, thanks to an escapade like this one. Lucas worked from the ground level, tying the blanket's other corner to the window's crank handle. The blanket cut diagonally across the double windows. No way an evil witch was getting through there.

"You done?" Lucas asked.

Eli fumbled with the blanket. "Almost."

"Eli." Lucas gasped—he was good at gasping.

"What?"

"Greta's flying on her broom! She's coming in fast!"

Eli tied off his corner and jumped down. Together, they grabbed their foam swords and pointed them at their new Witch Window.

"Get ready, buddy." Eli put on his most serious voice. "Time to take out a witch."

"Die, evil witch!" Lucas cheered. "DIE!"

The door opened behind them. The boys spun around together, dropping their swords. Mom filled the doorway, looking *very* unimpressed.

"Were we being loud?" Lucas asked.

"I'm pretty sure the neighbors heard you," she replied, cocking her head, giving them the *mom look*. "What's that?"

They glanced at their creation. "Witch Window," Eli said.

"It's crooked." Lucas used his hand to mimic a flying witch. "So when a witch tries to fly in your window, she can't. Crooked window means no witch. No witch means I don't get sacrificed."

"Yep, that would be a shame. And uh, what is this witch's name?"

Eli clicked his tongue. "Don't remember."

"Boys." The sternness crept in. "It's not nice to make fun of Greta. This is going a little too far."

"But she's so weird," Lucas said.

"She's been through a lot. And she needs your help. Why do you think she needs Eli all the time for chores?"

Lucas shrugged. "Cause she's an oldie."

"Because she's hurting. She had a bad accident. She lost her husband." Mom shook her head. "She's a sweet lady. And you're being disrespectful."

"Sorry," Eli and Lucas muttered together, both fully aware of their vast collection of Greta Horror Stories . . . and the vast amount yet to be made.

"However." Mom leaned in, her cigarette breath mixed with spearmint gum. "I met this woman yesterday at the salon. Deborah. Total evil witch. And we still have plenty of regular windows for her to fly through."

Lucas smiled. "More Witch Windows?"

"More Witch Windows." Mom applauded. "But a little quieter this time."

Lucas picked up his foam sword. "The good witches rise up!"

"Yes they do." Mom laughed, tucking her hair behind her ears. "I'll help you, Lucas. We have a few windows to cover, then it's right back to bed. And Eli, your dad wants to see you in the kitchen."

Mom and Lucas left the bedroom, conversing about leaving Alex's windows the same so the witch could get him instead.

Eli didn't follow them. Outside, the storm raged, and he caught himself in the crooked window's reflection, his thin jumpsuit like a suit of armor. He didn't want to have this conversation. But he had no choice. He had a feeling that things were about to change, because Chase and Tyler had made their stance clear: they hated Eli for what happened at the dodgeball tournament back in April, and they wouldn't stop—Mom and Dad knew it, so did Eli—they wouldn't stop until Eli was seriously hurt. It was only a matter of time.

Eli couldn't outrun them forever. Eventually, very soon, he'd be forced to do something. And it wouldn't make for a good story. Lucas was too young to understand, but all those stories about good and evil were wrong. Everyone was part monster, part hero. Even Eli.

He zipped his jumpsuit up to the collar and left the room. From the corner of his eye, he saw the blanket over their window shift, suffering from a hastily tied knot. Without a sound, the blanket fell.

Chapter 4

Greta sat in her rocking chair, head pounding with a ghastly headache. She stared at the empty, cold wood stove in front of her, and like everything else, it reminded her of Clive. Maybe that had been part of his smell. Wood and ash. She hadn't thought much about it before, but seeing the stove now made her heart incredibly lonely.

When she hit her head on the deck outside, the lost memory came back to her again. This time it didn't slip away.

After lying on the deck in the rain for what felt like a long time, she crawled back inside her house. She peeled off her wet clothes and donned her bathrobe. Standing in the kitchen, she bandaged the cut on the back of her head. Despite the migraine, despite needing a hospital visit, nothing mattered more than the new memory.

After the accident, the doctor told her everything would either slowly come back, or most would come back at once. The doctor said a lot of things. Most of it wasn't helpful. Brain damage wasn't exactly a mastered field. To Greta, it felt more like magic than science. Some memories had returned, but they were vague and too short to draw conclusions from.

After a year of struggling to remember basic facts about her life, Greta finally had a new memory about herself. One she would not forget. One she could not share with another soul. It had latched itself into her brain like a parasite. Like the other prodigal memories, this one felt real. It *clicked* inside her. A missing piece had come home. And it terrified her.

It can't be real, she thought. As if lying to herself worked. As if it erased the reality of what happened.

The new memory was an old one. An old Greta and Clive adventure.

No, it's not real, she thought again, but her stubbornness was fading.

She left her rocking chair and paced through the living room, pain buzzing inside her skull. She touched the bandage on the back of her head. The bleeding had stopped, but there was blood on her robe.

It could be real, her thoughts said, using the voice of her younger self.

You could test it? That voice again. *After all, what better way to prove a memory than to recreate it?*

What a nonsensical idea! She found herself in the kitchen again, grinning stupidly at the thought of *testing* something like that.

Why not? Why not test it and find out?

"But how?"

The answer came.

Procedural memory.

The doctor told her about procedural memory. About how some things don't go away. Language, riding a bike, playing the piano. If she started to try something, she would know if she'd done it before.

First, before she tried *anything*, she needed to see the memory again.

Greta closed her eyes. Her mind used to be an empty house, with one occupied corner of the living room. That corner had been her memories, leaving the rest a blank void. After hitting her head, the house in her mind had grown into something else. A callback to her teens and twenties, she suspected. When she closed her eyes, she didn't see a little ranch style home, but a haunted house, alone in a pitch-black field.

Her haunted house was a three-story mansion. The windows glowed with red light, spiderwebs covered broken shutters, and smoke curled from the gaping mouths of chimneys. The front door was cracked open, the welcome mat bloody.

Wanting to explore her renovated mind, Greta pushed the door open and faced a narrow hallway. Lights flashed, chains rattled, some poor soul deep inside the house screamed and screamed and it sounded so much like herself.

Step after step, the house swallowed her. Paintings covered the walls—depictions of her and Clive on their old porch, or on their motorcycles, or in their kitchen. A painting of Clive on top of her, naked, with her legs wrapped around him. A painting of Young Greta standing in a creek with upturned jeans, holding a crawdad in her palm. A painting of them riding bikes down a country road.

Since waking up in the rocking chair, Greta had closed her eyes and visited the haunted house three or four times. Each time she walked through those halls—those pathways in her mind—they had a new painting to display. New memories came to life with vivid color—memories destroyed in the accident, rebirthed on those walls.

In her mind, the hallway led her to an open room with a high ceiling. A massive chandelier hung from it, reflecting the glow of lanterns placed around the room. The next hallway sloped down, leading to a cavern with a walkway down the middle. The walkway had railings on each side, and exhibits all around, like a museum. She hurried down the walkway since she'd seen the exhibits already.

A car and a white truck mashed together in a head-on collision. A shed with a padlock on the door. A suburban house with a manicured lawn. The opening of a cave in Kentucky. Some exhibits she remembered, others were foreign. She would unlock their importance in time.

The walkway led her to a small circular room with three doors, each labeled with a black and gold plaque.

Death.

Dreams.

Clive.

The door called *Death* rattled gently. Greta was afraid to touch it. She wanted it to stay locked. *Dreams* was also locked, but she didn't care. Her new memory, the one she needed to see again, was behind *Clive*. After all, the memory involved him.

She opened *Clive*, unsure what to expect. The new memory was doing strange things to her house. With every visit, the rooms and furniture were different.

Behind *Clive*, she followed the winding path through cheap replicas of their farm and wax figures made to look like them. Countless memories. But she didn't have time for the ones she already knew. She kept on, through the haunted house, until she found it.

The new memory.

She faced a brightly lit kitchen with granite countertops and a tile floor. Young Clive and Young Greta stood by the sink, washing out wine glasses marked with fingerprints and red lipstick. Judging by their age, this must have been thirty years ago, at least. A third person joined them—a young man in a disheveled suit. He wore an expensive watch. The three of them engaged in conversation, but Greta couldn't hear the words. Somewhere deep in her haunted house, that same woman screamed again.

Young Greta kissed the man in the suit. The man laughed it off, his face turning every shade of red.

Young Clive smiled from the sink. He nodded. *Go on*, he motioned. *She wants you.*

The man in the suit kissed Young Greta, this time with aggression, maybe a hint of violence. Young Greta wore an off-the-shoulder shirt that the man pulled down to her waist. Between her breasts, a faded scar traveled from her stomach to the top of her chest. A memento of escaping death as a child, a precursor to the second open-heart surgery, decades later, that re-opened the scar, installed a ticking valve, and sewed it shut again.

Young Greta led the man out of the kitchen, pulling him by his belt. They disappeared behind a wall, like actors leaving a stage. The memory didn't go that far. Instead, it lingered on Young Clive. He watched Greta lead the man away. When they were out of the kitchen, Clive reached for the knife block and withdrew the largest one. Holding it, testing the weight, Young Clive left the kitchen with it firmly in his hand, following the direction his wife had taken.

Greta opened her eyes. She was back in her living room, holding the moss-green case for her glasses. The memory replayed in her mind—so clear and vivid, she had no reason to doubt it. She'd helped kill someone thirty years ago. A man in a suit. She and Clive were killers. *And they got away with it.*

Greta steadied her trembling hands. What if she made it up? What if the memory in the haunted house came from a dream instead of reality?

Test it. I have to test it, she thought. She didn't trust the memory. She didn't trust a lot of things nowadays. The doctor told her procedural memory worked. If she killed someone once (maybe *more* than once), she could do it again. Just like riding a bike.

Greta opened the moss-green case and withdrew her reading glasses.

She sat on the couch.

She shoved the glasses deep into the couch's crevice, where all things, important and meaningless, ended up.

Greta closed her eyes. She walked through her haunted house, back to the new memory. She watched it again, positive of the outcome. They butchered the man in the suit and got away with it.

Taking the landline phone from its cradle, Greta dialed Mindy Wright's cell phone, as she had so many times before when she needed Eli's help around the house. Normally, she paid him to come do chores, and rarely did she call this late—but this was, after all, an emergency.

Because she had to be sure. She had to test it.

Chapter 5

Julie froze, unwilling to consider why Aunt Susan had brought up the night her mother died. "Why do we need to talk about it? We both know what happened, what else is there to say?"

"You need to talk about *her*. Before there's no one left for you to talk to."

I'm not doing this right now, Julie thought. She started reading *David Copperfield* on her own, in her head.

"Julie. You need to tell someone what happened. If not me, then someone else."

"You *know* what happened. Everyone knows what happened."

Aunt Susan shook her head. "I read the police reports. I talked to those officers, and even they never fully knew."

"That's not true—"

"They pieced it together, Julie. They had all the evidence they needed." Aunt Susan paused and chewed on her next words, as if softening them. "But you never told them, or anyone, *what happened*."

"I was nine, I must've told them. Why wouldn't I?"

"I was there, honey, and you were in shock. I became your guardian—you never talked to them without me."

Julie shook her head. "I don't want to talk about this."

"Julie."

"Stop." Julie stood up, tucking the book under her arm. Memories cropped up, threatening to pull Julie back into the bad places she didn't want to visit, back to that night, to the things she never told anyone.

"I'm sorry I never helped you talk it through." Aunt Susan's voice broke. "I lost my sister. I gained a daughter I wasn't equipped to take care of. And it was easier for me to raise you if we weren't always thinking about what happened to her."

"*Why* are you bringing this up?"

"Because I'm dying, Julie. And all I can think about are the things I've avoided for years. And it's killing me." Tears spilled down her cheeks. "I'm sorry I didn't help you more when you were younger. I was selfish. I didn't want to deal with it, so I avoided talking about her. And that was exactly what you needed. You *need* to tell someone. It's been eating you alive for twenty years, honey. It's not going away. And the harder you try to hide who you really are, the worse things will be for you. I know. Trust me."

Julie exhaled, air hissing through her teeth. Her aunt was right. She'd never explained *everything* about that night. Her mother's last night on earth. And she wasn't about to.

Julie lifted the book, trying to keep the tears from falling. "Can we just read? Please?"

"I can't keep my eyes open forever," Aunt Susan said. "I have to close them sometime. When I'm gone, no one else will know what you went through."

"You can't force me to talk about that right now. Not after ignoring it for years! That's not fair." Her voice came out so high and pathetic. She was a kid again, scared to death of police and strangers, scared of sleeping and the nightmares that preyed on her.

Aunt Susan nodded. "I'm just trying to warn you. All day, I've thought of every mistake I ever made. It's all I can think about. Don't be like this." She laughed through her tears. "Don't be like me. All your problems will wait you out. I promise. They'll be there in the end." She smiled. "I used to think I'd look back on a beautiful life. That on my deathbed, I'd think about the moments most precious to me. I didn't think my mistakes would follow me all the way here, at the end of the world."

Julie sat on the metal folding chair and reopened the book.

"Julie?"

Julie looked up. She licked her upper lip where sweat had gathered. But she didn't trust herself to say anything.

"Can you open the window?"

"It's raining."

"I need some fresh air. Please."

Julie unlocked the window and cracked it open, making a mental note to close it after Aun Susan fell asleep. She sat back down and began to read aloud. The wind howled outside. The curtains gently swayed, and the breeze swam around her, filling the room with warmth. The air tasted like rain and freshly cut grass.

Julie read, but her mind was elsewhere. It wandered to those dark places—like that Friday night when Julie watched TV in the living room while her mom showered.

She kept reading, watching as Aunt Susan's eyelids drooped. Resentment coiled inside her. It was her aunt's advice, years ago, that held her back from telling people her life story. When she changed her name to Julie, Aunt Susan didn't blink. She understood. She thought it was for the best. A chance at a normal life.

Julie tried to focus on the words, but they didn't matter. Aunt Susan was practically asleep, and Julie couldn't stop the memories.

Her hands shook so much, she struggled to read. She forced herself to keep going, despite the wave of anxiety slowly drowning her.

Aunt Susan was the only person who knew Julie's real identity. And once the cancer finished its long and brutal takeover, the truth would die with her.

She looks like mom, Julie thought, no longer resisting the memories. She saw her mom's last breath, and how she looked at Julie with so much confusion in her eyes. In Julie's mind, her mom tried to form a single word on her lips. Julie's birth name. But the storm outside swallowed her mom's voice.

And somewhere far away, the wind screamed Julie's true name.

Chapter 6

Eli sat across from Dad, matching the man's slouch and poker face. They waited each other out, weaponless gunslingers. A pack of spearmint gum was on the kitchen table between them. Dad pushed the pack in slow circles with his finger, clearing his throat a few times without saying anything.

Dad wore glasses and a sweater and somehow always had his shirt tucked in like James Bond. Eli even bought him a fancy watch two years ago for Father's Day. It completed his look, and he wore it every day.

"Hey, you haven't shown me your new library books yet." Dad cleared his throat once more. "Let's see what you got."

Eli took the stack of books from the kitchen counter and set them down, side by side, on the table. Fantasy, sci-fi, and post-apocalypse were his top genres. With horror and mystery sprinkled in when the mood was right.

When a phone started ringing, Dad flinched but didn't check his pockets. He examined the pile, his eyes glazing over their covers. Despite Dad's love for reading, he didn't venture to other worlds or future societies. He stuck to nonfiction and classics. "*Five* books? You're going to read five books in three weeks? Eli, this is child's play."

In the living room, Mom's hushed voice answered her cell phone.

"They didn't have some of the books I wanted," Eli said.

"I know. I'm teasing." Dad smiled, but not fully. He pushed the pack of gum in circles again. "You didn't get me a new biography, what's up with that, huh?"

Eli shrugged. "They didn't have any good ones."

Dad nodded solemnly and pushed the pack around, his Adam's apple twitching, ready to clear his throat for the millionth time.

"Eli?" Mom's voice came from the living room, rising above Lucas's rambling and blanket sorting. Half of the living room windows were now witch-proof.

Eli didn't like the look on her face. Not one bit. That look said she needed him to do something he wasn't going to like.

"Greta called. She can't find her reading glasses, and she's very upset." Mom paused, eyebrows raised, like this was thrilling news.

Eli rubbed his eyes, sighing. Couldn't Greta go one day without needing his help?

"I'll drive you over," Dad said, scooting his chair back, sounding like he'd rather do anything else.

"No thanks, I'll walk." Eli opened the hallway closet and pulled out his rain jacket.

"You sure, sweetie?" Mom glanced out the window. "It's still raining."

"I have my jacket." Eli sighed again, slipping on his rainboots by the front door. He was no stranger to the walk from their house to Greta's. Even after the sun had set.

"Take your phone, okay?" Dad pulled a soda water from the fridge. "Call me if you need anything. Don't forget your flashlight!" He smiled at Eli, happy to skip a hard conversation. Like father, like son.

Eli jogged back into his room, pocketed his phone and heavy-duty flashlight, and returned to the front door.

Mom rubbed his shoulder. "Thank you for doing this. Greta will be so grateful."

He doubted it.

Dad appeared by Mom's side, handing her the pack of gum from the table. She took it without looking.

"We'll talk when you get back, okay? Maybe tomorrow." Dad slurped his soda water.

"Okay." Eli flashed them a big fake smile and stepped outside. Even if going to Greta's was annoying, at least it spared him from whatever was supposed to be happening at the kitchen table.

Eli stood in the rain for a moment, tilting his head back so drops fell down his face. There was a sweetness to summer thunderstorms. He could've stayed there for a long time, but he had a job to do. At the end of their short driveway, he turned right instead of left, feeling the wind push against his back like a gentle guide.

He jogged down the sidewalk to the Main Street bridge that crossed the Little Miami River and connected their sliver of town to the rest of Darling. He leaned over the railing, breathless at the sheer strength of the water. To his left, Darling slept soundly while the river crept up its banks. A slow drowning. Half the baseball fields were underwater.

No surprise there, he shuddered. Just thinking about the baseball fields gave him the creeps. A storm like this could change those fields forever.

Leaving the bridge, Eli jogged past his home, past apartments and shoddy houses with crooked porches. He fought against the wind. He reached the bike trail and turned right, heading the same direction as the parallel river. He followed the bike trail for two minutes, then he stopped and glanced up a long hill.

At the top of the hill, Greta's house lights glowed through the trees and stormy gale. The bike trail was faster than driving. Plus, it was more fun this way. Eli wasn't scared of the dark (most nights) and the adventure fed his imagination. Even if Greta was old and boring, the night trips were especially fun once he got started.

Leaving the bike trail, he leapt across an overflowing ravine. Normally it was dry with rocks and dead leaves caked on the bottom. But not tonight. Good thing he had rain boots, because the hill was soggy, and his boots kept sliding down every few inches, leaving trails of exposed mud. Keeping the house lights in view, he picked his way through the honeysuckle, trees, and half-buried rocks.

As he climbed, his inner narrator started working, as if telling his brother Lucas a story. *There he was! Explorer legend Eli Wright—the fearless, handsome, ladies' man.* He conquered the slippery hill, fighting tooth and nail for every step. Dangerous precipices awaited every turn. Rocks gave way, dead tree branches snapped when he—

And he had reached the top—another victorious climb. *Now, explorer legend Eli Wright had to face his arch nemesis, an old witch, named Greta. And find the infamous, fabled, Reading Glasses.*

Eli smiled at himself as he approached the house. Making a game out of things helped lessen his aggravation. If Greta only knew what craziness went on inside his brain, she'd be scared of him.

He came up on the side of the screened-in deck and made his way around the front yard and flower beds. Off to the side, against the trees, was Greta's wooden compost bin. The wind had flipped the lid open. A little plaque hung on the bin, reading:

COMPOST ONLY
VIOLATORS MAKE GREAT FERTILIZER

Pretty funny, especially if you knew Greta. Eli closed the open lid and walked to the driveway. Before him, a slippery, stone walkway stretched from his rainboots to the front door. Greta must have been looking out the windows, because the front door opened, and her thin frame stood in the doorway. She waited for him, like a goblin guarding a narrow passage through the mountains. She held the doorframe to steady herself. Her face and eyes were shadowed by the light behind her. For a brief second, he wondered if that even was Greta.

Eli didn't like the way she waited, her bony arms and legs outstretched, like a spider standing up. But he disliked it even more when the lights vanished and the house plunged into total darkness, taking the woman with it. He could barely see her slink back into the dark cave of her home.

Eli ensured his jumpsuit was zipped to the collar. He had no choice but to go inside. Step by step, he followed the stone walkway to the open door and entered the house without light.

Chapter 7

Eli tried adjusting to the murky darkness inside Greta's house, but the shadows kept changing into impossible shapes. His primary concern was finding Greta. He didn't see or hear her move, but she was by the door seconds ago. The wind poured through the open doorway, whispering along the wood floor. Greta's house somehow always smelled like sawdust. This time, the smell mixed with fresh rain and a sweet, candle-like vanilla.

He shut the door behind him, silencing the storm. "Mrs. Shaw?"

"Over here!"

He turned his flashlight on. A beam of white light cut through the darkness, catching Greta as she fumbled through kitchen drawers for matches (who used matches anymore?). She was dressed in her bathrobe—a clothing option Eli had never seen her in before and hoped to never see again. Her shaved, skinny legs looked more like bones than flesh.

Greta shut the kitchen drawer. "Power's out. I'll grab some lamps if I can find them. I haven't lit those old things in years."

"Mom said you lost your glasses?"

She tilted her head to the side. "*Yes*. Yes, I did lose my glasses."

"Do you remember when you saw them last?" Eli directed his light around the room, a PI in search of a game-changing clue.

"Oh." Greta scratched her head as if not anticipating this question. She shuffled to the couch and rotated in a slow circle. "Shoot. Uh, I remember having them in my bedroom. But that's it."

"Okay, I'll check there."

Eli entered the bedroom, guiding the light from corner to corner, object to object, hoping for an easy break in the Missing Glasses case so he could get out of there.

He'd never been inside her bedroom before. He noticed a lot of Clive's things: old work boots in the closet, a hand-carved walking stick, a compass, and a shelf of books about eating roots in the wild and surfing and dangerous bugs in South America. The dresser was topped with a framed photo of Greta and Clive at least ten years younger, smiling in front of a monstrous redwood tree. Clive wore the same boots, held the same walking stick. Above the dresser, a corkboard hung on the wall, boasting a montage of polaroids and movie ticket stubs and parking passes to once-in-a-lifetime places. A polaroid showed the couple in front of the Darling Library. Their smiles giddy, their cheeks touching, they had no idea that night would be their last outing together.

Eli didn't like the image, especially with his hometown library in the background. He examined the dark blurry windows for something that wasn't supposed to be there (the Darling Library *was* haunted, and one day he'd prove it), but he suspected the library wasn't the problem in this photo. It was Clive. Even when Eli moved, Clive stared *right* at him.

Eli turned away, no longer trying to find glasses, but hoping to learn as much as he could about the woman who paid him to do chores. He found a collection of bird feathers, books about birds, and a pair of black industrial binoculars. So, Greta and Clive were oddballs. Not exactly a revelation.

A match ignited in the living room. An oil lamp burned like a small, dying sun. Greta adjusted the wick length, and the flame grew. She set the lamp on the coffee table between the couches and went to light another lamp.

She placed the second lamp on her dining room table and turned around. Eli paused, anticipating some recommendation for where to look. But her eyes were closed—shifting behind thin eyelids.

He thought she would open her eyes and catch him staring, but Greta only smiled, her lips parting in surprise, as if watching something funny in her mind.

Eli shifted away from the bedroom door and leaned against the wall. Everything was draped in darkness. Greta giggled in the living room. Her bare feet padded along the wood floor. Eli imagined her turning the corner, laughing, eyes bulging behind closed eyelids. What if closing her eyes was the only way to stop them from falling out?

But Greta moved into the kitchen, hopefully with open eyes. The dread in Eli's stomach slipped away. She was just weird, nothing more. Just a strange old woman.

Eli didn't find anything in the bedroom. Her glasses could be anywhere. In her car. In the library. In the front lawn. In the toilet. Greta's mind wasn't the sharpest. It wasn't her fault, of course. The accident had left her broken.

The bathroom also yielded nothing. Two toothbrushes, a hairbrush, and a cabinet full of Clive's things: a razor, open razor blades, shaving cream, scissors, an ear cleaning kit, pomade, and cologne.

Greta's living room had two couches facing each other, a coffee table, two rocking chairs, a few floor lamps, a desk, and a bookcase of stacked magazines and DVDs. One of the piles had a porn magazine hidden somewhere in the middle. Eli snuck it into the bathroom once, while Greta napped, and flipped through it, cover to cover. If he closed his eyes, he could still picture how the blonde was posed.

Eli glanced at the magazines and resumed his search. The bookcase was crowded with old mysteries, anywhere from Nancy Drew to the Hardy Boys to the Boxcar Children. Mostly kid stuff. Greta had Eli read those books to her sometimes, as they washed windows or planted flowers. He'd sit in the grass and read aloud while she packed mulch down around her hydrangeas. He told her they could read more advanced stuff—Agatha Christe, Edgar Allan Poe, or Sir Arthur Conan Doyle. But she thought he wasn't ready for those, and she liked the kid stuff anyway.

Eli moved on, wishing he was reading to her rather than looking for her stupid ugly glasses. Of all the chores she paid him to help with, reading to her was the best. It was surprisingly fun, and she became as enthralled in the mysteries as he did.

Despite the oil lamps, Eli used his flashlight to pierce the shadows, hoping the glasses would reflect when the light hit them. He stooped over Greta's antique wooden desk for a closer look. Seemed like a logical place to leave a pair of glasses. But the desk was mostly covered in papers. Adult-looking papers. Boring stuff.

He turned and almost ran into Greta. She towered over him, smiling. Her teeth were white and ageless. A bead of saliva clung to the corner of her lips.

"Do you want a snack?" she asked.

Eli quickly said yes, noticing dried blood on her robe he hadn't seen before, and he wondered if she'd cut herself.

Greta shuffled into the kitchen. A white bandage hung loosely from the back of her head, half of it caked in dried blood. She disappeared into the pantry. Items shuffled around. Something fell on the floor, followed by unintelligible muttering.

She hit her head, Eli thought. *No wonder she's acting strange.* Calling Mom and telling her Greta was hurt seemed like the best course of action. But it would be rude to do without asking Greta, and he was too scared to ask her anything.

"*Here we are,*" she sang, leaving the pantry with a bag of potato chips. "Why don't we take a break so you can eat? Hmm?"

"Okay."

"Sit, sit." She patted the couch cushions.

Eli sank into the couch, temporarily overwhelmed by its musty embrace. The pattern was old and hideous. On the far wall, tall windows reflected the room around him. He lifted a hand, waving to himself. In the window's reflection, Greta walked behind him. She set the chips in his lap and ventured back into the kitchen.

Eli opened the bag. Of course, he couldn't refuse potato chips. After eating a few, he brushed the crumbs from his shirt, letting the couch swallow them.

Wait!

He sat up straight, feeling his pockets. His EpiPen was still on his dresser. Not great, but Greta knew about his allergy. She'd be careful. He settled back into the couch, hunting for another chip.

"I'm preparing a snack as well!" Greta shouted way louder than necessary.

She carried a cutting board with a cucumber on top, set beside a wide knife. Like for cutting up a lot of meat. She stopped at the couch, eyes rotating from the couch to the coffee table to the couch.

"This won't do." Her voice fluctuated, like she was in a play and couldn't deliver her lines. "I'll use the table." The table was behind the couch. She set the cutting board down and picked up the knife.

Eli ate a chip and stared ahead, thinking about getting on his phone and checking the group chat to see what his friends were up to. Before he could grab his phone, he looked at the window across the room. In the window's reflection, Greta stood at the table behind him, bent over the board, slicing through the wet cucumber. The room echoed with chip-munching, veggie-cutting, and the monsoon coming down on the roof.

Slice, slice, slice.

Eli glanced in the bag and withdrew another chip. Everything went quiet behind him. He looked up to the window.

Greta wasn't chopping cucumber anymore. She stood directly behind him. Her head hung down, slowly rolling back and forth. Her arms swayed at her sides. Her window reflection had a blurry, featureless face. She raised her hands—one of which held the knife. It rose over the couch, over Eli, its silver smile widening.

Eli dropped the chip, too confused to move. Did the window make her appear closer? Because holding the knife like that was *not* a safe way to cut cucumber. The rain made the reflection look like a rippling pool, but Eli knew it wasn't distorting his view. If he reached back, he would touch her robe and feel her ticking heart. He would feel her dried, crusty blood, and the cold metal knife in her hands.

Tick, tick, tick.

Greta buried the knife in Eli's shoulder.

At least, it looked that way in the reflection. In reality, the knife swooped behind his shoulder. Its quick motion sent a small breeze over his neck. Greta raised the knife again and brought it down, stabbing the air behind him, practicing for the real deal.

Paralyzed, he couldn't look away from the window. Greta repeatedly sliced the air, stabbing an invisible person. Her other hand clenched her chest as if to keep her scar from tearing open. She made little grunting noises as she swung.

Eli dropped the chip bag and rolled forward, careful to not fall back and get pinned to the couch by his crazy neighbor.

She froze like a deer in headlights. Greta stared at the knife, then back at him. "Do you want some cucumber?" she stuttered, pretending to be confused and old and sweet as apple pie.

Eli shook his head. He'd never seen her pretend like that before. For all her quirks, Greta was consistently weird. But seeing her completely switch personalities made Eli want to run away and never come back.

"More cucumber for me, I guess." She grinned, taking a thick slice from the cutting board and biting into it with a wet crunch. The bandage on the back of her head had almost fallen off. It clung to her with a single piece of tape.

She's really lost it, Eli thought. It was the only thing stopping him from sprinting out the front door. *She needs help. Serious help.* The fun and games were over. This wasn't a silly story anymore—she'd nearly killed him.

"I can't find your glasses," he said, thinking, *Please let me go home.*

"You didn't check the basement." She set the knife down with an innocent shrug. "I was down there earlier."

Something like a fire alarm exploded in Eli's brain. *The basement?!*

"But the basement's scary," he said. Now was not the time for false bravery. Private Investigator? No thanks. He was retired, effective immediately.

"It's not scary! I'll be with you."

As if that made things better.

Greta's bandage fell to the floor—a bloody leaf. Eli pictured her brains slipping out the back of her skull and splattering like wet laundry, that aloof smile forever fixed on her face. They'd close the casket on that smile.

"Can I take a lamp?" he asked.

"No. Too dangerous on the stairs. Use your flashlight."

"What about you?"

"I'll be right behind you."

"Did you hit your head?"

Greta's hand twitched, as if to feel the wound. She caught herself, hand half-raised. "On the deck," she said. "The deck is slippery like the basement stairs. Be careful on them."

Eli clicked his flashlight on.

"Real quick." She shooed him to the basement door. "One quick look-see."

Eli opened the door. The wooden steps were cold, splintery, uneven, and had no railing. The image before him was so stereotypical of scary basements, he almost laughed. What did he think was going to happen? His elderly neighbor was going to murder him with a rusty axe and leave him bleeding on the cold concrete beneath her kitchen? The *stories*. All those insane stories he told Lucas made him paranoid. Greta was no monster. She was a victim of many things: memory loss, injury, concussion, maybe even brain damage. What sort of—

Tick, tick, tick.

Right behind him. The ticking of her heart, just beyond the purple scar, fighting, pumping, keeping her alive. Her robe brushed his elbows. Cucumber breath kissed his neck.

A hand pressed against his back, and he tipped forward. He dropped his flashlight—it's beam slashing the darkness before vanishing—hitting the steps and winking out.

He waved his arms, losing his balance, and fell—unable to grab the walls, unable to use the railing that wasn't there, unable to scream or cry or do anything except hold his breath and wait for the stairs to shred his face open.

But hands clutched his rain jacket. Greta yanked him back, their bodies colliding, and she held his shoulders to steady him.

"Oh my goodness," she laughed. "That was close! I told you the stairs were slippery." Her eyes were closed and squirming in their sockets.

Dizzy and nauseous, Eli pushed past her and stumbled to the couch. Greta opened her eyes and gazed at the dark basement, as if something stood at the foot of the stairs. Maybe it was waving to her, asking where the little boy went. Maybe it was Clive's ghost.

Greta shifted her head, staring at Eli with delirious delight. She looked as though she'd never felt more alive. Like she'd been trying to solve a mystery all day, and the answer had finally made itself known.

Backing up, Eli bumped into the sliding glass door that led to the deck. He wasn't about to try the basement again, and if the glasses were outside, he could finally leave. Moving his hand behind him, he pushed the door open and stepped outside. His rain jacket protected him from the waves of torrential water. The wind sailed through the screens, somehow stronger and meaner than before. He checked the soaking wood planks, careful not to slip like Greta did earlier. No sign of her goddamn reading glasses. His head felt feverish, and his body kept shaking, urging him to run.

Greta followed him outside, undeterred by the biting raindrops. She gazed through the screens, through the dark woods, staring at everything and nothing.

"I remember," she said. The wind played with her hair. "I remember now. How easy it is. It's like riding a bike."

"I hope you find your glasses," Eli said, moving for the sliding door. He couldn't do this, he couldn't spend another minute with her. His chest hurt, he had to get out.

Greta rocked on her bare heels. "I remember. I can't believe I ever forgot." Rain or tears dripped from her eyes. She closed and opened them. And with each opening came disbelief, as if stunned by what she saw with her eyes closed. "Eli!" She squealed with laughter. "I remember who I am!"

Eli ran inside. Grabbing his flashlight was not happening, so he dashed out the front door. The dark trees twisted, all bowing to the wind. Everything around him moved. Every leaf and flower and blade of grass.

What exactly did Greta remember? Did all her memories come back? With luck, she remembered the whereabouts of her glasses. Because she was on her own.

He ran past the deck as a voice rose above the thunder.

"I remember!" she screamed.

Was she talking to him? Was she talking to *anyone*?

She stood on the deck, looking skyward, her throat crooked and deformed. She opened and closed her mouth. "I remember!" She spread her arms out, embracing the heavens. Her robe came undone and flapped in the wind.

Eli stumbled down the hill, dodging tree after tree, staying on his feet despite the constant mudslides.

"I remember!"

He ran into the ravine, catching himself, soaking his shoes in the gushing stream.

"I remember!"

The storm carried her voice, the wind adopting it as its own.

Chapter 8

Julie opened her eyes.

She was in their trailer—the one she shared with her mom. Curled up beneath a dirty blanket, Julie looked around her room. There were no pictures or posters on the walls. A bean bag chair slouched in the corner, the tear along its side growing every day, beans spilling out like guts. The only other furniture was a dresser, painted white, but most of the paint had come off. Wallpaper looped around the room like a belt, showing beautiful, galloping wild horses.

Unlike the rest of the room, the wallpaper was still intact, except for the spot directly above Julie's head, where she had picked at it on sleepless nights, peeling those wild and free horses off the wall and crumbling them in her palm.

The door creaked. Julie pulled the blanket over her face, preparing for how her body would look in a morgue. A shadow fell over her. Fingers played with the blanket's edge.

Julie wanted to close her eyes but couldn't. She never had control of these nightmares. She was trapped. Asleep, awake, it didn't matter. She never escaped this part.

The blanket flew off and her mother towered above her, blood pouring from her mouth and neck and chest, black as ink.

Drops of blood fell on Julie's face.

"I'm so sorry," Julie whispered. Letting the blood wash over her.

Drip... drop... drip...

Drop. Drops on her cheek.

Julie wiped her face. She sat up, still in her childhood bed.

No, no, somewhere else.

She scrambled off her bed, looking for the wallpaper with wild horses.

It was gone. The walls were bare. Drops of blood still hit her face. She wiped them with her sleeve.

She was home. *Her* home. Not her childhood home, but the house she had bought and lived in as an adult.

Okay. Nightmare over. Good. She sank to her knees and felt the carpet, smelling it, anchoring herself so she couldn't forget.

She was *home*.

Now that she knew where she was, she had to figure out what she'd been doing. She'd been reading to Aunt Susan. *David Copperfield*. She remembered that.

She must've finished reading, gone to bed, and had a nightmare. Simple as that.

Then why was there blood on her face?

Julie touched her cheeks. They were wet. And not with tears, not with blood.

Drops kept sprinkling on her, making her shiver. It smelled like rain.

She looked up, her chest aching with fear. Her bedroom window was wide open with the curtains flung to the side. Rain poured through the screen, splashing on her, soaking the carpet. Outside, trees bent and shuddered like souls in torment. A cold white streak flew across the sky and thunder shook the floor beneath her hands. The wind howled through her open window, brushing her hair back, making the curtains spin.

"No, no, no." She sprang up and shut the window, whipping the curtains closed. The damp carpet bled through her socks.

Why would she *ever* open her window?

She wiped rainwater from her face and stumbled into the dark hallway. She flipped light switches, but nothing happened. No power.

Julie ran into the living room, berating herself for not setting aside flashlights. The wind sailed through her clothes, fingers, and hair. It pulsed around her, vibrating the air with a heartbeat's regularity.

The windows—two in the living room, one on either side of the picture window, and two in the kitchen—were open, curtains pushed aside. The house lit up in a pale white burst, and thunder snapped so loud, Julie's teeth rattled. She turned, staring at all the open windows, all the rain blowing inside.

Julie ran to each window, slamming them shut and turning the locks. She checked the screens for cuts or tampering. If someone had tried to get inside, she would know, but the doors were still locked, so the windows were opened by someone already in the house, and that terrified her, because only *she* could've done it. Whenever she woke up after a nightmare, she was typically screaming, crying, and in another room. Sleepwalking was normal. But this? Unlocking and opening the windows? She'd never done something so complicated and contradictory to her habits.

Windows secured, Julie straightened the curtains, and the house darkened. The wind was gone, the thunder muted. Her home was safe again. She pulled a towel from the cabinet and started to wipe up the rainwater when she heard something.

Whistling. Like wind through a keyhole.

The windows are closed, she told herself. But that wasn't true. She'd opened Aunt Susan's window before reading to her.

She checked the locks on the front door.

One, two, three.

Tap, tap, tap.

It was just a nightmare, she thought. Opening the windows. Just like *that night*. Old memories were filtering through her blood and into her dreams.

She stopped at Aunt Susan's door. The whistling came from behind it—from the window she'd left open.

Julie twisted the doorknob and gently pushed the door. It opened without a sound. Wind slithered past her.

She quickly shut the window, angry with herself for being so careless. Despite the wet carpet everywhere (which would grow mold, no doubt), the carelessness of an open window bothered her more. What if someone had been out there—*in the woods*—waiting for an opportunity?

How did Aunt Susan sleep through the storm? With the window closed, and the wind gone, the house succumbed to silence. The storm didn't feel as close or urgent anymore.

The room was pitch-black—the shadows darker and deeper than normal shadows. She feared if she stepped too close to them, she'd sink into an ocean of darkness. Julie stared at the shadows, feeling as though something was staring right back at her.

She turned around, trying to remember what happened. The conversation about her mother had turned her stomach, and she read aloud to distract herself—to distract them both. But that was it. Her mind stopped after that.

She edged around the bed, fixing the twisted blanket. Aunt Susan didn't stir.

She moved to the other side and paused. The metal chair she'd sat on earlier was overturned. *David Copperfield* was half under the bed, pages bent. Everything on the nightstand—a tissue box, a lamp, and Aunt Susan's phone, had been tossed on the floor. Julie looked at the bed, at the blanket wrapped around Aunt Susan's petite frame. Like a cocoon. Like she couldn't get warm enough.

Julie inched closer, feeling absurd. She tapped Aunt Susan's shoulder.

Aunt Susan didn't move. She was sleeping on her side, facing Julie, the blanket pulled over most of her face.

Julie pinched the blanket and peeled it back, meeting her aunt's open eyes.

Aunt Susan stared at Julie with her mouth stretched open, as if she couldn't breathe, or had seen something horrifying. Her eyes were wide and pleading.

Even with the strange look on Aunt Susan's face, she looked familiar.

She looks like Mom, Julie thought.

Then she staggered through the hallway and into the bathroom and vomited inside the toilet. She emptied her stomach, coughing and spitting bile.

She looks like Mom.

Julie gripped the toilet bowl, her chest heaving. Breathing was impossible. Her mind raced from her mother to her aunt.

Two dead women. Both died with Julie in the house. Why was everything knocked off the nightstand and onto the floor? Why were all the windows open? Why did Aunt Susan die with a look of terror?

She closed the bathroom door and locked it, then sat on the tile floor and pulled her knees up to her chest, afraid her dead mother would return with Aunt Susan by her side, both asking the same question: *Where were you, Julie?*

"I'm sorry," Julie whispered, shaking. She couldn't stop seeing that open window, curtains blowing in the wind. She felt like a kid again, hiding in Aunt Susan's bathroom, too scared to sleep. Or maybe she was always like this. Maybe she'd never outgrown that trauma she experienced as a little girl.

The little girl who never told anyone the truth.

Chapter 9

Eli sprinted down the bike trail, the darkness closing around him. Every shadow hid a zombie or a serial killer. Every lightning flash illuminated some deformed creature on the hunt. He'd never run so fast, never been so terrified. Greta's voice rattled inside his brain like an echo chamber.

I remember.

He reached Main Street and made for his house. He crashed on the front porch and barged inside. Mom sat at the kitchen table, twirling a cigarette between her fingers. A battery-powered lamp glowed beside her. The rest of the house was dark. The pack of gum from earlier was nestled in the breast pocket of her t-shirt. She raised her eyebrows when he slammed the door shut.

"Eli? You okay?"

He considered telling her everything right then. After all, Greta might've hurt herself, maybe they needed to go over there and drive her to the hospital. Maybe they'd wake up tomorrow and Greta would be dead from a head injury. Died in her sleep, peaceful-like. Eli couldn't decide, his brain tried to replay the events at Greta's house, and he felt so foolish and embarrassed, he didn't want to say anything. Didn't want to see the doubt on Mom's face when he told her Greta stood half-naked on the deck and screamed at him.

"Eli?"

Eli approached the table, water dripping from his rain jacket and onto the tile. Mom looked ready to say something about it.

"I don't want to get old," he said.

She held his cold, wet hand. "Me neither."

Eli hugged her, attempting to keep her dry. He mostly succeeded. He hung his rain jacket on the front doorknob, so the drops landed on the entry mat.

"Eli?"

"Yeah?"

"I love you."

"I love you too."

"Dad went to bed. He's probably reading."

Eli nodded.

"Did something happen, sweetie?" She cradled the cigarette in her palm, like a talisman. "Did you find Greta's glasses?"

"No. And everything's fine."

"Okay. Get some sleep."

Eli stopped at his parents' bedroom door and knocked, pushing the door open. Dad was sitting upright in bed, his back against the wall. An open book rested in his lap. His reading glasses stopped halfway down his nose. He wore a small headlamp—the one he used every night for reading. A literary workingman, mining books like caves. The headlamp projected a dim white light. Eli called it the 'searchlight' because its brightest setting could probably cause permanent eye damage.

"Going to bed," Eli said.

Dad stared over his glasses, his headlamp shining on Eli. He paused, examining the specimen in his light.

"You look cold."

"I need to change."

Dad nodded. "Can we have lunch tomorrow? You busy?"

"No."

"Then it's official." Dad winked. "I'll pick you up here. Goodnight, I love you."

"Love you too."

In his bedroom, Eli peeled off his jumpsuit and hung it up in the closet to help it dry. Buried in blankets, his little brother blinked.

"You should be sleeping."

Lucas shrugged. The mountain of blankets shrugged with him.

Eli sighed and went back into the closet. He removed two kites, one red, one yellow. He handed the red one to Lucas, who, with a grin, propped it up against the wall beside him and snuggled back under the blankets. Eli climbed to the top bunk and slid inside his sleeping bag. He set his kite against the wall.

Lucas and Mom had fixed the blanket over the window, making it witch proof again. The view, though cut in half, was the same dark river as before. Except there wasn't a tree monster this time, just Greta, crawling through the mud in her robe, head up, throat exposed. Crawling, crawling . . .

Lightning flashed. Silence suffocated their room. Greta came closer.

"You awake?" Eli asked Lucas.

"Mmhmm."

Eli forced himself to look anywhere other than the window. He looked up. The ceiling had a crack in it—a long, tiny cavern, probably belonging to tiny people. Was it a story? Not really. Not yet.

"What was the last Julie Baker story?" Eli asked.

"Miss Baker found that alien slug, remember? It ate the mayor."

The story replayed in Eli's mind, making him smile. He knew how to help Lucas sleep. "Ready for another Julie Baker tale?"

"Yes." Lucas shifted below, gently rocking the bunkbed's bones. Lucas was now on his side, in his usual sleeping position.

Eli cleared his throat. He had the perfect idea. Pitch: Julie Baker defends the library from the ghost of a voracious reader who refuses to leave.

Maybe not good enough for Hollywood, but good enough for Lucas. And that was all that mattered.

Eli began. "Julie Baker was closing the library one night. One *clear* night. On *Halloweeeeen*. When, all alone, she heard the sound of pages turning . . ."

Chapter 10

Owen couldn't decide what he wanted more: to take Carly's clothes off himself or to watch her undress for him. This conundrum had plagued him all night, through their entire date, and he still couldn't decide which was hotter.

"My shoes are soaked." Carly had given up avoiding puddles and sloshed into one, stopping at the deepest point, letting the water swirl around her ankles. The puddle danced with the falling rain. Carly smiled despite her shoes, her skin washed in the orange streetlight glow.

"What are you smiling at?" Owen hugged her body against his. They shared a large black umbrella, which was comically useless given the sideways rain and the floodwaters.

"I'm smiling at how cute you are." Carly kissed his cheek, tapping her tongue against his stubble in a way that made him shiver. Her body radiated heat. He hoped, after this stupid midnight crusade through downtown Darling, they'd go back to his apartment and celebrate his birthday properly.

"Can you tell me where we're going yet?"

Carly shook her head, grinning. "It's a surprise."

"Are you feeling it?"

She paused. "No, not yet. You?"

"Nothing."

At a hundred and thirty pounds, the edible would hit her first. Any moment now. Owen only had twenty pounds on her, but if past experience was anything to go by, he'd have to wait his turn while she floated away.

"I don't like surprises," Owen said as they started walking again. "We better be out in this hurricane for a good reason."

"Relax, mister." Carly patted his cheek with a clammy palm. "You'll find out soon enough." She wobbled, and he kept her steady. Too many margaritas from the Mexican restaurant they'd just left. She was a drink or two away from slurring—imagine his shock when she busted out the weed brownies before going on this walk.

"I like this new side of you," he said. "Reminds me of when we first started, you know? Before college."

She didn't respond. His alcohol-saturated brain considered his words. How potentially loaded and bitter they were. *Before college*. Because college (ironically) stole a lot of time, sex, and partying. All the things Owen lived for. How else can you endure forty hours of mindless manufacturing labor if you're not living life on the weekends?

They walked on the Main Street bridge, leaned over the railing, and watched the river run. She wore tight jean shorts and one of his old sweatshirts. He slid one hand down her back and over her ass.

"Holy shit," Carly said. "That water is moving *so* fast."

"Are you feeling it yet?" Owen gently nudged her.

She stared at him, concentrating on his face. "Oh my god, you have beautiful eyes. They remind me of my mom's eyes."

"Thanks . . . babe."

She leaned over the railing, out of the umbrella's reach. Water poured on her head and ran down her cheeks and mouth. "Look! I'm a fountain statue!" She opened her mouth, letting the rainwater dribble off her lips and down her chin.

Owen grabbed her arm. "Be careful."

Carly jerked away from him. "Why? Afraid I'll drown? Afraid I'll fall in?"

"Not in that order, but yeah. You're drunk and high, I think."

She giggled, cupping her mouth with her hands. He moved closer to keep the umbrella over her.

"I'm not going to fall in, stupid." She snorted, leaning against the railing, trying to catch her breath. "Why would I ever *choose* to fall in?" Staggering to the side, Carly fell off the sidewalk and into the street, landing on her hands and knees.

"Carly."

More laughter. She tried to stand and fell over again. Headlights came down the big hill—yellow rays beaming through the rain—approaching the bridge.

"Carly!" Owen dropped the umbrella and seized her shoulders. He hauled her up and yanked her back to the sidewalk as the small car blew across the bridge, throwing water on them both.

"Slow down!" Owen shouted, picking up his umbrella and launching it after the car. The wind caught the umbrella and blew it over the side of the bridge.

The car braked, casting blurry red light over the asphalt. Owen felt a drop of fear trickle through his guts, then the car slowly drove away. Apparently, they weren't worth the fight. Owen lifted his middle finger anyway, confidence restored.

Carly sat on the sidewalk, her back to the bridge railing, crying from laughter.

"It's not funny." Owen helped her stand. This was getting old. He needed the edible to kick in, so this felt less like babysitting and more like hanging out.

Carly hugged him. "That car was going *so* fast. Like a rocket."

"What are we doing out here? Why won't you tell me?"

"C'mon, grumpy." Carly took his hand and pulled him across the bridge and into downtown Darling. The baseball fields were almost completely submerged. Were the rumors true? They would know once the water levels receded.

"Babe." Owen stopped. Carly tried to keep walking and pulled on his arm. "Where are we going?"

Carly pointed several blocks down the street. She smiled. "We're going to the library."

"Okay. Why?"

Carly blinked, knocking raindrops from her eyelashes. "Because I want to have sex there."

Oh, shit. She knows. His throat dried up.

"Isn't that something you've always wanted to do?" she asked, leaning on him to keep from falling. "I'm going to quit working there, for obvious reasons. So, we better do it now, while I'm feeling brave. It's not something I'd normally do."

No, you wouldn't, Owen thought. But Carly's best friend, Becca, on the other hand, would do just that. He had sex with Becca in the library bathroom two weeks ago. Three times. Three separate days. Twice while Carly worked down the hall.

Owen stared at the falling rain, his mind collapsing. Maybe she didn't know? Maybe it was some freaky coincidence?

"Let's go, silly," Carly clutched his hand and kissed his wet cheek. "I know you want to." She tried to wink but closed both eyes instead. She marched onward, pulling him toward the library.

Owen considered making a run for it, but two things happened simultaneously:

First, they reached the library. Owen grew up in Darling. He played in the library as a kid—he knew every story by heart. People said the place was haunted, but he'd never believed it. But now, in this storm, his resolve began to crumble.

Second, the Darling Library started to float off the ground.

The library was an old building, with red brick, a pointed roof, and cream-colored trim. It was bathed in the orange streetlight glow, and the windows were murky black pools. From the earth to the gutters, dark green ivy scaled the library's right side. Twin chimneys stood on opposite ends of the roof.

The edible had landed, and now the entire library hovered above the ground, its doors and windows and eaves morphing, made of smoke. He suddenly noticed every single brick and how elegant and symmetrical they looked stacked on top of each other.

"What did we take?" Owen closed his eyes and tried the library again. It was back on the ground, looking fairly normal, but closing his eyes made him dizzy.

"We took Main Street." Carly smacked her lips, as if not used to their placement on her face. "It was basically a straight shot from the restaurant, kiddo."

Owen swallowed the giggles back down his throat. Between his mind melting from too much weed and his girlfriend about to revenge-murder him in the library bathroom, he had a lot to think about and not enough time to do it.

Carly fished a set of keys from her pocket and swung them around her finger. "Guess who's got the keys, baby? Stole these bad boys on my way out. Right under Julie's ugly nose."

I'm dead, Owen told himself. *She's going to kill me. She knows what I did with Becca.*

"Let's go, let's do it." She pulled him around the library's yard, toward the back. "We gotta go through the kid's room, cause of the cameras in the front."

They stopped at the back entrance. Carly sifted through the keys, trying a few without success.

Owen inspected the door frame, pushing against it with both hands. *They made this so strong.* He backed up, hands on his hips, taking in the entire Children's Room from the outside. Everything was so symmetrical. Did all buildings look like this? How much thought and planning and *history* went into making a single building?

"Hey Owen," Carly called from the open door. "Wanna get out of that rain?"

Rainwater. Owen pursed his lips, forcing his jaw shut. *Don't do it. Don't laugh. You won't be able to stop. There's nothing at all funny about rainwater.*

He shivered when he left the warm rain for the air-conditioned library. Water dripped from his clothes to the carpet. He was soaked down to his testicles, the same ones Carly would chop off any moment now.

Carly wandered through the Children's Room. He needed to consider her goal here—her master plan. But how could he when the entire library was so symmetrical? He thought the outside looked incredible. But the inside? Good God. He stared at the shelves, every single one. So beautifully made. So rectangular and perfectly placed, side by side. The adult book sections had long, boring metal shelves. The kids had sweet wooden shelves, like cute little cubbies for all their small books.

How long had he been staring at the shelves? Owen turned in slow circles. One circle took him ten minutes. He hadn't seen Carly in hours.

Owen tried calling her name, but his throat was too dry. His lips were cracked slivers of flesh. A muscle in his thigh threw a dance party. It burned inside his leg, like a little critter trying to get out. He limped through the hallway, eyes barely adjusting to the messy darkness. He ran into tables, a drinking fountain, and a bookcase with little glass doors. *Whoopsie!*

And he tripped on the carpet. The carpet! As if it had grabbed him with tiny polyester hands. He shuffled forward on his hands and knees, teeth clenched, chest heaving as he tried to think of *anything* other than laughing.

Carly emerged from Non-Fiction, wearing an open book on her head like a hat. Like the book was trying to eat her from the top down.

And that did it. Owen exploded with laughter. Nothing else mattered. Nothing even crossed his mind. For what felt like twenty minutes, he lay on the carpet, imprisoned by his own giggling.

Carly tugged on his shirt, and he somehow found his feet, and hugged the woman bound to take his life at any minute—any minute now.

Carly led him deeper into the library. The book on her head was gone. Her wet hair glowed in the red light of the EXIT signs. The security lights were either not working, or only a few had ever been placed. The Darling Library was old, and desperately in need of an update. The rooms were dark—the hallways were darker—aside for orange light drifting in from outside.

Carly led him into the foyer, beside the front desk. She pointed at a camera in the ceiling corner, lowered herself to the floor, and crawled behind the counter. Owen followed. Together, they reached the other side and turned right, into the office. Once out of the camera's sight, they stood up.

The office had a small window with a security light in the ceiling. The room was divided into four spaces, with four desks, and a closed door leading to another room with more offices. Carly walked up to a desk, pushing the chair aside.

Shhh, Owen tried to say.

Carly hunched over the desk, accidentally knocking a few items over, making a lot of noise. What was she doing? He tried to get a closer look, but his feet were roots, and he had planted himself in the carpet.

Carly turned her phone on to help her see and set the phone on the desk. Taking a pen from the penholder, she stared at a calendar hanging on the wall. Lifting the pen, she paused, staring down that calendar like it was the worst thing she'd ever faced. Her back was rigid and tense. She'd forgotten all about Owen. Not that he minded. It was better than death.

She placed the pen on the calendar, stopped, and pulled back. She shook her head, drove the pen against those little symmetrical paper dates, and wrote in large letters, *I quit!*

Who used that desk? Carly often complained about another librarian, Julie. It had to be Julie's desk. Carly dropped the pen on the floor and turned around, her face a smooth mask of indifference. She sat up on the desk, pushed the keyboard and monitor back, and spread her legs.

Owen unrooted himself and lumbered forward, drawn to her body like a bug to a lightbulb. They collided. He kissed her lips, her neck, her shoulders. Her hands trailed down his back, her nails digging through the fabric of his hoodie.

He touched her hips, her skin-tight jean shorts. Becca wore leggings when they did it in the bathroom. Black leggings, with a small rip on the waistband.

He kissed Carly again, totally lost and confused about whether she knew or not. He didn't care at this point—he needed her body.

The library bathrooms were for individual use only and equipped with locks. Perfect for hookups. He wondered what Becca would look like on some librarian's desk, wearing his sweatshirt.

"Hurry baby," Carly said, pulling him close. Carly hadn't acted like this since the start of their relationship. She was urgent, like Becca.

Owen gripped her thighs. They were smaller than Becca's, so were her breasts. He pictured Becca underneath that sweatshirt.

"Baby?" Carly grabbed his hands.

He glanced up. Becca had a prettier face. Prettier lips. "Sorry, Becca," he said.

Carly held her breath. Their eyes confronted each other, slowly working out what to say next. The seconds felt like minutes.

"What?" Carly asked. She dropped his hands.

"Nothing."

"You said Becca's name." Carly pushed him back and slid off the desk.

"No I didn't."

"Yes you did."

"I don't know why," Owen said. "My head is fried, Carly. I don't even know what's happening. What did I say? I think I blacked out for a bit—"

"Why would you say her name?"

"I swear, babe, I don't know. I just got confused—"

"You confused me with my best friend? Prick." She stormed past him, knocking him against the wall.

He tried to follow her. He shuffled into the foyer, immediately staring at the security camera. "Shit." He ducked behind the counter. "Babe?" His throat ached. He needed water. He needed a good night's sleep and a few snacks and another margarita.

Noises came from the hallway. Owen crawled behind the counter, reached the other side, and followed the sounds. The bathroom door slammed shut and quickly bolted. He remembered that sound. That *click*, right before Becca pulled his pants down.

Becca, Becca, Becca.

He tried twisting the handle. "Open it, babe!"

She cried behind the door, gasping for air.

"Please open it, baby," he tried again, knowing it was a waste of time. Knowing he'd rather have Becca than deal with this anymore. It was Carly's fault for ruining their relationship. Her fault for never wanting sex, never wanting to give up studying for time together. What else was he supposed to do? Becca wanted him. She basically dragged him into that bathroom—

The crying stopped. Silence filled the library again. She unlocked the door, but left it shut, forcing him to make the next move. Fine.

He opened the door, prepared to either say anything to help her forget what happened, or tell her all the things he had wanted to say over the last year. He'd decide what to do when he had to.

The door swung open, and he walked inside. "I want to be honest with you, because I think we need—" He stepped in a puddle. He strained to see in the darkness—aided only by the weak orange light coming through the hallway windows.

The puddle he'd stepped in was dark and thick. It made heavy smacking sounds when he moved his shoes through it. Carly sat on the edge of the toilet, her back against the water tank, her head laying on the tank's lid, her eyes pointed at the ceiling. His sweatshirt on her was darker than before. Her legs were coated in the same dark substance as the puddle. Her throat had a wet opening across it, like a second mouth.

Something stung the back of his neck. Something sharp. Something hidden behind the door.

He collapsed. He sank to the tile, tipping forward. He hit the floor and blood filled his nostrils and mouth. Another sting landed on his back, right along his spine. He screamed into the blood. Inhaling, drinking, drowning.

Then came the darkness.

Chapter 11

Eli jolted awake to someone screaming. He bolted up, convinced Greta had found him. His dream returned to him—the black and white circus of dead animals, Greta the ringmaster, holding her brains in the palm of her hand.

Her eyes had fallen out of her head, but she kept saying, *I see you, Eli*.

Eli quickly found the real source of the commotion: Lucas running around their bedroom like a maniac, holding his red kite, shouting for Eli to wake up.

Eli removed his phone from his pillowcase. He browsed through his notifications, scrolling through a few memes his friends had sent before grabbing his yellow kite. Despite a rather jarring wake up at 6:30 a.m., he'd been eagerly waiting for this moment.

He jumped from the top bunk and raced to his closet, but his jumpsuit was gone. A damp towel sat on the floor, directly beneath an empty hanger.

Mom worked in the kitchen, dressed in flowy shorts and a long shirt, looking like she'd rather have slept longer. On the counter beside her, breakfast sandwiches containing sausage, egg, and cheese were piled on a plate. The kitchen smelled like food and coffee, cologne and warm rain. Dad had just left for the office. Mom took one look at Eli and pointed at the laundry room.

Eli stopped the dryer and removed his warm jumpsuit. He zipped it up over his body, checking the scar to make sure a thread hadn't come loose.

"Eat something, boys," Mom called from the kitchen.

Lucas and Eli snatched their sandwiches and ran out the front door, kites in hand. "You're welcome!" Mom yelled behind them.

They stood in the front yard, already halfway through their sandwiches, not minding the heat or the grease on their fingers.

Their world had changed overnight. Heavy gray clouds covered the sky, like one massive sail pulling the Earth through space and time. The clouds moved with impossible speed, a dizzying race through the atmosphere, driven by hurricane winds.

The wind.

It was *everywhere*. It surrounded Eli's body, pressing against him, making it hard to breathe. He finished his sandwich, set his kite down, and stepped on it carefully. Lifting his hands to the sky, the wind flowed through his fingers.

Lucas clutched his kite with bewilderment. He faced the wind and leaned forward on his bare toes. The wind held him upright, even at an impossible angle.

"Look!" Lucas shrieked before losing his balance and toppling over.

Eli tried it. He stood against the wind, tipped himself forward, and spread his arms. It held him up at a slanted angle—it even tried to stand him up straight. He'd never felt anything like it. Eli stopped resisting and let the wind shove him backward. He rolled on his back, immediately catching his kite before it blew away. They stashed their kites against the house between a bush and the vinyl paneling.

Lucas ran through the front yard in circles, arms out like a human airplane. He leapt off the ground, lingering an extra second in the air. Eli joined in, jumping into the wind and letting it carry him. He didn't care if they looked dumb. He couldn't understand how people waded through this wind and went to work like nothing had changed.

They challenged each other by hopping on one foot and whoever stood upright the longest won the game. They took turns winning and losing. The wind didn't discriminate who it chose to knock down.

Alex watched them from the doorway, wearing his gas station uniform. How long had he been there? He laughed when they fell, and Eli felt a tinge of bitterness. Why couldn't Alex just stay and play games with them?

Lucas waved to Alex, throwing his arms out and flying through the front yard. Alex waved back and took a picture. Eli chased Lucas and pushed him. Lucas whirled his arms, unable to keep his footing, and somersaulted through the grass. Eli glanced back to see Alex's reaction, but he was gone. His car was pulling out of the driveway.

Eli fell on his back and lay there, chest heaving, sweating. The clouds rushed through the sky, coming from nowhere, going nowhere.

But that wasn't entirely true.

A portion of the clouds shifted above him and funneled into a track or a current. Did the sky have currents? Was the sky like the ocean? And where did the currents lead?

Lucas dropped beside him, following his gaze. "What?"

"The clouds are so weird." Eli sat up. The cloud current soared away from them, over the river, and over downtown Darling. If the wind had currents, were their kites like sailboats?

He jumped to his feet and retrieved his kite. Lucas did the same. They took off down the street to a park with a playground alongside the bike trail. The park was empty. A jogger ran on the bike trail, his every muscle straining against the wind.

They picked the most open spot in the park.

"This is going to be *insane*!" Lucas shouted, using his best diabolical villain voice.

Lucas was right. The wind would either shred their kites or lift them all the way to Heaven. Of course, it was getting the kite skyward that thrilled him—something about the launch, the climb, maxing out the string. There was nothing like it.

Eli was prepping his kite by unraveling the string a little to create slack when Mom entered the park with a coffee mug in one hand, the steam trailing behind her like a locomotive. Her presence brought Eli right back to last night. Mom had the same look—the *Greta needs you* look.

"Hey boys," she said, sipping her coffee.

"Hi!" Lucas spread his feet farther apart, planting himself to keep from tipping over. The wind was to their backs, always pushing.

"Wow." Mom glanced at their kites. "You guys are ready to go."

Eli should've told her everything last night. But told her what? He *did* have a history of creating frightening tales with Greta as the headlining star. Any 'story' he told Mom about Greta would feel like fiction in her mind. He didn't blame her. It was a boy-crying-wolf situation. Except the wolf was very, very real this time.

"Eli, Greta called," Mom said.

Greta called. A horrifying pair of words (it was now a tie between *Greta called* and *I remember*).

"Let me guess, she found her glasses?"

"She actually didn't mention them. She needs help clearing her driveway. I guess a small tree fell over or something. Can you head over? She's worried about needing groceries today."

"Uh. Yeah, I guess." He really, really wanted to complain. He didn't understand why Mom forced him to help Greta every day. She knew he hated going over there. He wanted to fly his kite and follow the wind currents, and she knew that.

Mom should've known Greta was having trouble. She should've gone with him last night.

"Greta will feel so much better with you there," Mom said.

"Mom," Lucas groaned. "We were gonna fly kites!"

"I'll help you fly yours," Mom said. "Eli will be back soon, and he can join us, okay?"

Lucas looked ready to hit something. His pout deepened.

"Hey." Eli patted Lucas's shoulder. "Have fun, stupid. I'll be back soon."

Lucas tried to smile. "Okay." He carefully set his kite down and started unwrapping the string.

Walking back alone, Eli carried his kite inside his house and threw it on the living room floor. He grabbed his phone and EpiPen and set out.

A few minutes later, Eli climbed the hill to Greta's house, passing the occasional muddy streak from where he'd slipped the night before. When he recalled the memory of last night, the details grew fuzzier. The only logical explanation was that Greta had suffered a concussion, resulting in her unusual behavior. It wasn't her fault. And he was blowing it all out of proportion, amped up on too many stories. Too many Greta-the-Witch tales distorting his view of her. Classic self-sabotage. In the cold light of this windy day, he could firmly say last night was far weirder than most, but not enough to do anything about it. With luck, Greta slept a long time, had a few good dreams, and woke up feeling like a new woman.

Cresting the hill, he first saw the screened-in deck. Fallen branches covered the roof, as if the storm had tried clawing its way in.

Passing the deck, he came around the front flower beds (what remained of them) and stood beside Greta's car. He scanned the driveway from the stone walkway to the road. No fallen tree. Plenty of branches and leaves, but nothing more. Greta could hit the open road whenever she wanted.

Greta's front door was open and shifting back and forth. Without much choice, Eli strolled the walkway, wondering why the old woman had called and told his mom there was a tree in the driveway. Did she move it already? Did she *think* she saw a tree? Was she having an episode like last night?

Because if so, no thanks. Eli was all set. Just because it wasn't her fault didn't mean he wanted to go through it again.

He reached the doorway and knocked. No answer. But the door was open, and she did that sometimes to signal she was busy doing something and couldn't come to the door. It was a poor habit in the summertime, given the number of bees and house flies around her property. Despite the heaviness in his stomach, Eli entered her house—it was far less scary in broad daylight—and he still didn't see her, but he heard the kitchen sink running.

"Mrs. Shaw?" Forcing himself to shuffle forward, he moved into the living room, one baby step at a time. "Mrs. Shaw?"

The kitchen sink *was* running. But the kitchen was empty. Eli turned the sink off when he heard a noise from the pantry.

"Don't be scared." Greta's voice wavered. "Before you look, just know that you don't have to be scared, Eli."

Eli stared at the sink, at a series of dark red trails caked on the stainless-steel walls. He gripped the kitchen counter, steadied himself, and looked behind him.

Greta stood in the pantry, not moving, just waiting for him to react. Dry, crusty blood ran down her robe. At least, it looked like blood. It could've been something else. Eli was no blood expert, but he'd seen a little bit of dried blood before, and this was the same, only *much* more. The blood coated her robe from the shoulders to the bottom fringes. Blood was on her neck, arms, and the top of her chest. If all that blood had come from her head wound last night, she would be dead.

There's too much blood. It's not hers, he thought. *It can't all be hers.*

Greta gave an apologetic smile. "Eli. I need your help."

No, no, no, no, please God, no.

"I made a mess of things. I was out last night, driving around, remembering things about me and Clive from a long time ago. I don't know why, but I followed these people. I didn't know them. They weren't paying attention. I nearly hit them with my car."

Eli shook his head. "What?"

"I'm getting there," Greta said. "I followed them and I . . ." Saying the words out loud made her pause. "I used the knife. I made *sure* their hearts weren't beating, and then I left them there."

This isn't real. It's not. It's not real, he thought. "I can't," Eli said. "I can't help you. You need to see a doctor, or someone."

"Please, please." She emerged from the pantry, reaching for him. "I need you to help me. I left them, I left the bodies. I was scared, I didn't know what to do. But if we don't get them, someone's going to see."

"No, I can't." Eli pushed her hands away.

She grabbed his shirt with stained fingers. "Eli. *You're not listening to me.* They'll know I did it, I need you to help me, please."

Something was very, very wrong with Greta. "I need to call my mom." Eli touched the cell phone in his pocket. "I . . . she told me to call her when I got here. It's a new thing. She's worried about me. So, I have to call her."

Greta let go of his shirt.

"I'm just going to call her," Eli stammered. "Let her know. Let her know I'm safe."

"You can't," Greta whispered. "You need to help me first."

He pulled the phone from his jumpsuit pocket. He clicked on his contacts, his fingers shaking, making mistakes.

Greta slapped his hand, knocking his phone to the floor.

She picked it up while he gawked at her. His hand stung from where she'd hit it. How did she hit him that hard when she was too weak to lift a rake? Everything about her seemed different. Like she was running on three energy drinks.

Greta slid the phone into her robe pocket. No longer asking. "I need you to help me."

Many things passed through Eli's head. Disbelief? Shock? Endless responses, yet nothing measured up to Greta in her blood-soaked robe. Nothing came to his lips. He didn't believe she'd hurt anyone. But the blood came from somewhere. *If* it was blood.

"I know you don't want to spend all day here," she said. "So we'll try and make this quick, all right? You help me, then you can leave." She picked up her landline phone, pressed a series of numbers, and held the phone to her ear. "But I have to make sure you won't run."

Eli watched, dumbfounded.

"Hi Mindy, this is Greta." She slowed her words down and deepened her voice, making it sound sickly and tired. "Yeah, yeah, he's here. He's already helping me . . . Yeah . . No, the tree isn't too big. He's almost done. But I was hoping to keep him a while longer. This storm destroyed my yard and my deck, and Eli is just so helpful. I'll pay him extra. I just don't want to cause trouble . . . Okay, thank you for being flexible. I'll ask him. Make sure he doesn't mind . . . Okay, thank you. Oh, and one more thing. There's a lot of cleanup to do. If Eli's overwhelmed, or wants to finish it sooner, could you bring Lucas by? Just in case we need his big muscles," Greta chuckled, clearing her throat. "You're wonderful, Mindy. Oh my, I would be lost without your boys . . . I'll call you if I need Lucas. Okay, thank you. Bye." Greta hung up the phone.

Eli stared at the front door. Everything was happening too fast. He hadn't considered running until now. He was far faster than her. Or he used to be. This version of Greta had energy like he'd never seen before.

Greta frowned. "You can't leave. I'll call Lucas over here."

Eli swallowed.

"I'll kill him."

His heart stopped. She wasn't serious. She didn't mean anything she was saying. Some mental collapse had hijacked her brain, making her imagine things. If he ran away, he could get her help. She needed help, and that was it.

That's all this is, he thought.

"Are you *listening*?" Greta moved closer. A stench wafted off her robe. "I'll kill him." She pointed at the deck. "I'll drown him in the hot tub if you don't help me. I'll hold him under."

Eli's stomach lurched. He felt dizzy enough to faint but somehow stayed on his feet.

"Come here." Greta opened the sliding glass door and walked onto the deck.

He followed her. Stepping outside didn't change anything. The wind didn't change anything. Nothing touched the twilight zone his mind now lived in—where the old friendly neighbor, who gave out chips and candy to young visitors, was willing to hold a child beneath hot water until his lungs were filled with it.

Greta picked something up off the glass table. The knife from last night. The cucumber knife, now covered in sticky red smears.

"I was going to clean it out here earlier, but I changed my mind," she said, lifting the blade up. "Isn't it something?"

Beside them, the hot tub hummed with life, ready to be drowned in. Greta held the knife against the wind, as if showing it off to an invisible guest. She put her lips together like she was going to whistle. Instead of whistling, she breathed through her lips, making a sound like rushing air, like how the wind sounded in the eaves. The wind howled, and Greta copied it. She broke into laughter, her eyes glowing. She looked twenty years younger. Oddly enough, somehow, Eli *liked* it. This was the version of Greta he'd always wanted to see. Sharper, faster, bubbly. He just wished she wasn't imagining things, like killing people. Or threatening to kill people, like his brother. He couldn't explain where the blood came from, but he wasn't positive it was blood to begin with. He'd follow along until he could escape and get help. What other choice did he have?

"I'll help you," he said, wondering how far he'd let things go.

Greta stopped whistling. "We'll need to grab a few things first."

"Where are we going?"

Greta squinted into the wind, smiling. "To the library."

Chapter 12

Julie awoke on the bathroom floor, curled up on the cold tile beside the toilet.

The house was quiet. She sat up and stretched her sore bones. Everything hurt, inside and out. She stood with a groan and leaned over the bathroom sink. In the mirror, her eyes were red and puffy. She barely looked like herself.

"Aunt Susan," she whispered, staring at the locked bathroom door. Was last night real? Was her aunt dead?

"No, no that didn't happen." She fumbled with the doorknob, finally unlocking and swinging the door open.

Oscar rolled on the hallway carpet, batting a paw at Aunt Susan's door, which was firmly shut, with a band of light glowing beneath it.

Had *any* of it been real? Did she imagine her aunt's death?

She knocked on the bedroom door, but no one answered. Julie went for the doorknob when she saw something move. In the crack beneath the door, there was a shadow. A pair of feet stood on the other side.

She backed up, feeling instant relief, almost calling Aunt Susan's name. Something stopped her. Oscar stuck his paw under the door, trying to scratch the shadow. She wanted to yank him back, but she couldn't move.

The shadow shifted away, and not in a walk like she'd expected, but a dragging, slow shuffle. Like it had two broken legs. Not a single sound came from the spare bedroom, yet something was in there, waiting for her to open the door. Something that wasn't Aunt Susan.

Julie waited. When the shadow didn't reappear, she forced herself to twist the doorknob. The door's hinges creaked, and opened, and the smell of death drifted out.

Julie looked inside the spare room. It told the same chaotic story she remembered from last night: the overturned metal chair, the lamp knocked off the nightstand, the book face down on the carpet, the pages bent.

And on the bed, Aunt Susan stared at the ceiling in horror.

Julie had prepared for this. She knew it could happen any day, and still, the sight of a dead body in her house made it hard to breathe. She couldn't approach the bed, she couldn't look away, she just stared at Aunt Susan and did nothing. It was like she was malfunctioning. If someone else had been there, what would they've said? Was she a sociopath? Or was something inside her breaking down, and it was too deep and too armored to feel on the surface?

Maybe something *was* very wrong with her. But maybe her hesitation came from elsewhere, like the disturbing scene in front of her. It looked like an altercation had occurred. Aunt Susan hadn't died peacefully, as they'd both hoped. No, Aunt Susan didn't pass away quietly in her sleep, she'd died screaming at the ceiling.

She sat on the edge of the bed and held Aunt Susan's cold hand. When she tried to remember last night, her head started to hurt. She had been reading, she remembered that. She'd been thinking about her mom—she remembered that too. But after that? She woke up in the middle of a nightmare, the windows wide open, the room in disarray, and Aunt Susan had died. No signs of forced entry, no obvious suicide.

It was the cancer. The cancer killed her.

Julie stared at the woman who'd raised her, the woman who was sinking into a mattress of her own fluids, the woman who'd gazed at something on the ceiling and died with her eyes open, too afraid to shut them, the woman who died alone.

Did she die alone? Or was Julie with her the whole time?

Panic swelled inside Julie's chest. Last night wasn't her first time blacking out. It used to happen often, when the memories of her mom's death were so unbearable, they felt like migraines.

Julie had to get out of there. She shut the door and walked into the living room, inhaling the fresh air. In her mind, she saw flashing lights.

The police would come for the body. They'd find Julie's real name. Aunt Susan never changed her last name legally. They'd look at Julie and wonder how two women had died in the same house with her, almost exactly twenty years apart. They'd wonder a lot of things about her, like why she lived alone, why she had no friends, why she never told anyone the whole story.

A car door slammed. Footsteps kicked the gravel outside, coming closer, moving faster. Julie covered her mouth, digging her nails into her skin to keep from screaming. When the front door rattled with knocking, Julie backpedaled into the hallway.

The knocking continued, growing more urgent. Julie approached the door slowly. She leaned against it, tapped the locks with her finger, and looked through the peephole.

Chapter 13

Eli couldn't explain Greta's change of character. They pulled out of her driveway—Eli riding shotgun while Greta rolled the windows down, letting the wind rush in, thick as water. She brushed the hair from her eyes, grinning like a little kid. She wore a gray t-shirt with jeans—an outfit he would've sworn she didn't own. His phone was tucked inside her pocket somewhere and impossible to reach unless he wanted to make things weirder than they already were.

The backseat was full of everything needed to clean up a crime scene: two shovels, two tarps, buckets, paper towels, wash cloths, bleach, trash bags, air freshener, rope, and her bloody knife. "Just in case," she had said. They left the trunk *empty*, which was a bad sign.

The items in the backseat clinked together with every bump. Eli's stomach flopped, as if they'd already done something wrong and were on the lam. He checked his mirror, waiting for red and blue lights to appear behind them.

"When does the library open?" Greta asked.

"Ten." It used to open earlier, before the pandemic in 2020 shut it down for eight months. It reopened with limited hours and never fully returned to the old patterns. The Darling Library was small, quaint, and could afford a small staff and laid-back way of doing business.

"We have just under two hours." Greta glanced at the clock. "We'll be fine. But we have to be quick." She shook her head. "I don't know what we were doing, me and Clive. I don't remember why we came to Darling and it's bothering me. It's *been* bothering me all year, but now the answer is right in the front of my brain, and I can't see it."

Eli never met Clive, but he saw them both in the library the night of the accident. Clive and Greta stayed at the library for hours, wandering the aisles, talking to librarians. He remembered their secret glances. The way they skimmed through shelves, looking, but not looking for books. Their eyes meeting. Their smiles. It was cute at first, their teenage energy. But after the accident, when Eli remembered that night, their smiles turned plastic.

"We came here for something," Greta said. "Clive and I came to Darling because there was something we needed to do."

They drove down the big hill, then over the bike trail and past the park. Lucas and his kite were gone. They drove past Eli's house, but it was too fast to see anything through the windows. Eli touched the car door handle, wondering if he had the guts to jump out. But the moment passed, and they were gliding over the river. The baseball fields were fully submerged, the water threatening to touch the nearest street.

"I'm remembering a lot, Eli," Greta said. "Entire years of my life are coming back. So many happy years. It's bizarre how surprised I am by my own history. I don't know why so much is coming back now. But I'm glad it is." Tears gathered in the corners of her wrinkled eyes. "I'm glad it's back. It's giving me a chance to meet myself again."

Eli tried to think of something smart to say and came up short. "I bet that's nice," he said.

"If I had some pictures, it would be easier. But I can't find my photo album and it's got just about everything in there. My entire life."

Eli's stomach sank a little. He remembered that photo album. "So the memories are just in your head?"

"Yes. I can see my memories up here." She pointed at her forehead. "My mind is a haunted house."

That surprisingly made a lot of sense.

"When I close my eyes, I see the places I've been. I see all the things I couldn't remember before. But there are still dark spots. Places I can't touch because I'm not allowed yet. There's locked doors and blank walls, which make me believe the story isn't over. More memories will be written."

As scary as it sounded, Eli wished his mind worked like that. Maybe not a haunted house. But a castle, or a small town, or a space station.

"It's very bizarre." Greta smiled. "I can see my memories, like I'm in a museum." She closed her eyes, then opened them. Then closed and opened them again. They were nearly at the library. She jerked the wheel to stay on the road.

Eli gripped his seatbelt, waiting for her to fly off the street and ram through a storefront window. Good thing most of the downtown stores were vacant. They reached the library (safely) and Greta drove to the back corner of the lot, close to the Children's Room. Eli didn't release his seatbelt until Greta parked and took her foot off the gas.

She leaned against the headrest and sighed, closing her eyes. "I could watch these memories all day. There's nothing like it, discovering something you lost. It's beyond words."

"We should hurry," Eli said. "The librarians probably get here early, before the open time."

"Do you want to see?" Greta cracked her eyes open.

"See what?"

"My haunted house."

Eli stopped himself from laughing. If Greta was *this* unstable, laughing could push the wrong buttons. "I don't see how that's possible," he said diplomatically.

"Give me your hand." Greta snatched his hand and held it. "Close your eyes."

He closed his eyes and held her hand. What if she was onto something? Despite the circumstances, seeing her mind as a haunted house would be insanely strange—in a good way. It deserved a shot.

"Do you see it?" Greta asked. She squeezed his hand. Her skin was softer and warmer than he would've imagined. "You'd know it if you saw it."

Eli saw only darkness. Colors morphed into shapeless blobs, and while he wasn't surprised at the lack of a haunted house, he was a little disappointed. He wanted to know it when he saw it.

"No."

Greta dropped his hand. "Were you trying?"

"I mean, yes?"

"I don't think so." She shook her head. "Try harder next time."

Next time?

Greta squinted at the library. "Looks like nobody's home."

Eli waited for it to dawn on her—how it was all a dream, how she wasn't a murderer (just an *almost* murderer). How they'd come all this way with a car full of really sketchy supplies for no reason.

But then Greta lifted a set of keys from the cupholder and swung them on her finger. "Good thing I have these."

Okay, having keys didn't make sense. Maybe she *did* break into the library last night. But there weren't any bodies there. This wasn't a movie. And if Eli ran, she wouldn't hunt him down because she wasn't dangerous, just confused. And he was a good runner. He'd get to his house way before her. Even if she drove, he could make it there first.

Maybe.

Maybe running from Chase and Tyler all summer long had prepared him for this. Sprinting down Main Street to save his life and the lives of his family.

He grabbed the door handle, his mind speeding up. Was he really going to do it? He didn't have a choice. Greta needed professional help. That was why she threatened him, why she said those things about Lucas and the hot tub. She didn't mean them. And he'd forgive her for scaring the hell out of him, once he was safe. Once she couldn't wave that bloody knife around.

He went to open the door when long, wrinkled fingers circled his wrist.

"I need your help, Eli," she said. Her voice was low, controlled, angry. "I can't do this alone."

He just needed to run. That was it. Run for help. Don't look back. Pull his wrist away and run run run.

She dropped his wrist and snatched his hair instead, turning his face around to look at her.

"Did you hear me?" Her face was twisted like she'd eaten something distasteful. But her eyes were wide and surprised, like she hadn't realized until now just how much she could hurt him. She didn't know when to stop.

She clenched her fist, almost ripping hair from his scalp.

"I'll kill them," she whispered, her voice barely above the wind. She released his hair. "Don't make me hurt them. They'll know it was your fault, right before their hearts stop. They'll know."

Eli blinked, a scream trapped inside his chest. He couldn't cope with it. His scalp tingled with pain. Greta smoothed his hair down and ran her thumb across his cheek.

"I'm sorry," she said, smiling. "I don't want to scare you. Just please come inside with me."

Eli nodded. He opened the car door and calmed his breathing and told himself the truth: *Greta is broken. This isn't her fault.*

Greta stood outside the car and grinned as if they'd just finished a fun little chat. "Let's make sure we can get in."

They walked to the back door. Greta tried the handle and the door opened.

"Look at that," she said to the empty library. "I didn't even lock up. How careless of me."

In the Children's Room, Greta scanned the little wooden bookshelves. "I don't think it was here. To be honest, it was dark, and it happened *fast*." She checked the children's bathroom, shaking her head.

The Children's Room had a stage in one corner. On the stage sat a puppet theater made of thin fake wood with red curtains as a backdrop. Eli wasn't a fan of puppets. He checked the stage and looked behind the theater. There were boxes of puppets, but no dead bodies. Greta's uncertainty fueled his confidence. No bodies? No problem, let's go home.

Greta waved to Eli. "Not here." He followed her out of the room.

They walked down the hallway. Tables and bookshelves lined the walls. Mostly Young Adult. Eli liked pulling books from this area and taking them to Adult Fiction, where he could hide at the wooden desk in the corner and read in peace. He'd never been in the library after hours with no librarians around. It made his heart skip—their secret mission.

The hallway had two single-person bathrooms, side by side. Greta approached one of the bathroom doors, moving in slow motion, as if following a memory.

She cracked the door, then opened it all the way, her lips peeling back. She breathed in, inhaling the stale air of death through clenched teeth. "I did this."

Eli edged forward, smelling the bodies before seeing them. Their blood matched the blood on Greta's robe from earlier. Dark and crusty. The woman sat on the toilet. Her head hung to the side, her neck partially open. Her hair was parted down the middle, exposing her face. Carly Waters. The part-time intern. For a split second, Eli wondered if Greta was still mistaken and Julie Baker had done the deed. Julie hated Carly. Any library regular knew that. But at the same time, Eli knew Julie. She wasn't a killer any more than he was.

A man lay in the corner in a pool of his own blood. It was Owen, Carly's boyfriend. Eli had seen him with her before. Owen's hoodie was ripped in the back. Dried blood stemmed from the tear like cooling lava after a volcanic eruption. Eli imagined the cut going down to the spine and the spine giving a white smile, grateful for the fresh air.

"We have to hurry," Greta said. "Let's bring the car to the backdoor and grab our things. We're running out of time."

Eli agreed. They didn't have much time. But he couldn't stop staring. He memorized the scene, feeling the images sink into the core of his mind and plant themselves there. He'd grow old and tired and grumpy, and despite a lifetime of memories, this one would visit again. And again. As many times as it wanted.

Greta hadn't been lying or confused. With her memory now sharper than ever, he didn't doubt her previous threats. He had proof right in front of him. She'd kill his family if he didn't help her. Starting with Lucas. Eli pictured his younger brother's open mouth under the water's surface. His lungs blocked, his black hair floating.

Carly had said *Hey* to Eli last night after his encounter with the bullies. He'd been embarrassed by her acknowledgement. She was young and beautiful and had freckles on her cheeks, and Eli had been crying like a little kid in his dumb Halloween jumpsuit and he wished she hadn't said anything to him. That was his last thought of her—*Please go away*.

Panic exploded inside his chest. He backed away from the bathrooms, crashing into a table of books. Greta said things but his mind ignored them. Carly's dead eyes looked at the ceiling, asking some higher being why it had to be like this.

"Eli, Eli." Greta gripped his shoulders. She shook him, her face hardening. "Listen to me. We don't have a lot of time. Help me grab the tarps. We'll move the car closer."

Eli followed her down the hallway. His brain hushed him, telling him all would be well. Shock would carry him through this.

Because Greta was right. They didn't have much time at all.

Chapter 14

"Julie! Let me in!"

Julie stood on her tiptoes, took one glance through the peephole, and undid the locks. Before she had a chance to talk herself out of it, she turned the doorknob and Tori fell inside.

"Holy hell." Tori stabilized herself against the wall, trying to brush her hair down. She grinned. "Thanks for saving me, honey. Have you been outside?"

Julie shook her head. She shut the door and locked it. *Tap, tap, tap.* "I have not, but I lost power."

"Same here." Tori adjusted her hair. "Does that look any better? I'm now aiming for a windswept look. Like I belong on a romance cover."

Julie smiled. "It's very windswept."

Tori laughed, throwing her hands up. "You know what? I don't even care. My day's already a dumpster fire and it's not even close to lunch time. Sophie was late to school this morning because the woman who normally takes her is hungover. And Stephen ran off to work after promising me he'd do the dishes. See what I have to put up with?"

"So you fired the drunk woman and did the dishes?"

"Hell no. He can keep his promise when his ass gets home tonight. And I can't fire the alcoholic because she's me. I'm the hungover drunk woman." Tori tugged at her long sleeves, a habit she picked up after getting hired at the Darling Library and was told to hide the tattoos on her arms.

Julie wandered into the kitchen, realizing she should show her friend around. Realizing, again, that her aunt lay dead in the next room. Why did she open the door?

"Anyway, enough about me," Tori said, whipping her hair into a messy bun. "How are you?"

Julie tasted blood in her mouth. She'd been nibbling on the inside of her cheek. "I'm good. I'm fine."

"I like your place!" Tori turned in a slow circle, soaking in the blandness, obviously trying to conjure up more compliments. Julie didn't think to open a curtain until now. They stood in murky darkness. She pushed the curtain in the kitchen window aside, tapping the two locks. Gray light filtered in from outside.

"It's pretty small," Julie said, regretting this on so many levels. Why did she agree to let Tori pick her up? Tori was a *work* friend. Not a friend-friend. No wine dates, no after-work drinks, and *no carpools*. Julie had lived by that standard since college, and apparently picked the worst night imaginable to bend her own rules. Her mind was working too sluggishly, any minute now, Tori would ask the inevitable question. And Julie would need to answer.

"I think it's cute." Tori shrugged, her smile contagious. "Though you should decorate the hell out of these walls. These walls could be my next project."

"I know, I'm just not good with that stuff."

"No offense Jules, but I can tell."

Think, Julie, think. What are you going to do?

Tori sat on the couch, flipping one leg over the other. She tampered with the stud in her nose, wincing a little, then looked down the hallway and lowered her voice.

No, no, no, Tori, please don't.

"Hey how's your aunt doing? Is she here? I thought I saw her car outside. I'd love to meet her."

Julie grabbed a glass of water and washed away the blood leaking over her teeth. The inside of her cheek was raw. She looked at everything except Tori, her stomach twisting with shame.

"She's good," Julie said. "She's . . . you know. She's having a hard time, but she's good."

Tori nodded sincerely. Julie wished she could take the words back. Tori was the only person in the world who would understand, and Julie just told a lie she couldn't walk back on.

Why won't you tell her, Julie? Is it because you're afraid she'll somehow make the link between Aunt Susan and your former life? Or is it because Aunt Susan is gaping at the ceiling like she'd been murdered, and you were the only other person in the house last night?

I can't, Julie thought. *I can't tell her. No one can know who I am. Ever.*

"I should get ready," Julie said, gesturing at her pajamas. "I'm running a little behind this morning. I'll see if Aunt Susan's up, we might have to reschedule you meeting her."

Tori waved a hand. "Take your time. And no worries, I'm sure she's tired."

Inside her bedroom, Julie shut the door and exhaled. There was no way out of the lie she'd just told. She was about to dig a hole she couldn't climb out of. But she didn't care. Her time in Darling was at an end, and not just because of her blackout, Aunt Susan's death, or the tug of fear that made Julie feel she had something to do with it, but because of Tori, who was currently in her living room. How did Julie ever agree to carpool? She didn't picture Tori coming inside, sitting on her musty couch, seeing all the locks and blackout curtains and bare walls. Julie knew her behavior wasn't how normal people lived, but she hadn't lived a normal life. Tori was already sensing that. How long until something tipped her off? How long until Tori put two and two together?

Maybe she was being paranoid, but Julie didn't know another way to live. She had to protect herself. She had to leave Darling.

She searched her closet for a suitcase, withdrawing an ugly lime-green roller she'd bought on sale years ago when she moved to town. She flopped it on the ground and opened the lid. It wouldn't take long to pack a few things. The clock on the wall read 8:45 a.m. They had to be at the library by 9:30, because doors opened at 10:00.

She opened her dresser drawers, yanked out stacks of neatly folded pants, shirts, and underwear, and tossed everything in the suitcase.

She changed into work clothes—loose jeans and a sweater, an outfit that made her look invisible. She cracked her door open, maneuvered into the bathroom, and finished readying herself.

Julie walked back into the living room, looking around for anything embarrassing she might've left out.

But Tori was gone. Oscar sat on the couch cushion, his fur rumpled from where Tori had pet him. Julie checked the kitchen, her heart hammering.

She pictured Tori opening the spare bedroom door, mistaking it for the bathroom, and finding Aunt Susan on the bed.

It was the cancer, Julie would say. *She was already dying*.

She peered down the hallway, immediately noticing the room at the end of the hall. The light was on, the door halfway open. She didn't even realize the power was back on until now.

Julie slowly walked forward, making no sound on the carpet, passing the spare bedroom without stopping. The room at the end of the hall was her personal library, a room where she kept two large, overflowing bookcases, a reading chair, and a cat tower.

Tori stood by one of the bookcases, arms crossed. She stared at the books, which were all neatly organized by genre, then last name. Multiple books by the same author were arranged in chronological order of publication (though a series was grouped together, despite breaking the order). Not the standard way to shelve books, but she liked it that way—dozens of mini timelines that told the author's story as much as the characters' within.

"Hey Tori."

Tori startled, breaking her trance. "Oh hey. Sorry, I shouldn't have wandered around, I just saw Oscar come out of here, so I thought I'd check out your books." Tori shook her head, biting her bottom lip. "Your aunt's in the other room, right? The spare bedroom?"

"Yeah, why?"

"I don't know. It's dumb. When Oscar walked out of here, the room was all dark and stuff, and the door was open a little and . . . I could've sworn I saw someone in here."

Julie held her breath. "What do you mean?"

"Clearly, I'm going crazy," Tori said. "I thought I saw this shape bend down, like it was petting Oscar. But then it stood up and looked at me."

Julie shook her head, thinking of the shadow beneath the door.

"I thought it was your aunt, but obviously, my imagination *really* got the better of me. This is why I shouldn't fall asleep watching *Forensic Files*."

"Does that happen a lot?"

"Oh yeah." Tori laughed. She walked down the hallway, relaxing now that she'd put distance between herself and that room. "It's crazy disorienting, especially paired with wine, you know? There's nothing worse than waking up, drunk off my ass, and someone on the TV is crying about a dead husband or wife or whatever, and it cuts to their covered corpse, and it's all bloody. I should start watching nature docs instead. I'd much rather wake up to a cute sea turtle. Although with my luck, I'd wake up to a snake swallowing a little mouse or something."

Tori rambled on and Julie let her. Light returned to her eyes. Her smile widened with each new story. Julie fixed herself a lunch bag while Tori sat on a stool by the kitchen counter, explaining a new show about storm chasers.

". . . . now *that's* disorienting," Tori said. "Waking up, the volume's insanely high, and everyone's screaming about a record-breaking tornado, and I'm thinking a twister is about to drop on my head."

Julie smiled. She'd miss Tori. And if the pain of losing her only friend was starting now, she could only imagine the loss she'd feel tonight, when she said goodbye. Leaving was the right decision, but it would still hurt. Julie wasn't *completely* callused.

"Anyways," Tori sighed, the strange shape in the room forgotten. "You ready yet? It's nine-thirty. Nancy *knows* when we get there late."

"Yeah, let's go."

"Tell your aunt I really wanted to meet her this morning, and we'll have to reschedule."

Julie nodded stiffly, thinking of the packed green suitcase. "I will."

Leaving the house, Julie slid into the passenger seat of Tori's SUV. She stared at her home, at the thick curtains blocking the picture window, at the narrow space where the two curtains met in the middle. It had to be her imagination—a reaction to what Tori said earlier, but she could swear something stood in that small sliver of darkness, watching her leave.

Chapter 15

Eli threw the last full trash bag in the back of Greta's car. They jumped in the front seats, Greta twisting the keys she'd left in the ignition.

The engine sputtered to life.

Eli's clothes were soaked through to his skin. He rubbed his forehead with his sleeve, mopping up the sweat. He unzipped the jumpsuit down to his stomach, unpeeled the top half, and folded it behind him. The wind made his t-shirt ripple. It ran warm fingers along his overheated skin. Greta leaned her forehead against the steering wheel, fighting for air.

The clock read 9:29 a.m. They needed to go before someone showed up.

Bzzz.

They stared at each other. "Was that my phone?" he asked Greta. She felt her pocket, her bony fingers resting on his phone, and shook her head.

Bzzz.

The vibrations sounded like text messages. Greta and Eli looked back at the trunk, and Eli imagined Carly's and Owen's cell phones back there, stored in their pockets, vibrating against their cold, dead legs. Their parents, siblings, and friends—all texting, calling, leaving voicemails.

Where are you? Are you ignoring me? You're late. Text me back.

It was only a matter of time. Eventually, they would be considered missing. That meant an investigation.

Police.

Publicity.

Volunteers.

A small town unified by tragedy. But for Eli, the young couple were not missing. They were in the trunk, and he'd helped put them there. He closed his eyes and swallowed deep breaths to keep from throwing up.

They'd rolled the bodies onto tarps and dragged them, one at a time, down the hallway, through the Children's Room, and out the back door. Greta backed her car up to the door's threshold, and the bodies were then leveraged, poorly, into the trunk. Getting Owen off the ground required their combined strength and several failed attempts.

It took some maneuvering to get them in the trunk. Greta said something about *rigor mortis*, and how it wasn't done setting in. Eli didn't know what bodies experienced in the hours after death, and he wasn't sure he believed Greta knew what she was talking about, but the bodies were barely bendable, and their discolored skin felt *loose* like a rumpled bedsheet. He wished he didn't know what loose skin felt like.

After that, they cleaned the bathroom with paper towels, chemicals, sponges, and dumped it all in trash bags. They did what time allowed. The bathrooms were old, like the rest of the library, and had deep cracks in the tile around the walls and cabinets holding the sink. But they didn't have time to scrub every tiny crevice, so they cleaned the obvious parts. At no point did Greta falter. Not when she scrubbed the tile on her hands and knees, and not when she dragged the bodies down the hallway. She clearly didn't need Eli's help with so many chores around the house. She had more energy than Eli had seen in any adult in a long time.

After the initial shock, Eli didn't cry or vomit, which surprised him. He wouldn't be able to eat for a while, and if he sat alone and his thoughts took over, tears would come. But frantically cleaning to avoid getting caught had helped him focus. Now that he was back in the car, the wind making it sway like a boat on the ocean, his heart kept beating, one ugly, bloody convulsion at a time, and it somehow kept him sane.

Their hearts were cold. Their phones vibrated. Loved ones were looking. Gray-haired parents and naïve siblings and busy friends, all taking a moment to wonder if everything was all right. When everything came out (because it would soon), they'd turn their attention to Eli and ask why he agreed to help. Why he didn't fight.

He'd tell them he was sorry, and that for as long as he lived, he'd never forget the way Carly and Owen were positioned in the bathroom, the way their skin loosened when he touched it.

"Oh . . . no," Greta said, staring at the library.

Eli dragged himself from his thoughts—from the bloody pictures in his mind. "What?"

"We only checked the bathroom," she said, opening her car door.

It was 9:31 a.m.

"What are you doing?"

"They were in the office," Greta slammed her door shut. "I followed them last night, they went to the office first."

"So?"

"So we didn't check! What if they left something?"

Eli opened his car door.

"No, no, stay here." She paused, pointing a finger. "There's room in the trunk, Eli. For you and for Lucas. Do not move from that seat."

Greta glanced at Main Street and hurried through the Children's Room door.

Eli shut the car door and folded his hands together in his lap and tried not to picture Lucas in the trunk. From his position, he could see the whole parking lot and the library's two main entrances. After moving the bodies to the trunk, they had parked Greta's car in the back corner of the parking lot, hoping no one would notice or care it was there.

A white SUV pulled in and parked in the opposite corner. Eli slid down until his knees hit the car floor and he twisted around so his head rested on the passenger seat. Slowly sitting up, he glanced through the window.

Two librarians, Tori and Julie, left the SUV. They grappled with the wind, struggling to walk straight. Julie glanced over at Greta's car, and Eli shrank back down, his mind reeling.

What if she came over? Greta only ever went to the library after dinner, before closing. She never showed up this early, and Julie would know that.

She's walking this way, Eli thought. *She's going to find me.*

He wanted to run out there and tell them what was going on. Julie would believe him, right? He could show her the trunk . . . she'd have to believe him. It was all Greta—he never wanted to help her hide the bodies. Julie was on his side. Of course she'd know he never wanted this to happen.

He lifted his head, but the ladies were gone. The library's front doors shut, sealing Tori and Julie inside with Greta.

Chapter 16

Julie entered the library first, holding the door for Tori.

"Thank you, ma'am." Tori dropped her phone on the front counter and turned the computers on. "Woah, you smell that?"

"Smell what?"

"*That.*"

Julie walked through the foyer, inhaling. "Bleach?"

"I think so. It stinks."

Julie looked at the windows in the foyer. They were tall, at least fifty years old, and not built to open. The maple tree outside danced in the wind, its branches tapping on the glass. Behind that, a small car was parked in the back corner of the parking lot, and it looked like the one Greta Shaw drove, which didn't make sense. She left last night. Julie remembered seeing her drive away in the pouring rain, and hoping Greta had made it home okay.

Julie stepped away from the windows. "I can try and prop the front door open, but the wind won't make that easy."

Tori waved a hand. "Gary must've spilled something when he cleaned last night. It'll go away soon enough."

Julie wasn't sure she believed that. Gary had cleaned the library every weeknight since the pandemic, and it never smelled the next morning.

Julie also set her phone on the front counter and hunted for the source of the smell. She maneuvered through small bookshelves promoting the newest and hottest books. Seven-day loans, no renewals. She straightened a few spines, re-shelved a book that was out of alphabetical order, and found no sign of spilled chemicals.

When she checked the hallway, the bleach grew stronger. On the left side, two single-person bathrooms were side by side. Both doors were open. Both would've been cleaned last night.

The bathrooms were empty and spotless, but the bleach came from the one on the right. Gary likely spilled something. No other explanation made sense. Julie wasn't closing tonight but would ask when she saw him next.

Then she remembered she wouldn't see Gary again. Today was it. Her last day.

Aunt Susan was back at home, still dead, waiting to be picked up. Julie needed to call someone. She didn't have to be there when they collected her. She *couldn't* be there. She—

"Hey Julie?"

Julie left the bathrooms and walked back through the foyer. Tori stood in the doorway to the office, befuddled.

"Are you quitting?"

Julie tried to keep her face straight. "What?"

"Your calendar."

Inside the office, Tori pointed at Julie's desk. Sure enough, someone left a message scribbled on today's date: Wednesday, July 31, 2024.

I quit!

"What the hell?" Tori said. "You did *not* write that."

It could've been a prank. The librarians had seen their fair share of humanity over the years. Overdoses, hook ups, graffiti, drug deals, affairs, everyone in Darling ended up at the library eventually, bringing their messy lives with them. And in the summer and long winter months, kids were often rowdy, young, and restless. Two teen boys once poured cement mix in their toilets. *Hilarious.* Stuff like that wasn't uncommon.

But it was especially bold, and stupid, to write a note inside the office, and Julie had no clue how someone could've done it without anyone noticing.

"The handwriting's terrible," Tori said.

They had security cameras, but only their boss, Chris, knew how to request the stored footage, and it wasn't worth all that work for something so minor.

"I'm glad you're not actually quitting." Tori laughed. "I'd be so depressed. *Who* would I talk to?"

Julie was trying to think of a joke or a way to change the conversation when she noticed something on the floor beside her desk, reflecting the fluorescent lights overhead. A cell phone.

Julie picked it up, instantly recognizing the polka-dot case. She didn't need the lock-screen picture to verify the phone's owner. She'd seen this case a thousand times, always in the tight grip of bright pink manicured nails.

The phone belonged to Carly Waters.

Chapter 17

Voices drifted down the hallway. Two librarians were inside: Julie and Tori. Both wonderful ladies who, over the last year, had assisted Greta in every way imaginable. Most weeknights, Greta would go to the library after supper, sit in the Reference Room, and read encyclopedias about the 1990s. Either Julie or Tori would help her sit, find the right book, and pick up where she left off. Because bless their hearts, they knew all about the accident and her memory troubles. She never checked out the encyclopedias. Without Clive, reading at home had become a lonely task. She preferred the library, where the librarians were personable and the atmosphere friendly. Besides, the library was their last stop before the accident, and now Greta could hardly feel Clive's presence without it.

Greta hid in the Non-Fiction room, debating on whether to move closer or stay put. There weren't many places to hide.

She peered down the hallway. All clear on both sides. If she wanted to get out, now was the time. She'd already double-checked the Children's Room, the bathrooms, and Non-Fiction. Nothing had been left behind. Sadly, the librarians came inside before she made it to the office, and the young couple were in the office last night. Fighting or screwing each other (it was hard to tell). Greta hadn't planned on killing last night. After Eli ran off, she went for a drive, barefoot, in her robe, with the knife sliding across the passenger seat. And what if she'd been pulled over? Poor, injured Greta

Shaw, wandering the town again. It wouldn't even make a good story for the officer, he or she would've just felt bad and taken her home.

But she didn't run into trouble. If anything, Darling protected her. It gave her two isolated, intoxicated young people. She saw them on the road and followed them into the library, waiting for *something* to stop her, but nothing tried. And how good it felt to move through life with unhindered confidence.

It was shockingly easy, following the pretty brunette into the bathroom, dragging the knife from one side of the girl's neck to the other (only realizing after it was done that the girl was the library's intern). Greta had never felt more alive, and now she knew: procedural memory was real. Last night was not the first time she had killed someone. There were others, she just couldn't remember them yet. So far, she only recalled the young man in the suit. More would come, very soon.

Until then, Greta couldn't hide in Non-Fiction forever. One of the librarians, Julie, had noticed the bleach smell. Greta heard her snooping around the bathrooms, sniffing for the source. Luckily, Julie wouldn't do anything about it. She wouldn't think twice. Ordinary people were excellent rationalizers. That was what made them ordinary.

With the librarians working, Greta had limited options. She would hope for the best and pray the young couple had left nothing behind, and the bathrooms wouldn't give anything away. Sure, all that blood would be easy to find, if someone looked for it. But would anyone have a reason to look?

She considered leaving, but curiosity pinched her. The girls were talking about *something*.

Greta turned right out of Non-Fiction, followed the hallway, and knelt behind the DVD shelves. Her body protested. It had been through plenty already, with all the cleaning and heavy lifting. Still, she ignored it. She strained her ears, the ticking in her chest as loud as a time bomb.

". . . I don't know," one of them said. "She works today, right?"

Tori emerged from the office, holding something. "Yeah, she's here at eleven, same as Nancy. I'm sure she'll be looking for it."

Tori turned, holding a cell phone. Behind the front counter, she opened a drawer and placed the phone inside, pushing the drawer closed with her hip.

If Greta correctly understood their conversation, then that phone belonged to the young woman, the intern. It would have missed calls. Texts. Voicemails. The librarians would get suspicious when she didn't show up for work, not even to grab her phone. Young people were obsessed with their phones. An investigation could materialize faster than Greta liked. Her work wasn't over yet, not until she remembered why she moved to Darling.

Greta stayed behind the DVDs shelf and waited for the librarians to give her an opening. Julie left the office and entered the Computer Room. Tori busied herself at the front counter, scrolling on the computer.

Getting that cell phone wasn't an option. Neither was staying put. Greta only ever came to the library in the evenings, and they knew her routine, and would find it odd if she showed up as the library opened. Greta needed to prioritize. Avoiding odd behavior, which people would remember, was near the top of her AVOID list. If she wanted to steal that phone, she'd have to come back. The librarians wouldn't suspect anything. Not yet.

But they will soon, a voice whispered to her. Yes, they would very soon.

Greta waited for Tori to turn her back. Although sneaking around the library could not compare to last night's hunt, it gave her a similar, intoxicating rush.

Julie yelled something about more paper. Tori checked a cabinet and said they needed to pull more from the closet in the hallway.

Tori turned, setting a book on the Holds shelf, and Greta jumped to her feet. Her knees popped and exploded with pain. She ignored them and focused on making it to the Children's Room, but Julie's voice echoed right behind her. The supply closet was in the hallway, close to the bathrooms. She couldn't make it down the hallway in time. Greta cut to her left, dipping back into Non-Fiction. She scrambled behind a shelf and crouched as Julie passed the doorway and opened the closet.

Tick, tick, tick.

Greta pressed a palm against her heart, feeling the thick ridge of her scar. Her heart struggled to keep up. She stretched out flat on the carpet, controlling her breathing, her body sighing with relief. Outside, she heard voices.

Kids. Boys.

Something was happening. Now she wished she'd driven away when she had the chance. She *did* leave a twelve-year-old boy alone, in charge of a car with bodies in the trunk.

Greta looked at the shelves around her, wishing Julie would hurry up. A book caught her eye. She crawled over to it, plucked it off the shelf and smiled to herself.

It was *exactly* what she needed.

The supply closet slammed shut, and Julie sauntered past, her shoes swishing on the carpet.

Greta hugged the book to her chest and slowly stood up.

Eli was going to *love* this.

She waited until Julie left the hallway before making her move. Head down, she rushed from Non-Fiction. The Young Adult tables on either side made it impossible to walk discreetly. Forced to walk in the dead-center, she reached the other end quickly.

"Greta?"

She stopped in her tracks and pivoted, unable to hide the guilt on her face.

Julie stood at the other end of the hallway, holding two reams of paper in her arms. She squinted at Greta, not believing her eyes. "Wow, you're here super early." She walked forward, shaking her head like this was all a pleasant surprise.

Greta didn't move, but her muscles tensed. No matter what, she had to appear normal. Poor, forgetful Greta.

"What are you doing out and about so early?" Julie asked. "You know, I thought that looked like your car in the parking lot! I was starting to worry you didn't go home last night."

Greta nodded, finding a smile. She stank of sweat and death and hoped Julie didn't step too close. Luckily, the bleach masked everything. From the blood under Greta's fingernails to the blood in the cracked tile.

"I made it home," Greta said, slowing her voice down. "But *what* a storm that was."

"I know." Julie frowned. "I'm glad you're all right. Anyways, I should get back to it." She paused, her slow brain finally working. "How'd you get in?"

Greta shifted, clutching the book with both hands. "The back door was open. I'm sorry, are you closed?"

"We open at ten." Julie trailed off. "The door was unlocked?"

"It opened for me." Greta smiled, hoping it looked real enough. "I don't know, I thought you were open earlier than this. I'm so sorry."

"No, it's okay!" Julie's puzzlement grew. "It's totally fine. I'll let you go, don't worry about a thing. Tori and I are just setting up. It's really not a problem, okay?"

"Thank you," Greta said, turning away.

"You like true crime?"

Greta rotated the book in her hands, running her palm over the smooth cover. *Famous Serial Killers*, the title declared. She looked back at Julie. "I love a good story. Usually the best ones are true."

Julie didn't respond. She looked uncomfortable. "Okay, well if you need anything at all, you know where to find us. And seriously, don't worry about being here early. I was just surprised the door was unlocked." Now it was Julie's turn to fake smile. "I'll talk to you later."

Greta said goodbye and hurried away, wondering what Julie suspected. Even if Julie believed something strange was at work, would she ever consider Greta was involved? No, never. Because old ladies like Greta were invisible. And while sometimes that hurt a little, today it was just fine.

Greta didn't have time to mull over what the librarians might or might not infer. She had bodies to bury and reading to do, because if her hunch proved right, she was no ordinary murderer. With Clive's help, she might've killed dozens of people, earning them a spot somewhere in a book of famous killers.

It was time to find out just who Greta Shaw used to be.

Chapter 18

After Julie and Tori disappeared inside the library, before Eli even had a chance to consider running home, two familiar faces came walking down the street behind the library.

Chase Thomas and Tyler Dunlop.

Eli touched the green stitching along his shoulder, hoping the guys weren't looking for him. After all, they spent a lot of time roaming downtown Darling for no reason, like animals in need of entertainment.

During the summer, Chase Thomas never wore a shirt. He had a ridiculous amount of peach fuzz and chest hair for a fourteen-year-old. His shoulders and arms were thick with muscle. He looked like a boxer. Wherever he went, he strutted, his chest swollen, his abs visible, and his hands were always clenched like he was dying to sock somebody in the face. Even the seniors left him alone. People avoided him, and he liked that.

Tyler Dunlop was the anti-Chase. Smart, tall, lanky. He had more acne than the whole freshman class combined. His eyes were sunken orbs, his lips puffy and cracked. His greasy hair often hung just above his eyebrows. Today, he wore a tank top with graphics of stacks of cash. His gym shorts were weighed down by the knife he always carried and the phone he filmed Eli with. If Darling regularly produced a breed of troubled youths, these guys were the mascots. Their families were broken and strung out, their houses shabby and cluttered. Part of Eli felt bad for them. He knew he came from a good loving family, and many kids in Darling weren't so lucky.

He slouched in his seat, but it was too late. The boys stood on the edge of the parking lot and locked eyes with him. They thought they could come to the library early and wait for him—here at the only place outside of home where he felt safe.

The guys entered the parking lot. Chase stuck his thumbs through his jean beltloops, his naked chest defined and tan, his underwear bunched above his waistline. Tyler had his phone out and kept twitching and blinking in a way that reminded Eli of a chicken. Dust skirted the blacktop, but the guys didn't even flinch. The wind didn't bother them.

Eli slouched a little more but kept eye contact. The windows were down. They could pull him out and beat him senseless if they felt like it. The way Chase stood there, a beatdown wasn't far-fetched.

"Looks like your mommy fixed your costume," Chase said, keeping his voice measured, careful not to draw out the librarians like he did yesterday. Tyler smirked, lifting his phone's camera. That little black eye gleefully watching.

Eli wished Julie would show up with a baseball bat and crack skulls like she did in the stories he made up about her, but he couldn't count on her again. He didn't want a repeat of yesterday.

"I'm sick to death of that costume." Chase turned to Tyler and shook his head. Tyler understood. He put his phone back in his pocket.

They're going to kill me, Eli thought. *They don't want it on camera*.

"I thought I told you I didn't want to see it again." Chase ambled over to the flower bed and squatted beside it, taking his time, and that reminded Eli of something.

Eli tried turning the keys, but the car was already running.

Chase shook his head and picked up a small granite stone out of the mulch.

"I hope that's not your mommy's car," he said. "She won't be happy."

It was the dodgeball tournament back in April. Chase had squatted just as he did now, the red dodgeball tucked inside his arms while he surveyed the killing fields. That was moments before Eli hit him with the ball that ended the game. It sent the town's small audience into a ruckus. Chase, dumbfounded, watched as the other team swarmed Eli with back-slapping congratulations. Darling's Annual Dodgeball Tournament. And Chase blew it because of his cocky squatting and holding the ball instead of throwing it. That cost him the game, and a small sliver of his reputation. He didn't throw when he had the chance.

"Chase, this is my neighbor's car. She'll be out here any minute!"

Chase turned the small rock, frowning. "Then get out of the car, dumbass."

No, this wasn't going to be like yesterday at all. Eli refused to walk inside that library again, defeated and crying and hurt. He pulled his legs up and slid over to the driver's seat. He shifted the driveshaft from park to drive but held the brakes steady.

"What are you doing?" Chase dropped the small rock and picked up a stone the size of a brick. The short stone wall around the flowers now looked like it had a missing tooth.

Last summer, Eli's dad took him to a big empty strip mall parking lot. The strip mall once housed a creepy bookstore, a bakery with burnt muffins, and a pricy antique store. Surprise, surprise, the bakery burnt one too many muffins and caught fire. And the fire ruined the whole strip mall, and the businesses moved out. Dad and Eli swapped seats in Dad's little car, and Dad said there was nothing to it. Turn the wheel, know where the gas and brake pedals are. Dad said empty parking lots were the best for practice. You couldn't hit anything.

Now, Eli clutched the wheel, hands slippery with sweat. Chase lifted the rock higher, licking his lips.

Eli set his shoe against the gas. The car thrummed beneath him like a living thing and began rolling forward. He didn't look at Tyler, or the front doors, or the road to see if anyone was pulling in. His vision narrowed. His heart roared inside his ears. His body pulsed with electricity, and when Chase cocked his arm back for a game-winning throw, Eli slammed the gas pedal to the floor.

When Greta's car lurched toward them, the arrogance dropped from their faces. Chase backpedaled, colliding with the library, his head bouncing off the red bricks. The parking lot didn't have wheel stops in the parking spaces, so Eli ran the car off the asphalt, through the grass, and toward the building. He hit the brakes as Chase and Tyler dove out of the way, the car's nose only inches from hitting the library. He switched to reverse and floored the pedal again. The car jerked back into the lot, tearing up grass.

Chase jumped to his feet and picked up the rock again. He threw his arm back and launched it.

Eli lost sight of the rock. He slammed the brakes, bringing the car to a sharp halt as the air exploded with a loud *crack*. The windshield splintered, webbing out, stemming from where the rock had landed and bounced off.

Tyler jumped up and down, cheering under his breath.

Eli parked the car, threw open the door, and stumbled out, knocking glass from his jumpsuit. He doubled over and spit repeatedly, until he was positive no shards were in his mouth.

"What did you *do*?" Greta approached her car, looking old and weary again. She held a library book in one hand and promptly tossed it through the open window and into the back seat. Her eyes darted between Eli, her car, and the two guys.

"Who are you?" Greta asked them.

They backed up, edging away from the lot.

"I asked you a *question*," Greta said, her lips curling. "Answer me!"

The guys turned and ran. Eli put his hands on his knees, sighing with relief. A slightly heavier rock would've gone through the windshield and smashed his face in, making Greta's car the proud owner of three dead bodies. At least the guys were gone now.

Eli looked to his right, but Greta was no longer in the parking lot. It took him a second to find her—in the grass ahead, running after the guys, screaming, "Come on Eli! Hurry! Let's *get them*!"

Eli took off after her. He'd never chased anyone like this before, and watching the guys run away made him smile a little. He *wanted* to catch them. He *wanted* Greta to hurt them.

"Don't you ever touch my car again, you little pricks!" Greta stopped on the sidewalk, chest heaving. She bent over and gave a hoarse cough.

Eli slowed down beside her. Chase and Tyler were three blocks away, just now turning around and allowing themselves to breathe again.

"Old bitch!" Tyler shouted, flipping them off.

Chase stared at Eli, sending a silent message: Eli was dead to him. It would be only a matter of time before Chase tried again, but with something bolder, something stronger than a garden rock.

Greta coughed a few more times and broke into deep, infectious laughter.

"Did you see their faces?" She wiped her eyes. "Oh, boy. I needed that. That felt good. I haven't run like that in years. Sign me up for the one hundred meters next Olympics."

Eli smiled. "I've never seen them look scared before."

"I mean, what were we going to do when we caught them?" Hands on her hips, Greta's eyes glistened with happiness. "What would we do? Beat them up?"

Eli shrugged. "Maybe you could. I wouldn't be much help."

"Nonsense." Greta started walking back to the library. "You're fast. And you look skinny, but I've seen you carry heavy stacks of wood. You're stronger than you think." She paused. "You're stronger than *they* think. Remember that."

Eli stared at the grass. "I don't think so."

"Why not?" Greta stopped. "Why do you wear this jumpsuit? You know who else wears jumpsuits? People who jump out of planes. They're strong. Not because they can beat someone up or throw rocks. But because they can do things people are too scared to do. Strength comes from the mind and the heart. Not muscle."

Eli stared at the library, thinking of all the times he'd run inside it, and how today was a little different. Past Eli would've only dreamt of doing what he did today.

Their walk back to the car was weirdly comfortable.

"You driving?" Greta grinned. "Now that I know you can drive, you'll be chauffeuring me from now on."

Eli shook his head. "No way, look what happened to your car."

"Suit yourself." Greta laughed, shaking her head. "It's not your fault, Eli. I almost wish you'd cut that boy in half against the library wall."

"You saw that?"

"You betcha. We could've tossed both halves of him in the trunk and been on the road before he knew what hit him."

She sat in the driver's seat, grabbed her purse, and slapped the windshield, punching a little hole from where the rock had hit.

"I can see perfectly through this. Which reminds me, one time, Clive and I were driving down the highway going west, right? Years ago. Some vacation in Wyoming we had planned. And we were driving along. And the speed limit out there is very fast, so we were going faster."

Greta closed her eyes. "And we were driving behind this dump truck, which was also going fast. And out of nowhere, this rock comes flying through the windshield. I mean, all the way through. The windshield shattered right in front of me, glass flying and everything. Just madness.

THE DARLING KILLER

Clive slammed the brakes and the car almost spun out. We were moving fast enough. One mistake and our car would've flipped and rolled thirty times."

Eli knew one thing about Greta: she always survived. He wondered how long she'd walk this Earth, out-surviving everyone else.

Greta pulled out of the library parking lot. "Hey, if the cops pull us over for the windshield, don't think about the trunk, okay?"

The trunk, the bodies, his batshit neighbor. It all came back after a brief intermission. They still had work to do.

As they drove, she told him about the librarians finding the phone. How they'd need to go get it at some point. Would Carly's phone unravel the whole thing? Surely someone would wonder why she hadn't come back for it. Eli prayed that was the case.

If Julie was anything like the woman from his stories, she'd figure it out. Sadly, those stories weren't real. But then Eli looked at Greta and remembered every ridiculous thing he'd made up about her, and thought, *not all stories are fiction*.

They left downtown and drove deeper into Darling's neighborhoods. Eli realized where she was headed when she turned left at a four-way stop. They were going to the Darling Cemetery.

Chapter 19

Julie turned over the "Open" sign, mulling over Greta's strange appearance. The poor woman didn't know where she was. Everyone at the library knew to keep an eye on her, but she was still independent. Still thoughtful and kind and a little eccentric. Her conditions had worsened as the year progressed, and everyone felt a little responsible for her. After all, she came to the library every night and read encyclopedias, and no one, not even Carly, made fun of her for it. Because it was heart-breaking to watch. Greta's last night with Clive had been at the Darling Library, and she'd spent the entire last year trying to get back the life she lost.

And true crime? What was that about? Greta exclusively read about the 1990s. Maybe she read something last night that sent her down a true crime rabbit trail. Either way, Greta's behavior bothered her, but the unlocked back door bothered her more. She *remembered* locking that door last night.

Now, Gary, the custodian, had keys. He might've unlocked it and forgotten to lock it up, but Julie couldn't waste time thinking about that or the spilled bleach any longer. She had to work. And forget.

Tori manned the front counter while Julie collected holds. Patrons drifted in. Today would be busy, especially if Darling's outskirts were still without power. People would need computers and Wi-Fi access. The library had probably lost power sometime last night, but not for very long (a perk of working downtown with the fire station and sheriff's office three blocks over).

Julie tried to busy herself. She restocked and reorganized. She did her best to stay ahead of the thoughts and memories following her.

Every time she saw Tori behind the counter, Tori grinned like a child, then would partially pull up her long sleeves, exposing her tattooed arms. Julie always laughed at that, especially when Nancy worked nearby, oblivious to Tori's *scandalous* past as a tattoo artist.

And Julie was going to walk away from it. From Tori. From the Darling Library. Maybe she'd return one day, her identity safe and sound, with fresh emotional distance from Tori, but what if that wasn't enough? What if Tori uncovered the truth somehow? Julie hadn't Googled her real name in years. She knew the results. She used to scroll through articles dedicated to her and her mom, all asking the same question:

Where is Maddie Burkes now?

Julie rarely thought of her real name. Her name was Julie, not Maddie. Maddie Burkes disappeared years ago. If only the memories had vanished with her.

Her mother lay on the carpet, blood dribbling down her chin. "Maddie."

"Julie."

Julie turned at the sound of her name.

Nancy's homemade bracelets rattled up and down her skinny arms. Everyone in Darling knew about her bracelets. They were a staple of the library itself. Nancy even gave them out as Christmas presents. Julie had a few of them stuffed in a drawer somewhere.

Nancy ushered Julie into the DVDs corner, swiping a stray lock of white hair from her forehead.

"Did Carly quit?"

"I don't know."

"I saw the note."

"I know, and she's supposed to be here by now."

Nancy frowned. "Did you say something to her?"

"No, why would I?"

"She wrote that note on *your* calendar."

"I don't know, we don't know it was her."

"Her phone was by your desk. Tori told me."

Julie didn't care whether Carly had quit or not. Nancy held a soft spot for the young girl, although Julie couldn't understand why. Carly never pulled her weight, and Nancy didn't let *anyone* slack off.

"She's not here, and it's . . . ten after eleven. She's never late." Nancy folded her arms. "Are you sure you didn't say anything?"

"Maybe she just quit," Julie huffed. "I honestly don't know. Interns quit all the time because this job isn't what they expect. And to be honest, she didn't try very hard."

Nancy opened her mouth, then closed it. Keeping her comment to herself.

"She'll at least come back for her phone," Julie said. "Ask her then if she wrote the message, and why she couldn't give two weeks like a normal adult."

Nancy rolled her eyes and walked away, still biting her tongue, which made Julie feel childish. She expected a quip, a passive jab, *something*.

A line had formed at the front counter because Julie's hunch had been right: they were busy, people needed internet, they needed entertainment. Tori flashed her *the look*, the *get your butt over here* look. Julie signed into the second computer and together they slowly worked through the line until Tori handed a receipt to the last patron.

Julie had thought the work would be enough. She'd thought it would numb the reality of leaving Aunt Susan back home, but it didn't. It made her feel like a monster—pretending to go through the motions with a dead relative in her spare bed.

"What's wrong, Jules?"

Julie shook her head, wanting to curl up in a ball and disappear. "Nothing."

"Did something happen?"

Julie almost said it: *my aunt died*. But the words caught in her throat. She had to get away from Tori, not move closer. The more she distanced herself, the easier it would be to say goodbye. She loved this little old library, but nothing—

Glass exploded in the foyer. A long, thin branch broke through one of the tall windows. The maple tree outside groaned and whipped back, and the branch snapped in half, part of it falling inside the library. It had left a baseball-sized hole in the glass, and Julie instantly felt the wind washing over her.

The patrons in the foyer waited for something else to happen. Julie expected the whole window to cave in. Cracks spiraled a few feet from the hole, but the window held, despite the strong wind whistling through it. Patrons muttered and laughed. They started conversations amongst themselves, commenting on the storm and the effects of the hurricane. The room returned to normal.

Julie picked up a dustpan and broom and swept up the fallen shards and the broken branch. She glanced at the jagged gap in the window. The wind brushed her hair back with warm hands wrapping around her head and sliding down her neck. She felt a gentle squeeze on her throat and her eyes watered.

The wind was *there*, last night. When Julie blacked out and woke up to the open windows and Aunt Susan's lifeless body. Something had entered her house after all, something able to slip through screens.

I know what you did, the wind whispered to her.

The broken window darkened as a shadow fell over it. There was nothing around her to cast it. The shadow didn't move. It loomed above her, watching, taking the shape of a man hunched over.

Something about it made her think of the night her mom died.

The night came to life with blinding clarity. Her mom had made mac and cheese for dinner, and Julie ate it in front of the television, watching cartoons. Her mom dressed in tight jeans and a low-cut blouse. Her going-out clothes. Open-toed shoes with pink nails. Blond hair curled to perfection, makeup in place, not too much, but not too little. *A delicate balance*, her mom used to say when painting makeup on Julie's face with old brushes.

Before her mom left, she kissed Julie's head, reminding her of the rules:

Clean the house.

Do the dishes.

Take every toy into your bedroom.

And don't come out, no matter what.

It was only years later, during Julie's blurry teenage years, when she realized her mom hadn't been ashamed of her. Her mom needed company, and having a nine-year-old at home discouraged some people. Other times, her mom didn't come home until the middle of the night. Or, her mom returned early and alone, and would knock on Julie's door softly and cuddle in bed with her, smelling of alcohol and cigarettes and perfume.

When her mom left that night, it was like any other Friday night. She recited the rules, kissed Julie's head, and said, *I love you*. And what beautiful last words those were; far better than her mom's final breath, saying Julie's real name with a look of utter confusion and sorrow.

Julie jerked back, tripping over herself. She dropped the dustpan and tried to catch it, slicing her palm on the glass. The shards fell at her feet. Everyone gave her pitiful glances and started to rush over, and Julie knew she couldn't do this. She had tried and failed. She never should've come to work, or lied to Tori, or pretended everything was okay.

Because the shadow was *looking* at her now, even though it didn't have eyes.

She had to leave Darling. And she had to leave now.

Chapter 20

They drove to the edge of Darling, to a hill overlooking the town. Darling Cemetery waited at the top, it's rows of headstones like a crown. In the middle of it all was a gazebo with picnic tables inside, and a green pointed roof that someone had spray painted *bad day* on. Greta drove on a small road cutting through the cemetery, slowly pulling up to a spot she knew. A spot she remembered.

Greta left the car without a word and wandered through the gravesites. Eli followed her. Up on the hill, the wind was at its peak. It dug its warm fingers into every inch of him—tugging, scraping, pushing. It whistled in his ears. It shook the trees down to their roots. He held his jumpsuit, pulling it tight to keep it from rippling.

The clouds ran above them. He even noticed the weird pattern from earlier. Except the current in the sky was different from his new vantage point. It was wider and funneling toward town.

Up ahead, Greta stood beside a gravesite, arms dangling at her sides. Eli kept his distance. He didn't need to see Clive's grave, nor did he want to disturb her moment of silence. She just stood there, an outline against a churning gray sky. She stood as still as Clive's gravestone. They seemed to be equals, the stone and her. Two pillars almost touching through the membrane that separated them. Each determined to outlive the other. Around them, the grass heaved in waves, like rapid breaths. The trees twisted and groaned. Dead flowers skipped between gravestones.

Eli turned in a circle as everything obeyed the wind's commands. Hawthorn trees were scattered through the cemetery. White flower petals flowed from the trees and blew past him, tickling his cheeks. More sailed by, crashing into his jumpsuit before slipping away after the others. The air above him was full of white petals. More appeared—dozens and dozens—filling the air like snow in the summer. The entire hill was a dandelion, its little white parachutes forced into the sky, blown by the hurricane winds.

He wanted to say something to Greta about it, but she was on her knees, sobbing. Her cries barely rose above the wind, as if the wind ate her voice as it left her lips. She rocked back and forth, comforted by invisible arms. Her cheeks glistened with tears. Her mouth opened and shut, half screaming, half weeping.

Did she remember it all? Did she remember every time Clive kissed her? Every time they held each other close? All their adventures. All their shared memories, forever in her mind, as vivid as graffiti on walls.

Eli tried to imagine what it felt like to lose someone after a lifetime together. And to forget it for a while and have it come crashing back in one suffocating memory overdose. He couldn't feel it. He hadn't lived long enough, and he knew that. He didn't mind being young. From his perspective, growing up wasn't all they cracked it up to be.

He shuffled through the grass to Greta's side. She didn't acknowledge him. Hunched over, planting her hands in the grass, she stared down. He patted her shoulder, hoping he wasn't overstepping. Greta reached up and put her hand over his, sniffling.

She touched the headstone. Felt it's realness on her fingertips. It's finality. Was she telling Eli she was okay? Or the ghost of Clive? Something brushed his shoulder and Eli looked behind him to see nothing there. Just the wind and the white petals.

Greta dropped Eli's hand and stood up, wiping her face with her arm. After a long gaze, she left the grave and followed the path toward the car, brushing aside wild strands of hair. She moved with more resolve, reminded of her mission. They came to Darling for a reason. She had started something with Clive a year ago, and Eli knew she was going to see it through.

Chapter 21

Greta hadn't taken a country drive since the accident. With the windows down, the wind spilled into her ears, whispering how proud it was of her. Greta didn't remember when the wind began using words. Only hours ago. The words dripped into her skull, like a slow fusion, transferring wind into the soft matter of her brain.

Poor Eli hated the wind. He squinted at it, not bothering to fix his tussled hair anymore. He looked like a mad scientist. So did she, for that matter. A couple of mad scientists on the run.

The drive wasn't long because Darling was small, and you reached the lonely countryside minutes after leaving Main Street. Broken pavement bled out into country roads, where acres and acres of trails, parks, and scenic routes were buried in honeysuckle and mosquitoes. The week Clive and Greta moved to Darling they hiked a few trails. Greta had those memories now, but she needed specifics.

She turned the car around several times, retreading the same roads, searching for the perfect place to stop. Between Eli and herself, the physical strength of their team was lacking. Dragging the young man and woman through the woods? Unrealistic. Greta didn't have all day to hide their bodies. Leaving Darling was by far the safest solution to the mess she'd created for herself. The only thing stopping her was the unanswered question she kept asking:

Why did we move to Darling?

Frustrated, Greta pulled the car over and closed her eyes. She felt Eli watching her, but he didn't question it. She ran through the haunted house in her mind, through the painted walls and exhibits she'd already seen. More memories had appeared. Farther in, the walls were wet and dripping with fresh paint. The depicted scenes were sloppy and hastily done. The memories were returning faster than her mind knew how to process.

She found a new exhibit, another memory given to her. Her heart fluttered. Deep down, she'd known there would be more bodies.

The scene played out with fresh actors. Young Greta cradled a man's head in her lap. Not the man in the suit. This was another man. Brushing his hair, running her thumb over his pale cheeks and lips, Young Greta kissed his head as he labored over his final breaths. There was something sacred about comforting dying people. Clive had his own reasons for watching them bleed. Greta just wanted to hold them when their hearts stopped. She wanted to hand them over into the afterlife. It was only later, after they'd collected a few bodies, that Clive taught her how to use the knife. After that, they traded off. Whoever was in the mood wielded the knife. Clive enjoyed watching her cut into flesh. It thrilled him, and she loved the way he looked at her when she did it. It felt like a drug.

Greta moved on from the exhibit. She ran through the haunted house—the house always directing her back to those three doors. She opened the door marked *Clive* and walked through. There she found the memories of the park. The trails they walked. The woods they lost themselves in.

Greta opened her eyes and resumed driving. She took the next street and drove for several minutes, coming upon a small park. She turned into it, taking a paved road about half a mile into the woods. A small parking lot appeared. Empty. She stopped the car and scanned the trees. Several trails branched off into the wilderness. Old picnic tables littered the flat grassy areas. Garbage skated along the ground as trash bags whipped around in their metal containers. A small playground stood off to the side—the swings moving as if used by invisible children.

"This is it. It's quiet." She drove off the lot and up a small grassy hill. Eyeing the land through the hole in her windshield, she pushed the gas, taking the car farther off road.

"There's a wide trail up ahead," she told Eli. "Wide enough to drive through. It'll take us away from this parking lot."

She drove through the field, past the picnic tables and trail signs. Up ahead, the trail widened. Sticks scraped the car's underbelly. The car wasn't meant for offroad use, so they bounced in their seats like pioneers in a wagon. Greta smiled. She liked that. They would survive a desolate trip like that.

Eli stared out the window, somber and quiet as always. Always using those inquisitive eyes and powerful imagination. She kept wanting to ask him how he was doing, as if he would answer her truthfully. Maybe that was an excuse not to ask at all. She was hard on him, she knew that. And yet he carried her burdens with astonishing resilience. Asking how he was doing could harm him. Force him to face his emotions.

They drove in silence. She took it slow, bringing the car down to a crawl until the perfect spot appeared. When it did, she stopped the car. The trail was littered with dead branches and leaves. Nothing but forest around them. Undeveloped, wild, lonely.

"C'mon." Greta moved out of her seat, holding the car door to keep from getting blown over.

Eli stood outside. The wind forced his hair in new directions. "What are we doing?" he asked. His voice was tense. Had it been like that all day? She knew he was living through things kids his age shouldn't live through. And it hurt a little to see the conflict in his face. The slow bloodletting of his innocence. But then, Greta remembered the bullies from earlier. The rock-throwing bullies. Eli wasn't as unprepared to handle bloody messes as he pretended to be.

"We're going to bury them," she said. No sense in sugar coating it. Eli had already gone through the worst of it. Burying them should be a piece of cake compared to cleaning their innards off a public toilet seat.

Eli grabbed two shovels while Greta surveyed the woods. "Let's find a spot," Greta said. They left the trail and wandered for a minute. Once they found a clearing, Eli struck the shovels in the dirt, and they went back for the bodies.

The girl was easiest. They pulled her from the trunk and dumped her onto an open tarp. Each taking a corner, they dragged her into the woods.

"I grew up in the country," Greta said, readjusting her grip on the tarp. "We had a big yard. And every fall the giant maple leaves would come down and cover everything. Big, beautiful leaves, all red and orange.

"Anyways, so we'd rake up the leaves every fall. And we'd make it fun, and have hot chocolate, and snacks, and maybe have a friend over. Not sure why a friend would want to help rake leaves, now that I think about it. But that's beside the point. It was *fun*. We would rake the leaves into lines and create mazes on the ground. Or make outlines of houses with bedrooms and furniture. And we had tarps like these spread out all over the place. We would rake the leaves onto the tarp, and fill it up good, then drag it all the way to the tree line, to our giant leaf dump."

Eli stared ahead, sweat lining his temple.

"That's what this reminds me of," Greta laughed, breathless. "We'd jump into the pile of leaves once we finished. It was a hoot."

Eli wasn't impressed with her story. Maybe he was tired of pulling the girl's cold body. Greta wracked her brain for more stories. Something more relevant perhaps, something he'd understand better. The book! The book from the library, of course.

They reached the clearing and dropped the tarp, taking deep breaths. Greta clutched the girl by the shirt and rolled her off to the side. "One down."

They repeated the process with the guy, though they had to take a break halfway. Eli's chest heaved rhythmically. Greta's bones felt like she'd fallen down a flight of stairs. Once they finished the trek, they dropped the man beside the girl. Together in life, together in death.

Greta lifted her shirt and wiped her forehead. She grabbed a shovel, stabbed the earth, and removed a pile of dirt. Eli's shovel joined hers. He grunted a little every time his shovel hit the ground.

Then he went to say something—his lips moving, trying to form words. "W-why... why did you kill them?"

The air rang with shovels striking dirt.

"I'm glad you asked, Eli. I was hoping to tell you more about it. I picked up a book from the library that might help."

He looked at her, confused and a little intrigued. Greta had him. He wanted to hear her story. He wanted to hear about a book.

"I killed them because I had to be sure," she said. "I had forgotten all of it, Eli. All of it. All my young years. Most of my time with Clive. It was gone. My mind was empty. But using the knife again brought those memories back. All day, they've been coming back. One after another. Some of them I don't understand. And I can't find the photo album we packed up before the move, and it's driving me crazy. All those pictures would've helped, but the album is poof... gone. Clive and I filled that thing with pictures from vacations, our farm, our old house. Everything. Even has my childhood photos in it. I bet there's one of me raking those leaves I was talking about."

Eli chewed on that. He remained quiet until he had a reply. "What book did you get?" he asked. Of course he was fixated on the book.

"I'll show you." Greta returned a minute later with the book and handed it to him. He set his shovel down, his eyes glowing with mild interest. That boy loved nothing more than a good story, and a book like this contained the *best* stories.

"It's all there." She tapped the book and resumed shoveling. Her hands already ached. "Go on. It's about famous serial killers."

Greta couldn't be positive she even existed within those pages, but she had a hunch.

Eli paused, glancing at the bodies. "Why would a book about serial killers help explain things?"

Greta shook her head. "So far, I've remembered at least three other deaths. And I know there's more. Maybe that book will help me remember the rest."

Eli sat down and flipped through the pages. "How do we know who you are? Or if you're even in this?"

"Clive and I worked together," she said. "Look for a couple, or anything based in Kentucky. That's where most of it happened. Probably look for uh, twenty, thirty years ago."

Eli flipped through the pages. "Wait, I know about this. The murders in Kentucky. You're the Kentucky Duo?"

The Kentucky Duo. The name greeted her like a nostalgic song. She felt a rush of relief. Of honor. Knowing they made it into a book of the greatest killers. "I'm half of it," she said. "The other half is buried in Darling Cemetery." Images of newspaper clippings flashed in her head. Of course they followed the news. They wanted to know what people were saying. They liked the nickname the press gave them. It was memorable.

Eli gawked, eyes wide. "Oh crap, I've actually heard of you. They talk about you on podcasts. There's a documentary about you! I've only seen the trailer. My mom used to love all that stuff. She wouldn't let me watch it, though."

"Smart mom." Greta shoveled more dirt. The work made her sweat, but the wind cooled her off. It held her gently, guiding her arms, whispering for her to dig deeper. Deep enough to fit the whole town in there.

Eli turned the page. "They never found you. Here, 'While the identities of The Kentucky Duo remain a mystery, independent researchers haven't given up hope of one day learning the truth.'"

"No," Greta said, moving again. "They never found us because we hid. We quit. We would've been caught if we kept it up." She made it sound so simple. So easy. *We were addicted to watching people die, and then we quit for twenty years.* As if quitting didn't nearly destroy their marriage. As if, only months after stopping, Clive didn't sleep with their neighbor and then bury her in the crawl space under the house. Greta had to clean the woman's house. Clean her own husband's prints off everything. And they were everywhere. Giving up killing sounded easy but it wasn't. How many nights did she and Clive take whatever drug would keep them home, on their couch, *not* hunting? They medicated in every way they knew how. It was enough for her, but never for him.

"What does the book say?" Greta asked. "When did the killings stop?"

Eli shrugged, trailing his finger down the pages. "The number of deaths rose during the early 90s. So, they stopped in the early 2000s? Somewhere around there."

No wonder she loved reading about the 90s. "But why exactly did they stop?"

"You should know, right?"

"I don't remember everything!" Greta laughed, chucking more dirt. "I still need a little help here, smarty pants. Clive and I went into hiding. I remember that. The last few decades we lived on a farm. It was a good place. I don't know why we left it to come here. I wish we hadn't."

She suspected they had killed a fair number of people. In time, she'd remember them all. Random things kept triggering new memories. Certain road signs, or trees, or even passing over the Little Miami River would send her back into her haunted house.

She was *positive* that all their victims were adults. Not only that, but they had a rule: no kids. A fact she would keep to herself, considering her initial promise to murder Eli's family. If he knew she wouldn't hurt a child, would he feel so desperate to keep his family safe? She needed him to be afraid, because once he lost that fear, who knew what he was capable of?

"According to this, you stopped because you were almost caught, and sketches were put out," Eli said, turning another page. "It doesn't say a lot more. We gotta watch the documentary." He shut the book and set it beside him. Then picked up his shovel and went to work. "What's it like?"

"What's what like?"

"Killing someone."

Greta slicked her hair back to get it off her forehead. "Do you ever think about how close we get to doing something awful? That line between safe and death is so thin. Anyone can stab their brother or sister. Anyone can drive their car off a cliff. It just takes a little effort. Grab the knife, jerk the wheel. One motion, and you've crossed the line. We dream about those things. About hitting someone hard enough to make them bleed. Pushing someone onto the subway tracks. But most people only dream about them. Some people, like me, cross that line. So, I guess killing someone is like living a dream."

"What happens when you wake up?" Eli asked. He always asked such intelligent questions for a boy his age.

"You want to dream again," Greta said. "You want to always be dreaming."

They shoveled in silence, listening to the birds. The wind came through the trees, whistling, seeping through Greta's ears like warm syrup.

Greta whistled back to the wind. "You wanna try?" She matched the wind's rising howl—like the sound the wind made on the eaves of houses.

Eli tried it and blew out regular air.

"You've got to really want it," Greta said. "Close your eyes, close your eyes."

He closed his eyes.

She whistled. "Now guess, was that me just now? Or the wind?"

Eli's face reddened with a smile. "I have no idea. You seriously sound just like it."

"If you talk to the wind, the wind will talk back."

The wind picked up, scattering leaves across their clearing. Greta wished it would tell her the truth. The wind *knew* why she moved to Darling, but it was too stubborn to tell her. She whistled to it again, begging it to answer her one question.

Why did we move here?

The wind howled, refusing to answer.

Chapter 22

Julie sat at her desk, tugging on the bandage wrapped around her hand.

Tori stepped back and inspected her handiwork. "You need me to redo it?"

"No, thank you though."

"That wrapping *is* overkill. My mama bear instincts took over. Sorry."

Julie shook her head, wanting to forget the way everyone had looked at her. She'd felt like they saw right through her. Like they knew she was broken. While Tori had escorted Julie to the office, Nancy tried taping a piece of cardboard over the hole in the foyer window, but the tape kept slipping, and the wind kept pushing, so she gave up and let the wind inside.

Tori closed the first aid kit and placed it back in a cabinet. She sighed, scratched her head, and gave Julie a *look*.

"Thanks for taking such good care of me," Julie said, meaning it as a joke, but the words choked her. "It was just a little cut."

Tori shook her head out of annoyance and love. Julie was pissing her off, and still, Tori never ran out of patience.

"What's going on, Jules?"

"What do you mean?"

"Did something happen?" Tori lowered her voice. She glanced at the doorway. "You were nearly unresponsive back there. I saw the glass cut you and you didn't even flinch."

"It happened fast."

Tori sat down and wheeled her chair over to Julie, looking her dead in the eyes. "Listen, I love you, okay? You know this. And if there's something you need to talk about, I'm here. I can't help if you don't tell me. You've been weird all morning."

"I spaced out. It happens."

"You promise? Can you promise me you're okay?" Tori's face was serious. Her eyes reflected a cold fear, though Julie couldn't pinpoint what Tori was afraid of.

The words nearly rushed out. Julie clenched her jaw to keep them from spilling like vomit. She knew what she wanted to say:

My aunt is dead, and I think I killed her.

She inhaled sharply, guilt slicing through her stomach.

And I left her there. She raised me, and I left her in my house to rot.

"Julie?"

The words came so close. She wouldn't be able to stop with her aunt's death, she'd keep going, until every secret from her past was out. Julie shuddered, wiped tears from her eyes.

Tori touched Julie's knee. "What happened?"

"My aunt," Julie whispered.

"Is she okay? What's wrong?"

Julie thought about Tori sitting on her couch earlier. Tori saw the inside of Julie's private world. The blackout curtains, the bare walls, the triple-locked door. Humiliation swept through her. She couldn't explain why she left her aunt there and came to work. What would Tori think? Tori would wonder what was *wrong* with her.

"She's worse," Julie said, the lie coming easily. "I really should check on her. I can't focus, I've been worried sick."

Despite years of practiced lying, Julie sounded like a kindergartener with toilet paper stuck to one shoe, insisting she didn't throw those books in the kid's potty.

Tori nodded, not giving anything away. She at least pretended to believe Julie.

"Take your lunch," Tori said. "Run home, check on your aunt, and take your time. Seriously, don't worry about it. Nancy knows the situation, she'll understand."

Julie smiled. "Are you sure? You don't have Carly, and Nancy told me that Cathy went on maternity leave."

"You have my approval. Git."

Julie stood. "You'll be fine?"

"I'm serious, girl. Get outta here already."

"But I don't have my car."

"Take mine."

But I don't think I'm coming back, Julie thought. "That's okay. I'll just walk. It only takes ten minutes or so. It's been a while since I've done that, and it'll be good to get some fresh air."

Tori shrugged. "Your choice."

Julie collected her things and made for the front doors, avoiding eye contact with everyone. She passed the broken window, the wind breathing on her like a hungry animal. This time, she didn't stop and stare at it. She could tell the shadow was gone, but had it ever been there in the first place? She pushed the doors open, taking one glance over her shoulder. No, she wouldn't come back. Not after coming so close to telling Tori everything. A single spilled secret is like a crack in the dam. It starts with one, then another, then the whole thing crashes down.

Nancy worked the front counter. Patrons browsed the newest fiction releases, plucking books from the shelf, holding them by the spine, and inspecting them like artifacts in a museum. Julie would miss all of it. Like the sign hanging above the DVD section, created by Nancy. In blue cardstock and black lettering, it read, "To whomever keeps stealing DVDs, we **will** catch you!"

Or the five-foot Christmas tree made from stacked books, complete with stringed lights and beads and ornaments. Nancy kept unplugging it, insisting the Christmas lights looked silly in the summertime. Julie insisted, in her head, that Nancy had no imagination, and turned the lights back on whenever she thought of it.

Tori leaned against the office doorway, hands in her pockets. She eyed the window suspiciously, not trusting it after it had cut her friend. She watched the window with growing uncertainty. Then she smiled at Julie, glanced at Nancy, and pulled her sleeves up a little, showing off her ink.

Let it go, Julie. You can't trust them.

Julie waved goodbye and rushed out before they saw her cry.

The wind twisted everything around her, making the world look like a Vincent van Gogh painting. As she walked toward home, the wind pushed against her as if to force her back to the library. Part of her wanted the wind to sweep her back because her heart was breaking.

Despite the wind, walking outside helped clear her head, and everything at the library felt like a distorted dream. The note on her calendar, Carly's absence, the bleach, the broken window . . . it was all part of a shift happening in Darling. Julie couldn't explain it, she didn't want to try. She wanted to leave before more memories returned, paralyzed her, and forced her to confront the truth of that night.

She'd soon be far away, and no one would know her real name or ask her why the police failed to acknowledge the odd timing of the 911 call.

The call came over two hours *after* her mom's estimated time of death. The police had asked Julie what happened between those points in time, and she told them she got lost in the woods outside their trailer. Apparently, that was all she said. She never elaborated on *what* she did for those two hours, and the police had no choice but to believe her story.

Even Aunt Susan never asked, although the question must've kept her up at night. Pestering her.

Because Julie didn't get lost that night. And the only person who knew that was her mom, who died on the dirty floor in their trailer, whispering her daughter's name.

Chapter 23

Eli's arms wanted to fall off every time his numb hands gripped the shovel. He'd done this a thousand times. A thousand times he inhaled, steeled himself, and launched dirt out of the waist-deep hole he stood in. Greta worked beside him, sweat dripping from the ends of her hair, her back and armpits dark. His jumpsuit was soaked all over again. He'd never sweat so much in his life.

Beside the fresh grave, the book on serial killers fluttered in the wind. He wanted to read everything about the Kentucky Duo, mostly so he could disprove her claim, because he didn't believe her. Though it didn't matter much either way, given their current predicament. Who cared what happened twenty years ago? It didn't make a single difference to Carly and Owen whether they'd been killed by a respected serial killer or a local crackhead. They were dead, they were gone. Eli couldn't form another perspective on the matter. They were just gone, and the clocks kept ticking and the wind kept blowing and the world didn't seem to care.

Greta leaned against the wall of earth encircling them, breathing in ragged sighs. "I need to stop."

Eli dropped his shovel and sat in the dirt, his chest heaving.

"We've made good time." Greta checked the sun's position. "Not bad. And look at this." She gestured at the grave, licking her lips. "We're quite the team."

"My half is bigger." Eli nodded at his mound of dirt off to the side.

"You wish, I added to your pile on accident. I'm senile, remember?"

"I thought your memory was back."

"Most of it." Greta smiled. "My head still hurts like the dickens. I'm sure I got a concussion, hitting it on the deck last night. At least no one can see it, right? I can keep my good looks."

"Should we check it?"

Greta sat beside him, groaning. "Take a look, doc."

Eli didn't want to touch her damp hair, so he used a muddy stick to push her hair aside. The wound looked like something that belonged on the inside of her skull. Disgusting, in other words.

"I thought you covered this with a bandage or something."

"It fell off. Besides, it stopped bleeding. How does it look?"

"Looks pretty good," he lied. Why tell her the truth? She wouldn't go to a hospital either way, and maybe if the wound was infected, she'd be too sick and weak to hurt him or anyone else. He was playing a long game here.

"Good." Greta didn't move. They sat side-by-side, knees almost touching, their backs to the dirt.

She sighed. "Back when Clive and I were young, we loved haunted hayrides, and corn mazes, and haunted houses. But one year, we were standing in line for a haunted bus ride. And this young woman in front of us was waiting for some friends who were in line behind us. She told us to go ahead in front of her. So, we rode the bus, and it was fun. And as we finished, we heard a lot of screaming from the bus behind us. We didn't think anything of it. It was a scary bus ride after all.

"The next day, we're eating breakfast and watching the news. This picture of the young woman who let us go in front of her was on the TV. She was dead. Their bus malfunctioned, something went wrong, and it flipped over. It crushed her. If that young woman hadn't let us go ahead of her, we would've been on the flipped bus."

We might've died, Eli waited for her to say. But she didn't. She didn't fear death. It wasn't in the cards, and he almost admired that about her.

Greta stood, stretching her back. "Let's go, my man, we have some work left. But we're almost there."

In that moment, two things happened:

First, a phone rang. Eli's phone. Greta pulled it from her pocket.

Second, footsteps echoed through the woods, barely above the sound of his ringtone.

Greta held his phone. "Why is your dad calling you?"

More footsteps. Someone was out there, about to run into them. Did Greta not hear them coming?

"Eli?" Greta waved the phone.

"We had a lunch date," Eli said, trying to find the source of the footsteps, inwardly begging Greta to shut up.

"Oh, *great*. Answer it. Make something up."

Greta tossed him the phone, which he barely caught. He answered it.

His dad's voice bled through the speaker, but Eli wasn't paying attention. Behind Greta, a few yards from the grave, stood a woman.

Greta raised her eyebrows as if to say, *what are you waiting for?* She noticed his panic and turned around, seeing the woman who had stumbled upon their clearing. Their crime scene.

The woman stared at them. She was roughly in her late twenties, early thirties. She wore hiking boots, jeans, and a tank top. Her ballcap sat slightly crooked on her head, hovering above a sweaty brow, sunburnt nose and cheeks. She stared at Greta and Eli standing in the freshly dug hole with their shovels, then at the bodies awaiting burial.

Eli waited for her to scream, or take off running, or something. But she went on total shutdown. There were too many wrong things happening. She couldn't process it fast enough.

"Hellooo?" Dad said through the phone for the tenth time. "You there, buddy?"

"Yeah." Eli pressed the phone to his ear, his hand shaking.

"Oh, good. Now, where are we with lunch?"

"Oh my god," the woman whispered, stepping back, turning.

Greta climbed out of the hole, shovel in hand. "I'm . . ." Greta trailed off, knowing it wouldn't matter what she said, because there was nothing to say at all. It wouldn't change the outcome.

"*Hello?*" Dad asked.

"Sorry, can I call you back?"

"What about lunch?"

The woman didn't see Greta as a threat, naturally. She stalled, letting Greta hobble closer, the confusion painfully evident on her face. "Are . . . they dead?"

Greta reached the woman, gripping the shovel with both hands. The woman figured it out too late. She backpedaled, tripping on sticks, her instincts too slow to save her. Why did she let Greta get so close?

"I'm busy," Eli managed. "With . . . Greta."

The woman screamed—a delayed choking sound, as if something were lodged in her throat. She tried to sprint, but Greta swung the shovel, clipping the woman's thigh. The woman gasped and tipped over, collapsing among the roots and mud.

"Oh, okay," Dad continued. "We can reschedule. Honestly, we can talk now. If you want. I wanted to do lunch and give us the space to talk about Chase, which I'm sure you had already guessed." He laughed weakly.

"Please," the woman sobbed, struggling to stand, a patch of dark red blood staining her jeans.

"What's that sound?"

"The TV." Eli climbed out of the pit, phone still to his ear. He had to stop Greta, this woman didn't do anything—she didn't deserve this! They could tie her up, or keep her quiet somehow, long enough for Greta to get away—anything, anything but this.

"Gotcha." Dad laughed again, even weaker. "I know this summer's been difficult with Chase. I don't know what got into him. Maybe it was that stupid dodgeball game—I mean, that was a mess. But he has no right to . . . to terrorize you like this. I went to his parents' house last night."

For a brief second, Eli focused on the phone call. Dad *knew* about Chase's bullying—for how long? And he said nothing? Did nothing? Not until yesterday's attack forced him to face the facts.

Eli's heart hammered in his chest. Did Mom know? Did she know the whole time?

The woman limped several feet before Greta struck the back of her head with the shovel. The woman grunted and crumbled back on the forest floor.

"And his dad was totally unhelpful," Dad kept going. "Dan denied that Chase would ever do that. Ever threaten anyone. His precious boy. Yeah right. I think the man knows what his son is up to, but that doesn't matter. He denies it. Chase's mom probably denies it, too."

Disoriented, the woman tried to crawl. Raising the shovel above her head and using the flat side, Greta brought it down on the woman's ballcap. The woman's head whipped down, bouncing off the Earth.

Eli almost threw up. He reached for Greta, hoping a calming touch would bring her back, but she swatted him away, not even looking in his direction. He quickly muted his phone and put Dad on speaker.

"Greta, stop," he hissed, frustrated tears blurring his eyes.

"But Dan is kind of a bully. And his son is apparently no different. Bullies run in the family, I've heard. Since his parents aren't going to help, I would suggest staying away from areas where Chase might show up. I know, I know, it's natural to fight back. I get that. But violence isn't always the answer. It only brings more pain."

Greta brought the shovel down again, this time with the sharp side. The woman went silent. Greta raised the shovel and drove another one home for good measure.

Eli spun around and fell to his knees. He dropped the phone, his dad still rambling, while Eli vomited on a pile of dead leaves.

". . . I just think it's best to avoid him," Dad was saying. "He'll move on and leave you alone. But I'm glad you're with Greta and not out there risking the chance of running into him. Don't walk through town, don't wander by yourself. Stick with Greta until you're back home, and we can sort it out."

Greta swung the shovel four more times—Eli counted each one, twitching with every soft slice.

"That sound okay, Eli? I'm sorry we couldn't talk this through over lunch. Maybe we'll talk more about it later."

That was the last thing Eli wanted. He unmuted the phone, swallowing leftover bile. "Okay, Dad. I'll see you later."

"Promise you'll be safe?"

"I promise. See ya soon." Eli hung up, slipping the phone inside his pocket.

Greta dropped the shovel and walked back to where Eli sat. "I'm done digging," she said, spitting the woman's blood from her mouth. Her shirt and jeans were speckled red. "We'll bury them all, then we'll leave."

Eli looked at the woman. It was impossible not to. Just like Carly on the toilet and Owen on the floor, he knew he'd never forget it. Not in this lifetime.

Greta patted his shoulder. "Help me."

And he did.

Chapter 24

Julie's front yard was littered with broken branches and trash, most of which had blown over from the neighbor's spilled garbage can. The roof suffered the same treatment. Everything, everywhere, was falling apart. Including her life—her internal walls that once protected her from the past.

Once inside the front door, she locked up (*tap tap tap*). The wind made the house rasp and creak, as if forcing it to settle prematurely. Julie hated the idea of a house settling. She pictured an old man sitting in an armchair, shifting his bones until he'd sunk as far down as possible.

In the kitchen, Julie unwrapped her bandaged hand. The cut wasn't deep and had stopped bleeding. She threw the bandage away and placed a small Band-Aid over it.

She turned down the hallway, flipping the light switch, satisfied with the warm yellow light coming on above her. Up ahead, the reading room was dark, the door half open, with Oscar inside and rolling around on the carpet. He paused, waiting for a playmate. Shifting to his stomach, he stared at something behind the door, ears twitching.

Julie whispered his name. Speaking out loud felt like an abomination in that quiet house. Like talking in a monastery dedicated to silence.

Oscar ran to her, his tail held high. She ran her palm along his back, smoothing his fur.

Tori saw something in that room, Julie thought. She forced herself to enter the reading room and check behind the door, even though she knew nobody was there. Sure enough, the room was empty. Why did this keep happening?

The spare bedroom looked the same. Aunt Susan's glassy eyes stared at the ceiling. The window was closed, the chair still toppled over.

The smell had worsened, and the sheets were stained around Aunt Susan's form because everything inside her was sinking to the bottom. Gravity at work. The sight made Julie nauseous, and she wished she hadn't come back. If she kept staring at her aunt, she'd break down and cry. Grief would overwhelm her and distract her from what she needed to do.

Julie straightened the room. She threw Aunt Susan's dirty clothes in a pile, picked up the chair, tissue box, and lamp. She put the battered copy of *David Copperfield* and Aunt Susan's phone on the nightstand. The phone lit up with notifications. Texts from friends. She'd been ignoring them for days, insisting she didn't want them to see her like this.

Cold. Tired. Dying.

Julie held her aunt's hand. "I'm sorry," she said.

She knew it was wrong—all of this. Leaving her aunt and running away. But she *would* call someone. They'd come get her. She'd express concern for her aunt and say she hadn't heard from her. Maybe ask for an officer to swing by the house. Leave a key outside somewhere.

Because she couldn't do police, and paramedics, and funerals, and cemeteries. She couldn't do those things—not after her mom. Not after the national coverage of her mom's death and Julie's heroic *survival*. She couldn't stomach it—she would have a panic attack.

Only one thing stopped her from calling the police immediately. Julie sat in the metal chair and tried to remember. Guilt ate away at her. So did the questions:

Why was the room in disarray when Julie woke up last night?

Why were all the windows open?

"I don't know," Julie whispered to herself. She willed the memory of last night to come, but her mind remained blank. She knew about trauma and its many malevolent forms. She knew blacking out and sleepwalking were not unheard of. But what had happened during that blackout state? Did Julie play a part in Aunt Susan's death? Or did she walk away when Aunt Susan needed her? Maybe she ignored her aunt's cries for help. Maybe she opened the windows so the wind could roar through the house so she couldn't hear Aunt Susan dying.

"I'm sorry," she said once more, turning away. Convinced the room looked *normal*, she continued packing.

She tossed more clothes into her suitcase, wanting to bring a book or two with her but hated the thought of going back into the reading room. She was being ridiculous. Ghosts didn't exist—only bad memories and bad dreams. Her mom wasn't *out there* somewhere, looking for answers. Looking for the *why*. She lived in Julie's head and never had a need to haunt anywhere else.

Hoping to curb her fear, she entered the reading room and turned on the light. Nothing looked different. No creepy shadows. No human-shaped hallucinations. All was well. Still, her heart raced. And she kept looking over her shoulder.

She took four books she hadn't read yet (any avid reader had a To Be Read pile and were lying if they said they didn't). She stacked the books on top of her clothes, zipped the suitcase shut, and set it beside the door. After she put Oscar's travel carrier out, she carefully placed him inside and closed it, despite his protests.

Undoing the locks, Julie gripped the doorknob and thought of something.

She should take *David Copperfield*. Continuing the story would honor Aunt Susan. She'd be proud, knowing Julie read it to herself every night until the story was done. Julie let go of the doorknob. Her gut warned her not to go back. The house was too dark and too quiet for lingering. If she left now, nothing else could happen.

Leaning into the hallway, she waited for something to move in the reading room. Nothing did. Satisfied, she crept into Aunt Susan's room, feeling absurd for trying to be quiet, as if her aunt were asleep.

It's not her I'm hiding from, she told herself, wishing she hadn't thought that. For someone who claimed to not believe in ghosts, she was certainly displaying the opposite.

The room was darker than before, as if a cloud had blocked the sun outside. Julie reached for *David Copperfield* when, in her peripheral vision, Aunt Susan blinked.

Julie backed away, *knowing* she imagined it, but Aunt Susan's face moved again. Her expression shifted. Her lips peeled back. Julie screamed, cutting it short by covering her mouth. The scream rang in her ears, a guttural cry in a silent house. She was seeing things. Just like in the reading room and on the broken window in the library.

Aunt Susan's face hadn't changed at all. Instead, a dark, shadow-like reflection had slid across her face, and now the reflection was moving. Aunt Susan's face was split down the middle—half pale, half dark. Her arms and legs were dark as well. Then *everything* shifted.

The shadow unlatched from Aunt Susan and slipped off her, melting into the corner. Her arms and legs were pale again. And the shadow, in the hunched shape of a human, watched Julie from the corner. Why had it been covering Aunt Susan's body? One word came to mind and refused to leave: feeding.

Julie didn't hesitate. She fled the room, running too fast. She bounced off the hallway walls, her entire body shaking with terror. Grabbing her suitcase and Oscar's carrier, she pushed through the front door. She didn't breathe. She moved. Running, dragging the suitcase behind her, she left the door unlocked. As she started her car and pulled away, the tires spitting gravel, she looked back.

The picture window had a stain on it. The shadow watched her leave, no longer in the same shape as before. Now it was bloated, like a hardworking mosquito. It was *full*.

Chapter 25

They buried the woman.

They had to grab her arms and drag her to the pit and dump her on top of Owen and Carly, who were already tucked inside. Their grave wasn't deep enough. *Something's bound to dig them up*, Greta had said. Nevertheless, they didn't have time to keep digging. It was already mid-afternoon, so it would have to do.

Greta tossed the library keys in the hole, and they hid the bodies with dirt, working with blistered hands and empty stomachs.

Eli was in a daze, throwing dirt one shovel-load at a time. It *looked* like a grave. It wouldn't fool anyone. *I'm glad you're with Greta*, his dad had said on the phone. When they finished, Eli carried the tarp and shovels and library book back to the car while Greta stayed at the grave, checking the area for anything accidentally left behind. Not that it mattered. She couldn't kill three people and get away with it.

He waited in the car, scanning the trail both ways. His hands still shook. His vision tilted a little from hunger and exhaustion. He held the library book on serial killers, too afraid to crack it open and see the crime scenes and bloody images. In real life, their eyes weren't blocked by a black censor bar. They were open. So still and so dry.

Greta took one long look at the woods before sliding into the driver's seat.

"We have to go," Greta said. "That wasn't supposed to happen. Give me your phone." She held out her hand.

Eli had forgotten all about it. He handed it over, and she put it back in her pocket. "What did your dad want?"

"We had lunch plans. I told him I was busy."

Greta managed to reverse the car and drive back to the parking lot. Since they'd last driven through, three vehicles had parked—a truck and two minivans. One of the minivans had two infant car seats in the back, and Eli prayed it didn't belong to the dead hiker. He pictured the babysitter calling, wondering why mom wasn't back yet.

A woman (who resembled the woman they buried) stood by the minivan, dressed for a jog. She stared down at her phone, typing.

"What if she's meeting her friend?" Eli asked as they pulled through the lot. "What if her friend was cutting through the woods to get back here?"

Greta nodded grimly. "Could be. But it doesn't matter, because sooner than later, they'll find them all. But don't worry, they won't find *you*."

"What?"

They left the park. Once on the open road, Greta hit the gas.

"They won't find you because no one will know you helped me," she said. "I won't tell them what you did. You're safe."

What I did? He wanted to feel relief, but his bones shivered. *Was* he responsible? Would people think he *wanted* to help?

I won't tell them what you did.

How he helped bury the bodies. How he watched Greta butcher that poor hiker. How he threw extra dirt over her grave.

The wind poured through the hole in the windshield, making his eyes water. Greta didn't drive through Darling. Didn't want to risk a cop pulling them over. She looked like an actor in a haunted house—all that blood. In a way, she was, wasn't she? Didn't she live in the haunted house in her mind?

"Where are we going?"

"Home. I need to change."

They both needed to change, but Eli would wait until he was back at his place. If he ever made it back.

Did Greta intend to let him go? At the end of the day, would she leave his body in a shallow grave? If she bothered to bury him at all. She wouldn't tell anyone about his involvement because there was no need. Eli would disappear like the others. And be found sooner than later, like the others.

Greta pulled into her driveway and parked, peeling her sticky hands off the steering wheel. "Hungry?"

"Not really." His stomach had been screaming at him for hours, but food sounded disgusting.

"I have leftover soup." Greta smiled. "I'll re-heat it. Nice and warm."

But they won't find you.

Eli nodded. "Sounds good."

He followed Greta inside, still stuck in a dream state. Was this what shock felt like? Would he ever feel normal again?

After washing her hands, Greta put cold chicken noodle soup in the microwave. Eli sat at the dining room table and looked through the big windows at the dancing forest. More and more branches covered the yard. Entire trees had succumbed to the wind and lay in the Earth, broken and splintered.

Greta said she was going to change, then stood in her bedroom doorway and stared at him, silently reminding him of her promise. She would kill his family. Eli saw what she did to strangers. He didn't want to know what she did to those who betrayed her.

She smiled and closed the bedroom door.

An idea formed inside his mind. An image of his future self, free from Greta, free at last to return home. And he saw the path he had to take if he wanted that freedom. There was only one option.

He scooted his chair back, his mind racing. He had to do this right if he wanted to get away from her. And he had to try. He couldn't wait around for her to kill him or his family.

He quietly sprinted to the front door, opened and closed it softly, and ran outside. Beside her driveway, Greta's little single-car garage was filled with Clive's tools and random things leftover from their move to Darling. Inside the garage, the workbench had buckets of nails and screws, along with several toolbelts, each pocket carefully organized. Cobwebs had claimed the toolbelts long ago. Eli brushed them aside and checked each belt, not finding what he needed.

Beneath the work bench, homemade shelves held anything from machine parts to sanders to extra belts and wrenches of every size. Some of it had been there a long time, left by previous owners. He found the right shelf—the one with the hammers. Three of the four hammers were massive. The fourth was a ball-peen hammer and looked as old, if not older, than Greta herself. He tested its weight. Satisfied.

Unzipping the top half of his camo jumpsuit, Eli stuck the hammer in the waistband of his pants and zipped the jumpsuit back up, all the way to the collar.

He ran inside and shut the door. Inside Greta's bedroom, the sink in the master bathroom turned off. Drawers closed. Greta muttered to herself.

Eli slid to the couch and waited. A few minutes later the bedroom door opened, and Greta emerged.

He acted normal. Maybe better than normal—something like his old self. He smiled and thanked Greta for the soup, and she was touched by that, he could see the spark in her young-looking eyes. Did she see through him? Did she sense something off?

Maybe not, because she sat on the couch opposite him and breathed a sigh of relief.

He couldn't run away—her threats made that clear. He couldn't let her harm his family. In fact, he could be the only thing keeping his family safe. The only thing standing between them and Greta.

He smiled again, totally normal.

Greta smiled back, totally oblivious.

It was now or never. Eli cleared his throat. "Can I show you something?"

"Like what?" Greta stood up and walked around the room, opening the windows, letting the wind come inside and blow receipts off her desk.

"It's in the basement." Eli walked to the basement door, praying the hammer didn't fall through his pants. "It's important."

Greta cracked the front door, taking a deep breath of summer wind. "You can't tell me what it is?"

"Not really." Eli opened the basement door. He pushed it against the wall, feeling it shift in his hand as the wind tried to shut it. "It's a good thing, I promise."

Greta nodded. "Okay, Mister Mysterious, lead the way."

Eli took the steps carefully, not wanting to knock the hammer loose. Greta waited at the top of the stairs, then she followed him down, not asking any more questions.

Because she trusted him.

Chapter 26

Julie fought to stay on the road. Her small car veered between the white and yellow lines, the wind trying to force her off. She clutched the wheel and glanced back at her shrinking mailbox.

She kept picturing the shadow and how it had spread itself across Aunt Susan's body. Julie couldn't shake the image of a vampire, only this type didn't feed on blood, but on something else. Something unseen.

Then she remembered the shadow in the library, moving over the broken window like a drop of color in a pool of water. No one else seemed to notice it. If she didn't believe in the supernatural, how could she explain the shadows?

She couldn't.

Both shadows, at the library and on Aunt Susan, could be written off as hallucinations if not for what Tori said earlier. Tori thought she saw someone in the reading room, and maybe she did, if the shadow had been there.

If Tori could see them, did she see the one at the library? If the shadows were real, supernatural beings, then what did they want? What did Julie's house and the library have in common?

She drove past the library with a lingering look at the dark windows, ignoring the stab of guilt in her stomach. In five minutes, she'd be on Interstate 71 North, moving toward Columbus. She'd need to form a plan, a story, before calling the police about her aunt. But she couldn't focus on that.

Julie couldn't stop thinking about the shadows. The more she replayed the memory, the darker the shadow became. It wasn't an innocent spirit hovering over Aunt Susan's corpse. It was *preying* on her, like a vulture from the afterlife.

It sounded ridiculous in her head and would sound even crazier if she tried to explain it to someone.

Still, Tori *saw* a shape in the reading room. And if Tori saw it, then they were real, and not in Julie's head.

Julie clicked on Tori's name in her phone and listened to it ring. It finally went to voicemail, and an automated man told Julie to leave a message. Julie hung up before the *beep*.

Approaching the 71 North on-ramp, Julie slowed down, aggravating a driver behind her. The car whipped around her and flew on by.

She pulled off on the side of the road. If the shadow in the library was anything like the thing in her house, then she didn't trust it or want it around her coworkers.

Pressing Tori's name again, Julie put the phone to her ear and stared at the on-ramp.

"Please pick up."

Tori didn't answer, and Julie started to feel sick to her stomach.

Something's wrong, she thought. Unless she wanted to go back to the library, she had to give up and wait for Tori to call her back. Julie dialed the library's main line, hoping Nancy wouldn't pick up.

"Thank you for calling the Darling public library, this is Nancy, how can I help you?"

"Hey Nancy," Julie said, smiling to herself, hoping it would trigger a friendly tone in her voice. "It's Julie."

"Oh, okay?"

"Is Tori there? I'm on my lunch, running an errand, and I needed to ask her something."

"I don't know where she is," Nancy said, sounding tired.

"What do you mean?"

"Julie, I have a line at the counter, I don't know where she went, maybe she took her break too." A pause. "Bye."

The call ended.

Julie stared at her phone, pleading for a text or a call from Tori. She glanced at the on-ramp one more time, Nancy's words inside her head:

I don't know where she is.

How could Nancy not know? Where would Tori have gone?

No relationships, remember?

Whatever was going on with the library and the shadows was far beyond her anyway—what could she possibly do? Tori was smart and capable. She'd be fine.

Julie, on the other hand, needed to take care of herself.

Just go, Julie. You don't owe those people anything.

The on-ramp called to her, and Julie listened. She merged back onto the road, drove under the highway sign for Columbus, and she didn't look back.

Chapter 27

Eli waited for Greta to catch up. She came down the stairs carefully—like the wounded, elderly neighbor he used to know—and shrugged at him, slipping her thin hands inside her pockets.

The basement was unfinished, and his shoes echoed in the cold, dark room. The overhead light was out, and Eli hadn't taken the time to fix it yet. He regretted that. The only light in the room came from the open door at the top of the stairs. The light flowed down the steps, illuminating a rack of metal shelves along the wall. He glanced around for the flashlight he'd dropped last night, but it was too dark to see. Eli stopped at the shelves, bent down, and pulled out a cardboard box from the bottom shelf. He'd placed it there months ago when sorting through the basement's junk.

Setting the box down, Eli withdrew a thick photo album. Its blue color had long faded, outlasted by the shiny gold trim. He cracked it open, catching sight of polaroids and three by five print outs, carefully placed in plastic sleeves. He had looked through it before, hoping to find something interesting, mostly just snooping, but the pictures were normal—no different than his parents' old photo albums.

"Oh my Lord, our album," Greta said. "You found it!"

"I found it a long time ago."

Her mouth dropped. "Why wouldn't you say something? I spent entire months searching for this, you know that."

"I'm sorry." He paused, the words building in his throat. "I didn't want you to have it. I knew that you really needed it, and when I found it, I wanted you to keep looking. I was mad. I didn't want to help you clean out your old stuff, but my mom made me. When we met you at the library, that was only what, a week after your accident? My mom basically offered you my help without asking me. Like it was some character-building chore. Of course I was annoyed about it."

Greta's face shifted, from wonder to confusion to pain. Now that he had started, stopping was impossible. It spilled out. The dam had broken. All because he was terrified of what he was about to do.

"I hate coming here," Eli said. "I hate helping you with chores. I hid the photo album because I didn't want you to tell me every little story about you and Clive."

He wanted to hurt her, and he could see it working. It didn't give him the satisfaction he imagined, but after everything she'd put him through, she deserved it.

A tear spilled down Greta's cheek. "I'm sorry," she said. "I didn't know any of that. I thought coming over had always been your idea. I didn't know. That's all I can tell you, Eli." She took the photo album from him, running her palm over it.

Eli shifted to his right, trying to move behind her. Greta opened the album, a glow of pride and relief on her face. This was it: her life, her memories. As she leafed through the album, her joy turned bitter. She held the album low enough for Eli to see over her arm. She skimmed through pictures of a road trip, with her and Clive sitting on a cliff with their feet dangling over the edge.

"I don't remember these," she whispered. "There's so much I still don't remember." She flipped the pages faster, trying not to cry.

Above them, the basement door wavered. It slowly moved away from the wall, now halfway shut. Eli imagined the wind at the top of the steps, baring shiny teeth, ready to slam the door. Eli moved again, standing directly behind Greta. He unzipped his jumpsuit slow enough to barely make a sound and removed the hammer from his waistband. It didn't feel the same. Up there, it was still a hammer. Now it was a weapon. He zipped his jumpsuit all the way back to the collar.

The basement door creaked, slowly shutting, then swinging back open. The wind roared outside. Eli's heart thundered in his ears. He lifted the hammer, aiming it at the back of Greta's head. He didn't need a lot of force. He wanted to knock her out, not kill her. The back of her head was wounded. If he hit the wound, would her brains spill out? Would her body fit inside the compost bin if he pushed down hard enough?

A swift knock on the head would turn her lights off. Just like in the movies. Then he'd run, call the police, call Mom, and tell everyone *everything*.

He swallowed, hoping he wouldn't throw up. He lifted the hammer higher as a breeze blew over his arm and ruffled Greta's hair.

Greta jerked her head around as the basement door *slammed* shut, cutting off the only light source. In the pitch black, two things reached Eli's ears: the distant, howling wind above them, and Greta's ticking heart.

"What are you doing?" she asked. Something hit the floor. She had dropped the photo album.

Eli stepped back. He didn't know the basement layout by heart. He didn't know the positions of the old bicycle, the table, or the workout bench. Dumbbells littered the floor somewhere. A floor-to-ceiling metal support bar waited, in the dark, for him to collide against.

"What are you doing?" Her voice came again, but from another direction.

"I'm sorry!" He shuffled backward, waiting to hit something.

"Sorry," she whispered. "Sorry, sorry, *sorry*." A shrill laugh echoed around him. "Oh, Eli. If you only knew."

Eli's shoes clipped something heavy, like a cinderblock. He shifted around it and kept moving. The hammer slipped from his fingers—a dull slap on the concrete floor.

"Did your mom ever tell you about what happened to Clive?" Her voice again, somewhere new. Was she circling him?

Eli crouched, walking on his hands and feet, hoping to move quieter. He jammed his fingers against a dumbbell and sank to his knees, clenching his teeth.

"We liked taking country drives, like the one you and I did today," Greta said. "Most Friday nights we'd be out there driving around, playing music, or one of the games we liked playing in the car. This time, we'd just left the library and wanted to drive around before going home. We wanted to explore Darling. Our new home. We didn't see the truck swerve until the last minute. By then, it was too late. It happened so fast, that truck. Like it was on purpose."

Eli froze. Something brushed by him—a faint movement of air—a quiet *ticking*. Her voice was behind him now. Or over to his left? Not easy to pinpoint, given the echoes. Eli slowed his breathing. He stood up straight, debating if he should run, hands out, to find the stairs.

"Clive was driving, and when the truck hit us, the front end of our car folded in and crushed him—he died instantly, or so they tell me."

Eli walked forward, arms outstretched.

"I don't remember the actual accident," Greta said. "But I see it, in my haunted house."

He pictured her in the dark, eyelids closed—eyes squirming beneath them.

"I see it *so* clearly," she said. "When I woke up, they asked me if I remembered anything from the scene. I said no, I didn't. They told me Clive was hit the hardest, but his head was propped-up. They said it shouldn't have been propped-up like that."

Eli didn't want to walk in the dark anymore. He didn't want to accidentally stick his hands in the gaping mouth of a propped-up head.

"But what *really* shocked them," she said, her voice closer, "was the message."

Her breath fell on his cheek—warm and putrid. Thin fingers wrapped around his arm. Her other hand grazed his jawline before sliding up to his forehead. "Someone wrote the word *sorry* on both our foreheads." Her finger traced his forehead, spelling out *sorry*. Eli didn't want to touch her, but something forced him—the same thing that forced him to go off about hating her. He reached up and touched her face.

"*Sorry*," she whispered. "They wrote *sorry* on our foreheads, on my husband's nearly decapitated, propped-up head, with a Sharpie. A Sharpie!" That shrill laugh again. "Can you believe it? They never found the driver—just cans of beer rolling on the floor of the truck."

Eli ran his fingers up her cheek, to her eyes. She didn't stop him. She knew exactly what he was doing. Her face was warm and feverish, and with an irresistible and morbid curiosity, he touched her closed eyelids. Beneath them, her eyes twitched and pulsed like twin hearts beating.

Eli twisted out of her grip and ran. He smacked into the wall, stumbled to his left, and banged his shoe on the basement steps. Sprinting up, he reached the basement door when a hand grabbed his ankle.

"Are you *sorry*?" a voice growled at his feet.

Eli twisted the door handle, letting a sliver of light in. Greta was crouched on the steps with one hand wrapped around his ankle. She opened her eyes.

"Are you *sorry*, Eli?"

Eli kicked her, knocking her down a few steps. He ran through the living room and out the front door.

"I'll kill them!" Greta followed him outside. "I swear I'll kill them if you leave!"

He didn't stop. He ran around the house, past the screened-in deck, and stumbled down the hill.

"ELI!"

He believed her—he believed every word—but he had to reach his family first and do whatever it took to protect them. He knew he was putting them in danger, but it was too late to turn around.

Greta screamed his name again.

And Eli ran with the wind at his back, guiding him home.

Chapter 28

Greta watched Eli from the screened in-deck, feeling the control slip through her fingers, seconds passing. Precious time. And she just stood there, staring stupidly at a little boy she couldn't catch. He'd known that all day. How fast he was compared to her. Yet he hadn't run until now.

She ducked inside and grabbed her landline, punching in Mindy Wright's cell phone number and waiting until Mindy answered to start sobbing. Real tears formed in her eyes, matching her panicked voice. She was going to give Mindy a heart attack.

"Eli's been h-hurt," Greta cried. "Can you come here as fast as possible?"

Mindy didn't even say goodbye. She hung up and that was that. The drive would take four minutes. Three, if Mindy pushed it.

Greta looked out the window. Eli's small frame was almost to the bike trail. He'd piece it together. He was smart. There was a *small* chance Mindy would see him on the bike trail, depending on how fast she moved in relation to Eli.

Just a small chance. A little glance down the bike trail, and Mindy would see her son sprinting for her, with a fear in his eyes that Mindy would never, ever forget.

Greta smiled, thinking of how close they were to unraveling everything—and it was much too early for that. It made her nauseous. Her entire body ached at the thought of almost getting caught. A small part of her wanted that brave little boy to catch his mother in time.

But if things worked out, then she had to sell it. Eli hurt himself, didn't he? Mindy was about to show up, expecting her boy to be hurt.

Greta walked into the bathroom. The first aid kit was in a plastic box beneath the sink—that was good—she'd need it.

After looking over Clive's things, she grabbed an open razor blade and held it gingerly between two fingers.

So small, so sharp. And easy enough to hide.

Greta tucked it safely inside her palm and walked outside, waiting for Eli to come back. And he would come back. Because it was a day unlike any other, and she was feeling very, very lucky.

Chapter 29

Eli broke out of the trees and jumped over the ravine, his shoes skidding on the bike trail pavement. Two bikers, one in front of the other, raced by, casting brief, curious looks. He sprinted forward, the bike trail impossibly long before him. *It's too far*, he thought, pushing his legs harder. The wind washed over him like a blanket, propelling him forward. It *wanted* him to run home.

I've killed them, he thought. *I've killed my family.*

He should have stayed. He should have done what Greta, but it was too late now.

Main Street up ahead: twenty yards. Another minute of sprinting and he'd be at the front door, ranting hysterically to convince them of the danger. How long until Greta showed up with her kitchen knife? Would locking the front door be enough to keep her out?

Ten yards left. A car flew past the bike trail—cruising way over twenty-five miles-per-hour—his mom's car, with Lucas in the backseat. Either they were going somewhere, and it was random and totally unrelated, or Greta had called his mom. Considering she was driving up the hill, to Greta's road . . .

Holy shit.

Spinning around, he ran back the way he came—the wind in his face this time, making him work twice as hard. Eli pushed through it. His chest and throat burned. What did Greta say when she called Mom? What would make her drive so fast?

Eli turned left and started up the hill. The wind knocked him sideways, no longer his ally. It wanted him to fail. It wanted his family to die. He scrambled to his feet and climbed, tree after tree, root after root, clutching rocks with his fingertips.

Nearly at the top of the hill, something shifted from behind a tree. A pale woman in gray clothes. A witch with long fingernails, waiting like a spider.

Greta.

She caught him. He tripped and fell hard, sliding on dead leaves. Greta went down with him, arms wrapped around his torso.

"I told you, Eli. I *told* you what would happen."

"I'm sorry—I won't run again, I swear."

"I don't believe you!" she hissed in his ear. "Your mom is here. I told you what would happen."

"I'm sorr—"

She clamped her hand over his mouth. "*Shut up.*"

He struggled against her, trying to bite her hand, but she held him down, squeezing his neck. "I'm sorry," she said. "I needed a reason to get her here fast. I can't change it now. She'll know I lied."

Eli froze. What was she talking about?

Hot pain shot through his arm. He jerked against her, but Greta held on tight. Screaming into her hand did nothing. The pain washed over him, spreading like fire. He glanced at his arm, at the open razor blade digging into his skin, cutting through his jumpsuit, making him bleed.

Somewhere up the hill, a car door slammed. *Mom's here*, he thought, and he tried to scream again.

Greta tossed the razor blade down the hill and squeezed his face in her hands. "Do you want her to die?"

No, of course not. Eli clenched his teeth and stopped screaming. Greta had won. Was he done paying the price for running away? Or was the razor blade just the beginning?

She let go of his head, letting him sink into the twigs and leaves. "Mindy! Down here!"

The next few minutes were a blur. Mom slid down the hill and picked him up and kissed his face. She carried him inside Greta's house, even though he kept saying, *I'm fine, I'm all right, I can walk.*

Mom set him on the couch and inspected the wound through his jumpsuit. Greta hovered nearby, tears on her cheeks.

"I don't want to ruin this," Mom said, tapping his jumpsuit. "Can you pull your arm out of the sleeve? Otherwise I'll have to cut the sleeve off."

Eli managed to pull his arm out. Lucas sat on the opposite couch, hands in his lap, unsure if he should smile or cry.

Greta placed a first aid kit on the couch and stepped back, letting Mom do her thing.

"Greta told me you hurt yourself." Mom cleaned his cut with an antiseptic wipe, sending fresh pain through his arm. "I'm glad she called me immediately. Lucas and I were about to go to the store."

"I told him to stay here and wait for you," Greta said, dabbing her forehead with a napkin. Playing the part beautifully. "He didn't listen. I had to go catch him."

"That was stupid." Mom shook her head. "What if you had fallen down that hill?"

It was Greta, Eli almost said. *She cut me.* What would his mom say? She wouldn't believe it. Even he barely believed it and he was *there* when his neighbor shanked him.

"I'm sorry," he said, catching Greta's eyes.

Greta nodded with approval.

"You should be," Mom said. "I thought it was way worse, from how Greta put it." Behind her, Greta shrugged a little.

"Luckily," Mom continued, "it's really not a bad cut. I don't think you'll need stitches. It's weirdly thin, though, and not very deep."

"Some of those metal shelves in the basement are sharp," Greta said. "I'm so sorry, Mindy. I never thought someone would get hurt cleaning them."

Mom bandaged Eli's arm with gauze and tape. "It's not your fault, Greta. These things happen. It's not the worst injury I've seen from this little man. I'm just glad he's okay. All right, you're all done. I'm sure Greta can give you a little medicine for the pain. You feeling all right?"

Eli nodded, not trusting himself to say anything.

Mom stood up. "Can I talk to you for a second?" she asked Greta.

They went out onto the screened-in deck and shut the sliding door behind them, leaving the two boys alone.

"Is Greta in trouble?" Lucas asked, sitting with his legs crossed.

"Yeah," Eli said, thinking of all the many-sided answers to that question.

"Where you been all day?"

"With Greta."

Lucas nodded, staring at the two women outside. "You going to fly your kite at all, or what? It's prime time, bro."

Flying a kite. What a simple, fun pastime. It hadn't really occurred to Eli that at some point, the nightmare would end, leaving him dead, or at the playground, flying a kite like all the normal kids. He wanted to give Lucas an answer—anything to encourage his brother. He wanted to tell Lucas that yes, he'd be around later. But maybe he wouldn't be. Maybe Lucas wouldn't be either.

Lucas leaned forward. "Has Greta been *weird* today?"

Eli exploded with genuine laughter, unable to stop it. Lucas joined in out of obligation. When Eli finally controlled himself, and his laughter died out, tears welled in his eyes. Not laughing tears.

Lucas frowned. "You okay?"

Eli nodded, finding his most realistic smile. "Yeah. I am. And you know what? Greta *has* been weird today." He sniffed and wiped his hand across his eyes.

The glass door slid open, and the women returned.

Mom clapped her hands. "Boys, Greta's offered to babysit you two while I run to the store. You going to be okay here, Eli? Greta has medicine for you. And we both agreed, no more sharp objects."

"Babysitting? We're not *babies*," Lucas said.

Eli glanced at Greta. He knew what she wanted, and he knew the cost of disobedience. "Yeah. That sounds fine. I'll be fine."

"Awesome." Mom ruffled his hair. "I'll be back soon." She kissed Eli's head and tried to kiss Lucas, but he wiggled away, swatting at her. She tickled him until he begged for mercy, then kissed him anyway. "See you boys soon."

Greta escorted her to the front door.

"You sure you're okay with this?" Mom asked. "I don't want them to be a handful."

"I feel awful about Eli's arm," Greta said. "Please, take as much time as you need, especially after that scare you had. I'll keep a close eye on them. No one will get hurt, I promise. I'm sorry again."

"Don't be. I'll be back. Call my cell if you need me." Mom waved goodbye and left the house, zipping her jacket up before the wind caught it just right and carried her away.

Greta shut the front door and locked the deadbolt. Lucas glanced back at Eli, eyes wide, jerking a thumb in her direction as if to say, *What's her deal?*

As Greta shuffled toward them, Lucas kept glancing at Eli, raising his eyebrows, like he expected a cauldron to appear any minute now. For the first time ever, Eli regretted telling Lucas all those Greta stories. Because they weren't *just* stories, were they?

Greta bent down, hands on her knees, and gave Lucas a clownish grin. "Guess what?"

Lucas shrugged, eyes bugging out of his head.

"I have special permission from your mom . . . to let you swim in the HOT TUB!"

"Yes!" Lucas jumped up. "Let's go! Oh yeah!"

Eli blinked, his arm warm and throbbing.

Greta gave them both a crooked smile. "I think it's going to be a really fun time."

Chapter 30

Julie didn't take the highway. She pulled a U-turn and drove back through Darling, stopping at a pet boarding house downtown, a place she'd never walked inside but passed every day on her way to work. She dropped Oscar off (just for the day), and although she hated leaving him with a stranger, she couldn't take him to the library, and going home wasn't an option.

She then drove four blocks to the Darling Library. With its faded brick walls, thin windows, and old chimneys, it *looked* like a place ghosts would gather. And despite the numerous stories and folklore claiming the library was haunted, Julie had never believed it.

Until now. *If* the shadows were real, *if* Tori could see them as well.

Inside the library, the foyer was empty. No patrons, librarians, not even kids. The wind whistled through the broken window, filling the library with warm, thick air.

"Hello?" she called. The wind carried her voice down the hallway.

A wheel squeaked. Footsteps shuffled. Nancy came out of Fiction, pushing an empty book cart.

"Where's Tori?"

"I told you. I don't know. I guess she left."

"Did you call her?"

"I tried, and she didn't pick up." Nancy blinked slowly, like she'd woken up after a long nap. "What's going on? Why did you call in here on your break?"

Nancy leaned against the book cart, expecting a satisfying answer. And she deserved one, but Julie couldn't tell her the truth. Not yet. Not without proof. "Tori was asking me about my aunt. I just wanted to update her while I was out."

Nancy nodded. "Try her phone again. I think she picked up some orders from the stacks. Then she left."

"I'll find her," Julie said. "Thanks, Nancy."

Julie hurried down the hallway, checking the corners and windows for shadows. The hallway led into the Children's Room, but before the Children's Room, a few doors were scattered on the left side. One of them led to a recreational room where they had a Book Sale set up. Long tables full of mass market paperbacks, labeled neatly by genre. The other was a utility closet they shared with Gary. And the last one (which they kept locked) led to the basement.

Julie tested the doorknob, finding it unlocked. Tori went down there (how long ago?) and didn't come back up. Julie opened the door, feeling the wind swell past her ankles and seep down the steps.

Julie descended one step at a time. Basements in general didn't bother her, but library basements were different. Besides holding supplies and leftover props from activities, it was where they stored extra books. Books set aside for the book sale, or additional copies, or new releases were put in the basement as a holding system. Nancy struggled to clear it out. The result: a lot of stored books.

They referred to it as the *closed stacks*. Or more often, just *the stacks*.

Julie reached the cement floor and wondered, not for the first time, why they hadn't tried to make the basement less creepy.

There were rows of metal shelves with dozens of books tucked away. A booklover's paradise, if not for the spiders, naked lightbulbs, and costumes.

Medieval gowns, mermaid tails, and pirate hats. The basement held all the junk they'd used in the past, back when they ran weekly entertainment for the kids. They still did puppet shows, but the skits and silly dress-ups had been discontinued. Now the costumes entertained no one and rotted down here with everything else.

The old puppet theater was propped up in one corner, its red curtains faded and torn. All the puppets, of course, hung from the ceiling rafters, twisting in slow circles.

Julie remembered why she hated this basement in particular: the ceiling was too low, the shelves too close together, oh, and the *puppets hanging from the rafters.*

"Tori?" She stepped down one aisle, her shoulders brushing the spines on either side. The ceiling pressed down above her head, as if it wanted to cave in.

Julie paused, collected herself, and moved again, running her palms along the books, trying not to think about the cave-like dripping sound coming from somewhere.

She turned a corner. More rows extended away from her. Some filled with books, others left empty. The shelves needed to be spaced out. They didn't even use them all.

"Tori?" her voice echoed back to her. She looked over her shoulder. The puppets *swayed* as if blown by the wind or disturbed by something squeezing past them.

She turned and her shoulders briefly wedged between the shelves. Books towered over her, almost leaning *forward*. She freed herself and stumbled on the rough cement. Working in an old library thrilled her a little too much now. She wanted a modern one—all color and light, self-checkouts, and a basement with even floors and plenty of lighting (or no basement at all).

She turned down another aisle and stopped. Tori stood at the other end, her back to Julie. She stared at the far corner of the room, where the basement went directly under the hallway bathrooms. Nothing on that side except for pipes. From Julie's vantage point, it was dark and empty. The light switch on the wall was flipped ON, but what had happened to the bulb?

"Tori?" Julie whispered. Why was Tori staring at the darkness?

Tori twitched. She turned around, doing the same slow, groggy blink as Nancy. She pointed over her shoulder at the space beneath the bathrooms.

"What are they?"

Julie dug her fingernails into her palms to keep from screaming. "Tori."

"What are they?" Tori looked like a little kid in adult clothes. How long had she been standing there?

Julie looked over Tori's shoulder. In the dark corner, shapes morphed together. Shadows flickered in and out. They were gathering there—not one or two, but dozens of them, swarming like bugs. Julie couldn't comprehend what she was seeing, but she didn't need a closer look. They needed to leave, right now.

Julie stepped closer and the shadows stopped moving. They didn't like that. They didn't like *her*.

Well, too bad. Whatever they were, whatever they wanted, they were intruders. They could not have the library and they certainly could not have Tori. Julie took another step, hoping they'd shrink away like frightened animals.

But the shadows broke apart, each taking that same hunched over, human-like shape. They melted into the bookshelves, the corners, and blended in with the pipes on the ceiling. They became invisible.

Then they moved together, a blanket of darkness slowly spreading.

Julie ran forward, clutched Tori's hand, and yanked her back. Uprooted, Tori fell, and her palms slapped the concrete. Julie picked her up and dragged her down the aisle. The shelves tugged at her clothes and scraped her skin. She glanced up, back, and forward, expecting the dark cloud to overtake them.

Their shoes thundered on the stairs as they moved upwind, aiming for the doorway filled with daylight. Once they got out, Julie slammed the basement door and leaned against it, knowing it was futile. Tori shook her head, thinking the same thing:

If the shadows were following, a closed door wouldn't stop them.

Chapter 31

Lucas stood in Greta's living room, hands on his hips, wearing nothing but massive swim trunks held up with a fraying shoelace. Lucas raised his arms like a gymnast after a superhuman jump. "How do I look?"

Before Eli could answer, Greta returned from outside. She opened the sliding door, clutching the handle so the wind couldn't push her over. "It's *ready!*" she sang, her high spirits climbing higher, her toothy smile not fooling anyone except for Lucas.

"All right!" Lucas ran outside and slid inside the hot tub, giving Eli two thumbs up. Greta followed him outside, resting her elbows on the tub's rim, watching him play. Glued to the couch, Eli just watched because he couldn't stop her. After Greta sliced his arm and lied to his mom, he was beyond scared of her. He couldn't compete with that level of crazy. Neither could he predict her anymore. This new version of Greta didn't think like the old one. She didn't think like anyone. Greta had said there would be consequences if he ran, and cutting him on the hill wasn't a consequence, it was merely fixing the problem at hand.

Drowning his little brother was the real punishment. Greta would hide it somehow or kill Mom when she came back from the store or kill them all just to buy herself a little more time.

Greta laughed at Lucas and splashed a little water on him. He grinned and dunked his head under the bubbling surface. Greta dropped one hand in the water, maybe feeling its warmth, maybe prepping to hold Lucas under.

Eli trembled. He stood on shaky legs, making his way to the glass door. Lucas broke the water's surface, waving at Eli, spit running down his chin. Greta stood behind Lucas, both hands in the water now.

Eli shook his head.

Greta glared at him, as if to say, *I told you what would happen*. She reached for Lucas as he ducked under again, his hair floating up, almost touching the surface.

Eli slammed his palm on the glass, screaming. He yanked the glass door open, but Greta met him in the doorway and shoved him back inside. Lucas came up, droplets clinging to his eyelids. He turned in a circle, looking for them.

Greta pulled Eli into the pantry. "I told you." She heaved him against the shelves, knocking over pasta boxes and pancake mix, holding onto the shoulders of his jumpsuit, almost clenching hard enough to reopen the green scar on his sleeve.

"I'm sorry! I'm sorry I didn't listen! I won't tell anyone, I won't run away, I'll do what you want!"

"But I *told* you, Eli. You almost ruined everything we've done today, because you ran when you knew what I would do."

Greta let go of his jumpsuit, her face dark and unhappy, as if forced to eat something bitter. "Clive and I had a rule, you know what it was? We said no kids. Not a single kid would suffer because of *me*! But I swear to you, I will kill him if you run again. You won't go home until I'm convinced you're keeping this secret. I am *not* spending the rest of my life in prison because of you."

Eli nodded, over and over. "I know. I know. I'm so sorry." Tears streamed down his cheeks. He'd never sobbed in front of anyone before. And what happened with Chase yesterday didn't count. Crying was a private matter—best done in small corners, surrounded by books, or in the shower. But he held nothing back. He slouched against the pantry wall, his chest heaving. He pictured Lucas in the hot tub, floating face down, motionless. The image made his heart ache and his throat fill with hot pain.

Greta didn't hug him, even though he wanted her to. She left the pantry, arms crossed, and disappeared into her bedroom. She shut her door softly, with remorse—upset at Eli for putting her in this position to begin with. After all, she had a rule: no kids. An old, sacred rule that Eli nearly made her break.

Eli sat down and cried. Several ants wandered the floor, scouting for crumbs. He mashed them with his fingers and wiped their guts on the wall. His throat hurt from all the crying. He ran his hands over his face, clearing the tears from his cold wet eyes. When he finished, he stood up and went outside.

Lucas leaned on the hot tub's rim, playing with the jet speeds. "Hey," he said. "Where you been?"

"Nowhere. Having fun?"

"Oh yeah!" Lucas kicked his legs, creating a small rain shower. "Sure you don't wanna join?"

Eli shook his head, wiping his nose on his sleeve. "Nah. I don't want to wear a dead guy's swim trunks."

Lucas howled with laughter, slapping the bubbling water. Greta stood in the living room, watching them play and laugh without her. She sat on the couch, flipped one leg over the other, and smiled at them.

Go on, her smile said. *Play like everything's normal.*

Eli splashed water in Lucas's face, earning a dose of warm water thrown back at him. They were trapped on the deck. Lucas didn't know that, and Eli intended to keep it that way. Big brothers were supposed to protect little brothers, so he splashed Lucas again, smiling.

Greta watched them through the glass, sometimes closing her eyes. She appeared to be napping, but Eli knew better.

She was trying to remember.

Chapter 32

Julie locked the basement door (as if that did anything) and took three steps back and waited for the shadows to crawl through the cracks.

"They *look* like us," Tori said, leaning against the wall.

"You saw one. At my house, remember?" Julie tried to slow her breathing. "Remember what you saw in the spare room? It was a shadow, like these, and it was still there when I went back." She thought, *It hovered over Aunt Susan's corpse like a fly on a carcass.*

Tori knelt on the thin carpet as if about to puke. She'd always claimed to be attuned to otherworldly things. She told Julie stories, usually when they closed the library together on slow rainy nights. Tori knew when people were hurting, or missing their loved ones, or keeping heavy secrets. She just knew. She claimed she had seen a ghost as a child, and it touched her, and that she *felt* it's touch. Ever since then, she had bad feelings when she entered certain houses, or was around certain people. Tori didn't have to debate the reality of what they saw down there—she believed it instantly.

Telling Nancy wouldn't do any good, because not a single bone in her body would believe them. The shadows were invisible when they wanted to be. Clearly, they didn't want attention. If they were at both Julie's house and the library, were they everywhere else? Were they just following Julie? Or Tori? Was there anything linking Julie's house and the library aside from the two of them?

Wind filled the hallway, rustling the YA paperbacks stacked on the tables. Tori opened her hand to feel the wind passing through her fingers. She then stood, walked up the hallway, and paused in front of the bathroom with the (now) faint bleach smell. She crossed her arms, not willing to step inside.

"I think something bad happened," Tori said. "Maybe it draws them?" She shook her head. "I can't believe I'm trying to understand this. There's nothing to understand. They're shadows. Just shadows."

"But I saw one in my house," Julie said. "*You* saw it when you picked me up."

Tori looked at her, those piercing eyes doing that *I-see-your-soul* thing, on the verge of asking, *Did something happen, Jules? Is your aunt okay?*

But she didn't ask. She knew the answer would be a lie. For the first time, Julie wondered how much Tori had gathered in one day. Would Tori even be surprised when Julie skipped town? Or would it confirm everything she'd sensed about her quiet, troubled co-worker?

"How long was I in the basement?" Tori asked.

"I don't know, I just got back."

Tori edged closer to the bathroom and peered in. "I would stay out of here. I don't think it's safe. I don't think the library's safe."

Julie cleared her throat. "In the basement, you were just watching them. Were they doing anything? Saying anything?"

Tori nodded. "They acted like people, but they were all clustered under the bathrooms like—"

"Like flies?"

"Yeah, sorta. They didn't say anything, but—and I'm going to butcher this because it's crazy and can't really be explained—I felt this urgency. It's like when you see a hungry animal. It doesn't need to tell you it wants food, you can just tell. Does that make sense?"

Julie nodded. It made sense, and it terrified her.

"I knew what they wanted just by looking at them."

The bathroom was empty. No shadows. No evidence of anything in there, other than that faint trace of bleach. Julie thought about the shadows beneath the floor, writhing like bugs.

"They wanted me to let them inside."

Julie's skin crawled. "What do you mean?"

Tori shrugged. "They wanted *me* to let them through. Or let them inside. I don't know. I don't know what's happening." Tori's face crumbled. She didn't try to hide the tears on her cheeks. She leaned against the wall and clenched her eyes shut.

Julie decided to do something she'd never done before. She hugged her friend, wrapping her up in the tightest, most loving hug Julie Baker could muster. Tori smiled against her shoulder.

Chase and Tyler loitered by the DVDs, watching them. Tyler smiled. He whispered in Chase's ear, and Chase grinned.

Julie let Tori go, not breaking eye contact with the boys, eventually forcing them to look away. But the boys continued to whisper. Tyler pointed at Tori and said something that sounded like, "What's wrong with her?"

Julie wanted to slap them, especially after what they did to Eli yesterday, ripping his jumpsuit like that. She'd never seen Eli look so miserable and defeated.

"Need to take a break?" Julie asked.

Tori sighed. "Yeah, that's a good idea. I'll sit in my car." Tori stopped herself from saying more, because she probably wanted to say it again: *I don't think the library's safe.*

Tori walked outside, hugging herself against the wind. Julie stood by the broken window, staring at the hole in the upper right corner and the maze of splintered glass running down the window. The cracks were longer now. The wind smelled like grass and garbage.

Nancy stood beside her, gazing at Tori's SUV in the parking lot. "Carly still isn't here. She hasn't picked up her phone."

While Carly was still the prime suspect for leaving that note on her calendar, Julie couldn't shake the notion stuck in the back of her mind. Carly should've picked her phone up. Or sent Owen to pick it up. That girl was addicted to her phone. Maybe she didn't know where she'd lost it and was looking everywhere but the library.

Nancy waited. She wanted an apology and an explanation, and she deserved both. Julie and Tori had hardly worked the last hour, but for a good reason neither of them could explain to Nancy right now.

"I'm sure Carly will pick it up." Julie wanted to say more, but Nancy walked away. She had every right to be angry at them.

But Julie had more important things to focus on. Not just Tori, or the shadows, but the boys who had migrated to the computer room. They huddled around one desk. Tyler threw his feet up and leaned back in his chair. He had a drawstring backpack in his lap, weighed down by a single heavy object. He gave Julie a sheepish grin and looked just like any other shy teenage boy. If Julie hadn't seen their hatred firsthand, she'd smile back.

She knew better—they weren't there for fun. They were on the lookout. Julie considered calling Mindy Wright and asking her where Eli was. Maybe warn Mindy to keep Eli far away because Tyler had something in his bag, and it was bulky and rolled around when he adjusted it.

Julie looked out the window. In the parking lot, the lights of Tori's SUV were on. Tori's phone was on the counter in the same spot they typically left their phones. In the driver's seat, Tori cracked her door open and held it there, not getting out yet. Just getting fresh air, just letting the wind in.

Chapter 33

Lucas sat on the couch, back in his clothes, his hair drying in convoluted waves. Eli sat beside him, and together they watched Greta and Mom talk in the kitchen. Greta heard all about how great it was to get some shopping done, and Mom heard all about how much fun Lucas had in the hot tub.

Oh yeah, what a truly wonderful day everyone was having. Eli wondered if Greta would slip up and say something alarming. Of course, she did no such thing. She spoke gently to Mom, keeping the forgetful-old-lady routine. Everyone knew about her unreliable memory, and their ignorance was Greta's strongest weapon. When it would all start to unravel, Greta would plead not guilty, even with hard forensic evidence. She'd cry and say she didn't remember anything, and everyone would believe her.

Lucas tapped Eli's shoulder. "Are we going home?"

"I don't know. I'm sure you are."

"But our kites!"

"I'll be home for dinner, at least," Eli said. "We'll fly after. I promise."

"Pinky promise?"

They linked their pinky fingers. "I'll keep your kite safe," Lucas said, sliding off the couch. He shuffled into the kitchen and told Mom he was bored.

Mom came over to the couch. In the kitchen, Greta towered over Lucas. She hunched down, extended a bony arm, and offered him a piece of candy.

Lucas gobbled it up. Greta pinched his cheek like their grandma used to before she died.

"How's the arm?" Mom asked.

"Doesn't hurt," Eli said.

"You get a little medicine?"

"Mmhmm."

"Good." She sat beside him. "Greta asked if you could help her finish the basement shelves before you go—she *swore* you'd be home by dinner." She glanced over her shoulder. "Between you and me, though. It's okay if you don't want to stay. Those shelves *did* stab you after all. And you've been going all day with her, even if it's good money."

Eli smiled. "I'll be fine. My arm's not even hurting. It won't take long for us to finish up."

Mom stared at him, calculating. Calculating what? Her next words? His facial expressions?

"Did your dad call you?" she asked, changing the subject but somehow not changing the subject. Her eyes shifted, hunting for a lie.

"Yeah."

"And?"

"He told me to stay away from where Chase hangs out."

"He wants you to stop walking to the library?" Her voice sharpened. "*The library?*"

"I don't know, I guess."

"Did you guys get lunch?"

"Nope, he called me. I was still with Greta."

"What did he tell you?"

When Eli recalled that conversation, he saw the hiking woman's expression. He saw Greta with the shovel. Then he remembered something his dad said. "He said that violence isn't how you deal with bullies."

Mom shook her head. "The problem, honey, is that if Chase pushes you into a corner again, what will you do? Sit there? I already sewed your jumpsuit. I'm not sewing up skin next time." Her eyes burned holes through his face. He wanted to melt into the couch and live with the crumbs.

"In fact, if he ever tries to corner you again, and hurt you, I want you to punch him. In the throat, if you can."

"Are you serious?"

"Yep." She patted his knee and stood up. "You're not going to avoid the library, you hear me? And me and your dad can't watch you every second. I know your dad's going to have a problem with this, but I'll talk to him. We'll figure out a system that works for all of us. But Chase can't keep doing this." That last part, Mom said more to herself.

He can't keep doing this.

Eli nodded, unsure of what to say. She hugged him, and he hugged her back. He wanted to tell her he was sorry for everything that had happened today. He was sorry for helping Greta with the bodies. *Don't believe what they say about me*, he almost said. *I wanted to stop it.*

Mom said goodbye and took Lucas out to the car.

Greta sat on the couch opposite Eli. "We're almost done."

"With the basement shelves?"

Greta rolled her eyes. "It was a dumb excuse. I shouldn't have used the thing that tried to kill you as a reason for why you have to stay."

You tried to kill me, he wanted to say. "I guess it worked anyways."

Greta frowned. "Are you okay?"

It was a pretty stupid question, all things considered. The image of her reaching for Lucas would haunt his nightmares forever. Nevertheless, Mom and Lucas had left the premises, and Eli could breathe a little easier with it being just the two of them again.

"Why can't I go home now?"

Greta thought about it. "I need to know you won't tell anyone."

They'll find you without my help, he thought. *We dug a shallow grave.*

"But, I also told your mom I'd have you home by dinner at six-thirty, so we have to work quickly."

"What do you mean?"

Greta clacked her teeth together. "There's one more thing I need from you. And I don't think you'll be happy about it. In fact, you're going to hate it."

Eli doubted it was worse than burying three people in the woods. "What is it?"

Greta leaned forward, grimacing and fake smiling all at the same time. "Let's go to the bedroom."

Chapter 34

Julie finished scanning a stack of YA fantasy books, earning a greedy smile from Lucy, one of the library's most voracious readers. Lucy thanked her quietly and rushed out the front door.

Lucy had been their only patron (aside from the bullies—who weren't real patrons anyway), and now the library felt empty again. As Lucy's car flew down Main Street, Julie wondered if her swift exit had more to do with the library's aura than her excitement to binge the latest fantasy series.

Did Lucy sense something off in the library? Julie certainly did, but she couldn't put her finger on what exactly, and there were no obvious shadows to blame. She found herself staring at the foyer carpet for a long time, feeling almost immobilized. She kept going back to last night, to the part she couldn't remember. Her plan to flee Darling kept hitting roadblocks. Julie's shift ended soon, but with Cathy having her baby, and Carly MIA, who did that leave for closing? Nancy and Tori?

Julie didn't want to stay and close the library. She didn't want to sit at her aunt's funeral, hear the kind words from her aunt's friends, and be forced to stare at a dead body stuffed inside a half-open casket. Julie had only ever been to one funeral: her mother's. And that brought enough pain to last a lifetime.

Trying to ignore those thoughts, Julie walked to the broken window. Tori was still in her SUV, the door still cracked open. Tori was hunched over in the driver's seat, not moving. Maybe just resting.

The front door opened. "Hello?"

Mindy Wright held a book in her hands. It was a book on business strategies and entrepreneurial habits—the same sort of books Mindy had checked out all summer because she was either working on a killer startup or using the books to keep tabs on her son.

"Hey Mindy," Julie said, moving back to the counter. "Bringing this one back? How was it?"

Mindy set the book on the counter, sighing. "Oh you know, I took some notes. Reading about a business and actually doing it are two very different things."

"I can imagine. Are you checking out a new one today? If you're here for Eli, I haven't seen him, unless he snuck in somewhere."

"Oh, no." Mindy waved. "Eli's been busy with Greta all day, helping her with chores after the storm."

"Oh." Julie's mind sparked. A red flag appeared. Before she could chase the thought, Mindy continued.

"I'm just here for me," Mindy said slowly. "I . . . also wanted to catch you and say thank you."

"Thank me?"

Mindy nodded. "For Eli. For yesterday. Patrick told me what you said and how you made sure Eli was safe after those boys attacked him, and seriously, I can't thank you enough. He's had a hard summer. And we've gone back and forth on how to deal with everything, and with you being here . . . I know he's safe."

Julie felt a ripple of pride in her soul, followed by intense guilt. After all, didn't she plan to leave all this behind? Who would stand up for Eli if she ran away?

Mindy smiled. "Eli's got the wildest imagination. I've never met anyone like him. He makes up stories about you. Yeah, you probably don't know. I'm sure he hasn't said anything. Why would he? But he tells Lucas these stories about the library, and you're always the hero. You're battling monsters left and right, you're protecting people from alien invasions or something." Mindy laughed.

Julie laughed with her. Tears waited in the wings for their entrance cue. She held them back, that small ripple in her soul now a surging tide.

"This is a lot for me to spring on you, and Eli would be so embarrassed if he knew I told you. But I wanted you to know that you mean something to him, and to this library. So, thank you, again."

Julie swallowed, blinking away those stubborn tears. "I'll keep looking out for him, I promise."

Why did she say that? Was she trying to make this harder for herself?

Mindy must've sensed someone behind her, because she turned around and spotted Chase and Tyler in the computer room, blinking like a pair of watchful owls. The muscles in Mindy's neck twitched. She cleared her throat but said nothing. The boys waited, not breaking eye contact.

Then Chase made a mistake: he smiled. Was it a nervous smile? A malicious taunt? It didn't matter. Mindy rushed into the computer room. Julie followed, realizing she didn't want to stop Mindy. She wanted to watch. With the wind swirling around them, it felt like they were outside, like only the four of them remained in their lonely desolate town.

The boys jumped back, shoving their chairs away. Chase's little smile vanished.

"Leave Eli alone." Mindy jabbed a finger at them. "Touch him again, and I'll break your fucking arms."

Tyler backed up against the wall, his mouth comically dropping. Chase stood his ground, but the arrogance had drained from his face.

With a final death glare, Mindy walked away. Julie caught her in the foyer and thanked her.

Mindy sniffed. "I'm not sure what came over me. Sorry about that. Have a good night, Julie." She pushed through the front doors, stuffing her shaky hands in her jacket pockets, digging for that half-empty pack of smokes.

Julie looked around in shock. *How* did that just happen? What the hell was going on with everyone today? Everything Mindy had said replayed in Julie's mind.

She hadn't realized Eli pictured her as a hero. Yesterday, she did what anyone would've done: she ran the bullies off. She hadn't thought twice about it, or about anything she did in the library. She showed up, she cared, and she kept an eye on the kids who needed watching. Kids like Eli were wading through the depths of adolescence and puberty. They were impressionable and young and curious, but she never assumed she meant something to them.

Yet, something else Mindy said bothered her.

Eli's been busy with Greta all day, helping her with chores after the storm.

Greta Shaw. The frail woman with the battered memory. The woman who had showed up before the library even opened.

A car door slammed, and for a brief second, Julie thought Mindy was coming back inside. But it was Tori in the parking lot, hugging herself and gazing at the library like a mountain too tall to climb.

Julie opened the front door. "You all right?"

Tori brushed her hair back. "Not really."

"Wanna talk about it?"

Tori nodded, biting her lip. "Those shadows really messed with my head, Jules. I mean, I don't know if I can go back in there."

Julie looked behind her and scanned the foyer. "I don't see them, but I doubt they left. Maybe they'll stay in the basement and leave us alone."

Tori squinted, holding a hand up to block the dust flying in her face. "Nancy will think I'm having a mental health crisis."

"Don't worry about Nancy. Do you want to head home?" Julie held her breath, hoping Tori would say she was fine and could close the library with Nancy because Julie still couldn't do it. Even with Eli depending on her and treating her like a hero, she could not stay in Darling. If anything, knowing how he felt made her want to leave even more. Then he would never see what a coward she really was.

"No." Tori's hair trailed behind her. She set her jaw, eyes blazing. "I'm not leaving it all up to you. We either stay and figure it out together, or we run together. That clear?"

Julie nodded, feeling another stab of guilt. She was a traitor, wasn't she? A deserter. She wasn't the woman Tori wanted her to be.

Tori took a deep breath and swung her arms by her sides like a swimmer before the plunge. Julie walked into the wind and stood by her friend's side. "You sure about this?"

"I'm sure."

They walked through the parking lot together, arms linked to keep the wind from knocking them over.

On the front steps, Tori glanced at the broken window. "What if we see them again?"

"We'll leave. Like you said, we do this together."

Tori smiled. "This is why I like you, Jules. You're not scared of anything."

Julie walked inside, pretending she didn't hear that last part. Tori made it halfway through the foyer when she stopped, doubled over, and vomited on the carpet. Julie stepped back, too stunned to do anything but stare.

Tori stayed on her feet, bent over at the waist. Chase and Tyler gaped with disbelief. First, Eli's mom threatened them, now *this*. Nancy emerged from Fiction, her book cart nearly empty.

Tori slowly stood upright. Bile dripped on her shirt. She breathed through open lips, her lungs swelling, her eyes expanding. Then she screamed.

Julie rushed over, avoiding the puddle on the carpet. She gripped Tori's hand, asking her over and over if she was okay.

"*Why did you bring me in here?*"

Julie shivered. She took a step back, still holding Tori's hand. "What?"

Tori groaned. "*Why did you bring me in here!*"

Something moved on the edge of Julie's vision. She looked at the ceiling, finally seeing what Tori saw: dozens of shadows. They stretched from one side of the ceiling to the other, sticking to the corners like black mold. The wind rose, turning into a high-pitched screech.

Tori's eyes rolled back as she collapsed. Julie barely caught her in time. This pleased the shadows—they congregated above Julie's head, forming a single ink-black stain. Julie stared at the swirling black hole, and for an impossible second, thought she saw a great lumbering shape in the darkness.

The shadows separated again—from the black spot came thin arms scratching at the walls, pulling themselves free of the colony. It looked like the ghost version of a rat king, and Julie closed her eyes briefly to keep from passing out. When she opened her eyes again, the shadows were halfway down the walls. And coming for her.

No. Julie looked at the unconscious woman in her arms. The woman whose life had become her responsibility.

They were coming for Tori.

Chapter 35

Eli didn't want to sit on Greta's bed, for obvious reasons, so he stood beside it, waiting for Greta to finish rifling through her closet.

"I'm struggling here." Greta pulled out two hangers, each paired with an ancient button-up dress shirt. "Dark green, or navy-blue?"

"Neither?"

Greta dropped both shirts on the bed. "You have to pick one."

"I don't want to wear Clive's shirts. That's disrespectful."

Greta uttered a sharp laugh. "What a joker you are. Disrespectful? You? Go on now."

Eli picked up the dark green shirt and proceeded to unbutton *every* button and then slip it on over his jumpsuit. Would he tell Lucas this part of the story? He was trying to picture what the future would look like, because he wasn't as convinced anymore that Greta meant to kill him. She'd spent too much time and energy forcing him to work for her and keep his mouth shut. Why go through the trouble? Besides, she couldn't get away with his sudden disappearance. His entire family knew he was with her.

"It matches your jumpsuit," Greta said, giving him that over-the-glasses look old people give young whippersnappers like him. "I like it."

"*Why* do I have to wear this?"

"Because I need your help." Greta put the navy-blue shirt back in the closet. "Clive and I came to Darling for a reason. I've thought about it all day, and nothing's sticking. I'm not sure why."

Eli would bet a million dollars that the answer to her question was online somewhere. Or in that Netflix documentary about the Kentucky Duo. But Greta had his phone, and he wasn't about to help her do research. If she wanted a wild goose chase, she could have it by herself. He had dinner plans.

"Anyways." Greta stood. "I'm hoping that shirt you're wearing helps me remember. You need to *be* Clive."

Eli hated where this was going. Suddenly, he saw himself in Clive's clothes, in Greta's bed. He shivered, forcing the thought away. The situation wasn't *that* bad. His task was simply to dress up like this lady's dead husband, pretend to be him, and jog her memory regarding their decision to stop murdering people. See, not *that* bad.

"We need to drive around. Do the things Clive and I used to. We'll return this book." Greta picked it up. "Because the library is important. We went there, the night of the accident. *What* were we looking for?"

Eli didn't want to ask, but Greta read his thoughts.

"If we drop the book off," she said, "and drive around, and if I still don't remember anything, I'll take you home. And we won't see each other again."

Eli hadn't expected a bittersweet feeling, but it gripped him. An intense fear of who he would be when he woke up tomorrow. Would he recognize himself? Would he miss Greta? Would he long to be around someone who knew what he had gone through?

Book in hand, Greta grabbed the car keys and made for the door. "Can you get the photo album from downstairs? Maybe something in there will help me. You can describe the pictures. I'm sure I haven't remembered *everything*."

Eli jogged down the basement steps and collected the photo album from where Greta had dropped it. He tried to ignore the recent bad memories formed down here.

Greta waited for him on the top step, and for the first time, he saw her not only as a weird old lady and an unhinged killer, but as a wife. A woman who had shared her life and body with a man. Greta smiled at him. "Ready, Clive?"

This is so weird, he thought. "Yeah."

She beamed with girlish enthusiasm and spun around, leading him outside. Eli followed—Clive's smell wafting from the old shirt.

They sat in her car, the windows still down.

Greta buckled herself in, turned the car on, and gave him a look of complete giddiness. "Are you ready, sweetie?"

He thought she had her eyes closed and was wandering her private haunted house and talking to ghost-Clive. But her eyes were open.

Wide, wide, open.

"I'm ready."

Chapter 36

Julie hooked her arms beneath Tori's armpits, hauled her up, and started dragging her toward the front door. If the shadows were forced to haunt buildings only, then going outside could deter them. Luckily, Julie was almost there, and the shadows were slow.

Ten seconds and they would be safe—

Tori jerked awake and swung her arms, breaking Julie's hold. Tori fell to the carpet, quickly found her feet, and stumbled into a display case.

"Tori! Stop!"

Tori didn't look at Julie or acknowledge that she had fainted. She stared at the shadows on the walls and ceiling and started shaking her head.

The two bullies and Nancy scanned the ceiling, hoping to see what Tori saw, but they came away confused and worried, especially Nancy. She edged around the other side of the book cart to protect herself.

Julie stood in the front doorway, propping the door open with her hip. "Tori! Come on!"

Tori dipped one hand inside her jean pocket and removed her car keys. "They're not shadows, Jules, they're people."

"Don't listen to them."

"Too many voices." Tori closed her eyes, her face twisting with pain. "No, no, no, I won't do that, I won't let you in!"

Julie felt something warm brush against the back of her neck, like a bed sheet settling over her. The wind picked up again, and this time, Julie heard the window cracking like a frozen lake. The whole thing was going to cave in.

Julie held her hand out. "Tori!"

Tori finally moved. She took one look at the car keys in her hand and bolted through the front door.

Julie moved just as fast, catching the end of Tori's shirt. Now they were stuck in the breezeway, the glass doors turning dark and smokey on either side of them.

Julie waved her free hand, trying to explain. "Let's call Stephen. He'll come pick you up, okay?"

"Let me go."

Julie felt that same bed sheet sensation on the back of her neck. But could the shadows harm them? Physically touch them? What if the shadows weren't trying to get Tori at all?

What if they *wanted* her to run?

Julie focused on Tori, trying to appear calm and in control. "Please, Tori, let's call Stephen. Give me the keys."

"I have to go." Panic filled Tori's voice. "*Let me go*." She shoved Julie back. Tori's shirt stretched and tore by the armpit, but Julie refused to let go.

"Tori—"

"I'm not staying here!"

"You *can't* drive! We'll go outside, I promise you, just please give me the keys. I'll drive you!"

"They want inside, Julie." Tori's cheeks glistened with tears, and their struggle paused. "They won't stop."

"I know, that's why we're leaving and getting far away from here."

"We *all* have to leave!"

"We will, we will! Nancy!" Julie reached behind her and punched the glass door. "Nancy, help me!"

"Don't touch me!" Tori jerked her head, as if shaking off a fly. She threw herself backward, crashing against the front door, bumping it open.

Julie couldn't keep doing this. The shadows were *everywhere*.

Tori grabbed the door frame and tried to pull herself through. The wind rushed inside the breezeway, as thick and restricting as gushing water. "*Why* are you trying to keep me here?"

Tori was right, they couldn't stay. But Julie had a sick feeling in her stomach. She wanted to hold Tori close and never let anything hurt her.

Julie's fingers slipped, and she let go of Tori's shirt.

Tori pushed through the front door, despite the wind, despite the shadows clinging to her—their black tendrils outstretched and curling like blown-out candles.

The air in the breezeway trembled with a silent, pulsing heartbeat. Julie felt a thump in her chest, and a blast of hot air, and she was out the door before the wind and shadows in the breezeway ate her alive.

Slowed by the wind, Tori hadn't made it far. Julie snatched her friend's hand. "Tori—"

"Stop grabbing me!"

"Listen, Tori, you're not okay right now. Your head is all over the place. Driving wouldn't be smart so please, please wait here while I get Nancy, and we can sort this out. The shadows can't even follow us out here!"

"Do you want me to die?"

"You know that's not true. Nancy, help me! Where are you!"

She finally spotted Nancy through the dark cloud in the breezeway, standing in the foyer, hugging herself. Not moving an inch.

"Nancy! Please!"

Tori yanked her arm back and Julie fell to her knees, gripping Tori's wrist with both hands. Then Tori's face changed. She held her keys in her free hand and flipped through them, finding the largest one and separating it from the rest.

Julie tried to say something—anything to get through to her friend, but she couldn't speak. She could only watch, strangely detached, as Tori drove the key into Julie's forearm.

Julie let go, she couldn't help it. Her hands twitched and before she could think, Tori had bolted into the parking lot, the car keys dangling from her fingers, dripping blood.

Oh God, please no. Julie didn't stop to examine her arm, she barely felt the slow wave of pain burning through her. She ran as the SUV's lights came on. She was almost there—twenty feet left.

Fifteen.

Ten.

Five.

White lights. Tori reversed without looking. Julie dodged to her left and tripped and sprawled on the pavement as the SUV roared past, the tires barely missing her fingers. She jumped to her feet and took off running and waving her arms. Tori's wide eyes filled the rearview mirror. Then she hit the gas and turned left on Main Street, swerving like a drunk driver. Julie ran across the street and onto the sidewalk, still throwing her arms up as if that did any good. Her lungs heaved, unable to catch up. She screamed Tori's name until it hurt.

Julie tried to run faster, but the SUV surged down Main Street, drifting into the other lane, then jerking back. Tori wasn't paying attention—she kept looking back, her terrified eyes in the mirror, to see if ghosts were following her home.

Ahead of her, kids played in an open field. Their soccer ball flew, catching that hurricane wind. The ball skidded through Main Street, and a young boy chased it, his blue shirt billowing in the breeze.

The boy caught the ball in his arms and tried to get out of the way, but the SUV moved faster than he expected.

And Julie watched, helpless.

Tori saw the child with the soccer ball—saw him make a run for the sidewalk—but there wasn't time. She swerved violently to avoid him. The SUV hit the sidewalk and jumped, its grille smashing into a telephone pole and crumbling around it. Glass exploded. The air echoed with crunching metal. The young boy dropped the soccer ball in the middle of Main Street and screamed.

Julie ran to the SUV, fighting against the wind, refusing to let it slow her down. It could have the library. It could have all of Darling.

But not Tori. Please not Tori.

Chapter 37

Julie's phone was back at the library on the front counter. But as cars slowed down and stopped, someone (if not a few people) would call 911. The paramedics would need to hurry because the SUV's front end was destroyed, and the telephone pole was resting against the shattered windshield, its black wires pulled tight. Julie approached the driver's window, steeled herself, and looked inside.

A lopsided gash ran across Tori's scalp, oozing dark blood down her face. A blood vessel had popped in her right eye—her green pupil an island in a smooth sea of red. Bits of glass and plastic covered her clothes. The space around the crash was quiet. The kids had paused their game to watch. The young boy had picked up the soccer ball again and didn't know what else to do but stand and stare. Cars slowed to a crawl, then stopped completely. Main Street came to a halt. All quiet, but for the wind.

Tori groaned and shifted in her seat, coughing and wiping blood from her eyes, trying to open her broken door.

"Oh God, don't move," Julie said.

Tori tugged on the door handle, the skin on her hand partially stripped off.

"Tori." Julie reached through the broken window. "Please, don't move."

Tori ignored her. She pushed herself out of the driver's seat and into the passenger seat. Opening the door, Tori staggered into the field. Her left leg rotated every time she leaned on it, forcing her to hop on her good leg. The soccer kids ran away yelling. People started approaching. Asking questions. Wanting to help the bloodied woman.

Julie beat them to it. She ran to Tori's side, catching her in her arms as Tori's leg gave out, and they sank to the grass. Voices came from the street. A young man in a backward ballcap and ripped jeans knelt beside Julie and opened a first aid kit.

"What do y'all need?" he said, unpacking the contents. "You know how to use this?" He'd emptied the kit and spread the supplies in the grass.

Julie pointed at the gauze and tape, trying to remember if a trauma wound needed anything other than pressure. The young man handed her the gauze, and she pressed it against the gash and ran the roll of tape around Tori's head. Julie kept shaking. She was messing this up, but she wasn't a paramedic. The young man's presence calmed her. He held Tori upright and said nothing and looked mildly bored.

Tori mumbled something. She focused on the SUV in front of her and blinked. Sophie's car seat was in the back. Red tears fell from her eyelids.

"Someone called for help," the young man said. "There's been a lot of stuff like this all over town, all day long. I hope they ain't busy."

The young man helped lay Tori's head down in Julie's lap. Tori stared at the sky, at the racing clouds.

"What happened?" Tori asked.

The young man shook his head and stood up. He walked back to his truck, answering the questions onlookers threw at him, keeping them at a safe distance.

"Just an accident." Julie cradled Tori's head in her lap. "You'll be okay."

"Does Steve know?"

Tori never called her husband Steve. "He doesn't know yet," Julie said. "He will. He and Sophie will come visit you in the hospital, yeah?"

Tori smiled. "Sophie will bring me a new picture. She draws new ones every Wednesday."

"I bet she'll bring you a bunch." Julie brushed Tori's hair away from the bandage, frustrated by the leftover strands stuck in the tape. She wanted to say more but nothing came to mind. She wasn't a comforter. People didn't approach her for advice or for help. She was utterly useless because she'd spent her life staying away from people. Keeping them at an arm's distance, not resting in her lap. Dying. She hadn't even been there for Aunt Susan, what could she possibly do for Tori?

Blood trickled from the corner of Tori's mouth. Julie couldn't imagine anything good about that. Not to mention her twisted and broken leg. Tori closed her eyes.

"Hey, don't do that. Stay awake. Talk to me about something. Anything."

Tori struggled to breathe. "Talking is hard."

Julie paused, the answer to their dilemma already on her lips. The thing she couldn't do last night. "How about a story?"

"About what?" Tori cracked both eyes open, one white, one bloody.

Julie swallowed her doubt and forged ahead. "About how my mom died."

Tori laughed a little, wincing, tears spilling down her cheeks. "Sorry, but not very comforting, Jules."

It would be so easy to lie, to make up a story just to distract her. Julie blinked away tears. She was sick of lying.

"Ever heard the name Kayleigh Burkes?"

Tori furrowed her eyebrows. "I think so?"

"That was my mom."

"But..."

"Yeah. My name is Maddie Burkes. Well, it was. I changed it, obviously."

"You're messing with me, right?" Tori squinted. "I've seen pictures of Maddie."

"Yeah, pictures of me when I was *nine*."

"You're messing with me, I swear." Tori shook her head. "That's not nice. Why would you lie to me at a time like this?"

Julie began. She started before she talked herself out of it. The story pushed against her heart and lungs, desperate to escape. Even if Tori knew what happened twenty years ago, she'd never heard this side of the story before. No one had.

"I was nine years old," Julie said, stroking Tori's hair. "Living in Kentucky with my mom in this gross trailer, as you probably know. Really rundown. I don't know, I think my mom thought she'd fix it up, and renovate, and make it into a beautiful home for us. But of course, that never happened. Instead, things spiraled. We weren't close to my mom's family. I never knew my dad. My mom never talked about him. And I think she was just lonely. She spent a lot of time by herself in her bedroom or going on walks. In some ways, I was pretty independent for a nine-year-old. I had to be.

"Anyways, my mom had this thing she liked to do. She'd go out on a Friday or Saturday night and leave me with snacks and a movie, right? Not exactly parent of the year, but those nights were fun, you know? They weren't bad. I didn't feel scared or alone because I had no reason to. Well, um, one night . . . she—we had this thing, where I would hide all my toys and clothes and pictures in case someone came home with her."

"I've never heard this," Tori said, eyes glowing. Sad, but glowing.

"Yeah, I know. At the time, it was a game for me. To hide from mom's friends, or the men she brought over once and never saw again. It was all a game. I guess she thought having a kid made her look bad out there in whatever bar or club she liked going to. One night, I turned off my movie, and I cleaned up the living room. I took my toys into my bedroom, and I shut the door. It was officially my bedtime because my mom was probably bringing someone over. So this night she brings home a couple. A man and a woman. I still remember their voices.

"They talked for a little bit. I could tell my mom was drunk because her voice got really high when she drank. They stopped talking, and I didn't hear anything for a while."

Julie paused. "The house was pretty quiet until she screamed. I remember her scream. It was high-pitched."

Tori grabbed Julie's hand and squeezed it.

"I was terrified. I mean, I was nine. What was I supposed to do? I was supposed to stay in my room. But then my mom kept screaming." Her voice cracked. "And they got louder—the screams. The man and woman were talking over it. Casually. Of course, I knew something was wrong. I should have stayed in my room, but I couldn't help it. I just wanted my mom to stop screaming. I wanted her to be okay."

"What'd you do?"

"I opened the door." The picture came to her with blinding clarity. "They were in the living room. My mom was lying on the floor with a knife in her stomach. The woman was sitting on the floor, still holding the knife's handle in her left hand. She had my mom's head in her lap, and she was brushing my mom's hair."

Julie realized Tori's head was in her lap, and she had been brushing Tori's hair. Tori also noticed the connection and smiled sadly.

"My mom looked right at me, and her eyes lit up. She looked so afraid. She whispered my name. *Maddie.*

"After she said my name, she started to fall asleep. That's what it looked like. She blinked really slow, just drifting off, like she did when I'd sleep in her bed after we'd stayed up late watching TV. The man and the woman looked at me. The man was naked and touching himself."

Julie's heart burned with shame, saying things she'd never said aloud before. "I couldn't look away from them. From my mom. That's when the woman held a finger up to her lips and shushed me. 'Don't be scared,'" she told me. "'You don't have to be scared, baby.'"

"That's when you ran," Tori said, because she knew the case. She understood a portion of Julie's fear and pain.

"I climbed through my window and ran into the woods. The man was yelling for me to come back, but my mom always told me to run to the neighbors if something happened to her, so that's where I ran. And her voice stayed with me, every second. I could hear it so clearly."

Tori smiled. "The neighbors were an older couple, right? Farmers?"

"Yeah. Nice people. I probably scared the daylights out of them, knocking on their door. Luckily, they hadn't gone to bed yet and were watching TV. After the police came to get me and check on the house, so many things happened. Things didn't stop happening. Police, questioning, news vans—and my aunt was there, just trying to shield me from it all. I talked to a sketch artist, and they put out posters."

"I've seen the poster. They never found them."

Julie shook her head. "As you know, the police were *convinced* it was the Kentucky Duo. They said the crime matched the profile. But, since the Kentucky Duo were never found, and no one else died after that, the police assumed the couple retired for good. Maybe because their faces were plastered everywhere? No one knows. Maybe they kept killing and got away with it."

"I can't believe you went through that. I'm so sorry, Jules." Tori closed her eyes and didn't reopen them.

"Hey, hey. Stay awake. The story's not over."

"You need to tell someone," Tori said. A tear escaped her closed eyelid. "Tell someone who will be there for you."

"I just did." Julie sniffed. "Come on, open your eyes. You haven't heard it all."

Julie thought about mentioning her dead aunt, but that could wait. Thus far, Tori didn't think Julie was deeply broken, and Julie wanted to keep it that way, if only for a moment.

"There was a gap," Julie continued, getting to the part with the sharpest pain; pain that cut her every day. "There was a gap in time, from when they stabbed my mom to when the neighbors called the police."

Tori opened her eyes. "I remember that. The police said you got lost."

"They assumed that. I never told them otherwise."

"But you didn't get lost."

Julie shook her head. "I was so scared, I hid in the woods for over an hour. I heard the couple calling for me. They tried for a few minutes, then they left. They knew the police would be coming soon."

Julie wiped her eyes. "Before I went to the neighbors, I went back to the trailer." She expected Tori to react. After all, this was new information. But Tori waited, hanging on every word, eyes open.

"I went inside, ready to see my mom dead, and she was still alive. She was awake. And crying. When she saw me, she kept trying to say my name again, but her voice didn't work." Julie paused, closing her eyes against the tears. "She kept trying to move but it hurt too much. She was shaking like a dying animal. And I was too scared to help her."

"Julie."

"I ran away."

"You didn't do anything wrong."

"I ran to my neighbors, and they called the police. Later, I overheard someone say my mom died minutes after they got to her. Just a few minutes."

"Julie, you were nine!"

She nodded. "I know. And I've never stopped wondering what could've been different if I hadn't been so scared. She died alone, Tori, and she didn't have to. I was there, and she still died alone. I couldn't save her, I couldn't even stay with her. It took me almost two hours for the police to get to her, and she suffered through every second of that just to stay alive for me."

Tori sighed and gently shook her head. "I can't believe you never told me."

"I tried to forget," Julie said. Far away, sirens echoed through Darling's streets, coming closer. "Part me feels like I killed her. And I've lived my entire life terrified the killers would find me again. After all, I'm the reason they went into hiding. That's what the police say. What if they tried to find me?"

"Come on," Tori said, smiling. "If those sketches you provided were accurate, they're old or dead. Probably dead."

"I know."

"No one's coming for you Jules. You don't have to hide. And it's not your fault." She closed her eyes again. "Don't get confused. *They* killed your mom."

A sheriff's car pulled into view, followed by an ambulance and a firetruck.

Julie helped Tori sit up. "Help is here, girl, you'll be better now if you just stay awake."

"I'm already better." Tori tapped her bandage. "It's just a scratch. But I do hope they give me all the drugs, please."

"I'll make sure they do." Julie kissed the top of Tori's head. "I'm not going anywhere, okay? I'll be there, once you're stable. No matter what."

The paramedics arrived and took over, and while Julie knew they were capable of far more than her, she didn't want to let Tori go. But she had to get out of their way and answer their questions. She held Tori's hand one last time before the ambulance drove off. The other responders worked on road cleanup and waited for a tow truck for the SUV.

Julie walked back to the library alone, feeling everyone's eyes on her. And no wonder they were looking. Her shirt had blood on it. Her hands and fingernails were streaked red, her face tear stained. She wanted to yell at them—did they find pleasure in heartache? Did they secretly long for the destruction of their perfect lives?

She stared at the library, at the dark windows, red brick, and off-white trim. She remembered Nancy on the other side of the shadow-filled breezeway, hiding comfortably in the foyer while Tori ran for her life.

Anger bubbled up inside, darkening Julie's vision. The shadows, the bullies, *Nancy*. They were all responsible. Julie begged for their help, and no one lifted a finger.

The wind gently pushed against her back, as if it wanted her to go in there and deal with the cowards hiding inside. Make them pay. Make them *understand*. If just one person had helped her, maybe Tori would be okay. She wouldn't be fighting for her life in the back of an ambulance.

Julie obeyed the wind and moved her feet. She didn't slow herself down or talk herself out of it. She opened the front doors and entered the library, knowing full well what she was about to do was wrong. She knew.

She just didn't care anymore.

Chapter 38

Traffic was a nightmare—some accident on Main Street had backed everything up. To reach the library, Greta had to swing around Darling's outskirts and get in from the other side. This took her by Darling Cemetery, which she briefly looked at without slowing down. It was a shame, burying Clive in Darling—a town he didn't know or like. She asked herself for the thousandth time why they had moved to such an unremarkable place.

She remembered the move: riding in the truck, walking through their new empty home, unpacking. She even remembered Clive's excitement. But it wasn't Darling or the house that excited him.

There was something else.

Greta drove toward the library, catching Clive's button-up shirt in her peripheral vision. Even his scent filled the car, undeterred by the wind sailing through the open windows.

Eli played the part well. His eyes were deep and thoughtful like Clive's. The two of them shared many traits: philosophical minds, mature for their age, the way they spoke and the words they used. Seeing that shirt brought a rush of longing, heartache, and emptiness, all at once, all fighting for control. She wanted to lean forward and smell Clive's shirt. Nuzzle against his neck and wrap her arms around his frame. Eli wouldn't like that, though. Too sensitive.

Eli quietly watched the world outside, as he always did. He had already leafed through the photo album and described the pictures to her. There were photos of her as a child, playing on the beach. Photos of a rabbit cage without a rabbit. Leaf piles. Homemade mugs. Coloring hard-boiled eggs. Camping. Hiking. Scene after scene of Greta as a teen, Greta with Clive, and then just Clive.

Greta tried to remember them all, but many of the scenes Eli had described didn't sound overly familiar. Nothing aided the ultimate question eating away at her, so she gave up quickly to avoid discouragement. She told Eli to toss the album in the backseat, and that not all hope was lost. The library was the key. It *would* have answers.

They pulled into the library's parking lot, and Eli scanned the surrounding streets and sidewalks. He was worried about the bullies, but not scared, not like he was that morning when they broke her windshield with a garden stone.

Tucking the book on serial killers under her arm, Greta walked inside the library with Eli beside her. He had taken off Clive's button-up and left it in the car. Apparently, he thought it was ridiculous to wear in public. As if he didn't wear a faded old jumpsuit every day.

The library was surprisingly empty. One of the librarians sorted through a book cart by Fiction. Just the one. If someone distracted her, Greta could slip behind the counter and grab the young woman's cell phone. She tried not to think about where the other librarians were and *why* they weren't at the counter.

They're out looking for the girl, she thought. She had wasted too much time earlier in the woods and at her house, and now they were onto her.

Was the front door open? She looked for the source of the wind, finding the broken window and the breeze wafting over her. She smiled and gave it a quick, low whistle. The wind howled in return. Whispers flooded her ears. The wind's voice was stronger in the library. So much stronger.

Then she glanced up. At first, she thought the library had a few burned-out bulbs. Patches of darkness colored the ceiling. But the darkness *moved*. Shadows stretched and morphed, almost like a bird murmuration.

It dazzled her, the way they hid from direct light. Greta didn't know their purpose and honestly didn't care. But if she were a shadow who disliked the sun, she would be waiting for nightfall, wouldn't she? When the sun went down later, the library might be a very different place.

Eli saw them too. Like Greta, he didn't look shocked or frightened. His face told her everything. He stared at the foyer like he didn't recognize it, like something had stolen his library, and he couldn't stop it. And it wasn't just the shadows, either.

The two boys, the ones who threw rocks, were in the computer room, watching Eli like vultures. Greta thought about going after them again, but those boys weren't scared of anything. That was the problem. Eli glanced back at Greta, and he looked so young. Like a little boy tasked with something unpleasant and was unable to escape it. Greta didn't know what he was thinking. Maybe he needed her to fight with him, as they had before. And run the ruffians out of town once more, whooping and hollering like jackals. And together, they'd accomplish something good. One good deed for the day.

But that had to wait. Getting the cell phone mattered most. It might not make a difference in the long run, but the cell phone indicated something was wrong, because young girls didn't just leave their phones behind. If the phone disappeared, the librarians would assume the young woman had come back for it.

It was still only the one librarian, Nancy, and she didn't say anything. She shelved and kept looking at the carpet, as if angry or upset about something. Maybe she didn't see the shadows (and if she did, she was wildly indifferent to them), maybe she was missing the young woman who still hadn't recovered her missing phone.

THE DARLING KILLER

The front doors opened, and Julie Baker walked inside, looking like she'd just murdered someone. Her shirt and hands were bloodstained, her hair messier than usual. She was also *gone*. Single-minded. Focused. Determined.

Everyone watched her enter, but Julie paid no attention to them. She walked straight to the book cart, reached over, and smacked Nancy's face.

Nancy fell against a bookshelf, too stunned to cry out or protect herself from another attack. Julie didn't try it again, although she looked upset enough to beat the life out of anyone who crossed her. No, she was finished with Nancy. She whipped around and locked eyes with the two teen boys. They were next. Greta and Eli were late to the party and had apparently missed something spectacular.

Then Julie saw Eli and her anger flickered out like an oxygen-starved flame. Everyone awkwardly waited for something else to happen. Nothing did, much to Greta's disappointment. There was something different about the library today. Everyone felt it.

Julie avoided their eyes, walked through the foyer, and disappeared into the bathroom.

Nancy stayed on her feet, rattled and obviously embarrassed. A partial handprint marked her face in bright red. She hurried into the office.

Now would be a bad time to check something out, Greta thought, smiling to herself. Good thing she only had a return. She'd never checked it out to begin with. She dropped the book of serial killers on the counter and slipped behind it, opening random drawers.

She had seconds to find the cell phone.

Chapter 39

Julie stared at herself in the bathroom mirror, at the bloodstains and disheveled hair, the dirt and tear tracks on her face and wondered if she would ever recognize herself again. Was she changing into someone new? Or simply revealing the woman she had always been?

She had never hit someone before. Her boss, Chris, would fire her once Nancy told him. Nancy could press charges. Get the police involved—the exact thing Julie had dreaded all day.

Look at you, she thought to the woman in the mirror. *You've tried to run all day, and all you've done is hurt people. You left your aunt to rot in her filth, after she raised you, after she tried her best to bring you out of your dark childhood. She had an impossible task and look how you've repaid her.*

Look at you, with Tori's blood on your clothes, all because you wanted to leave Darling. You let Tori back inside the library when you knew better. You knew it wasn't safe. You failed. You didn't protect Tori or the library.

Maybe worst of all was Eli's face after she hit Nancy. How could he tell stories about her, and believe she was a hero, when she just proved the opposite? It was obvious—he looked at her as he would a dangerous, unpredictable stranger. In that moment, she'd become no different than the boys who hurt him.

Julie leaned over the sink, too tired and emotional to cry again. She'd cried enough for one day. But her body shook, and she clenched the counter hard enough to make her fingers white and her nails start to bend.

How had she become this? This pathetic coward.

With soap and warm water, she carefully washed her hands. She then left the bathroom because she owed Nancy an apology, but when she turned the corner, Greta Shaw stood by the front counter. The woman jumped a little when she saw Julie and then awkwardly smiled.

"Greta, you're here again." Julie stepped behind the counter, trying to reassemble herself back into librarian-mode, despite the obvious mess she'd made of things.

"Did something happen?" Greta pointed at Julie's bloody shirt. "Are you all right?"

"Oh. Uh, my friend was involved in a car accident, and I helped her until the paramedics showed up. It happened down the street. Just a bit ago."

"My goodness." Greta rubbed her forehead, as if pretending to be upset, but not quite nailing it. "Is she okay?"

"I hope so." Julie paused, holding her breath. "Look I'm sorry, but things are rough right now. I need to go change and find Nancy. Is there something you need?"

"I brought this back." Greta tapped a book on the counter with one dirty fingernail. "I must've forgotten to check it out earlier. I'm very sorry for that."

"It's not a problem." Julie picked up the book, thinking about how The Kentucky Duo and her mother's murder was probably one of the stories inside.

"Do you like true crime?" Greta asked in a whisper.

Julie shook her head. After everything that had happened the last hour, she didn't care anymore. Why did she have to keep hiding? "I really don't like it. My mom was murdered a long time ago, and that stuff just glorifies it." Julie sounded like a complete bitch, but did that make her wrong? No, it didn't—she hated the way people treated true crime like fiction. It wasn't a juicy story, it was her life—twenty years of trauma served up in a cheap

Netflix thrill. Julie waited for Greta to argue or passively agree, but Greta said *nothing*. She just stood there, her face blank.

Julie hadn't expected this response. Wishing she hadn't said anything, she mumbled, "I have to go," and walked inside the office.

Nancy sat at her desk, her head in her hands.

Julie cleared her throat. "Nancy I—"

"Get out." Nancy didn't even look at Julie. She opened her phone, clicked on someone in her contacts, and held the phone to her ear. She was probably calling Chris to tell him what had happened.

Julie walked out, too ashamed to look anyone in the eye. She almost plundered the lost and found drawer for spare clothes but then remembered Tori's rain jacket on the coat rack behind the counter. Julie put it on and zipped it over her bloody shirt. It was a little small on her, but it smelled like Tori's perfume, so she kept it.

She expected Greta to be gone, off thinking about that weirdo librarian who brought up her mother's murder, because that wasn't something you did at your local library. It wasn't *proper*. But with Tori's blood still on her, Julie didn't give a damn about propriety.

As it turned out, Greta hadn't gone far. She stood in the foyer with her hands clenched by her sides, her head tilted up. Was it the shadows? Did Greta see them? Was Greta having a stroke or falling apart like everyone else had been all day? When did the Darling Library become so dangerous? The shadows were watching, always watching, but they weren't moving toward Greta as they had Tori. Julie had a million questions with no answers.

Julie rushed to Greta's side, gently holding her frail hands. "Are you okay, Greta?"

Greta's eyes were closed but very active. Then she cracked her eyes open and smiled at Julie like a little kid, all youthful and innocent.

"Oh, Julie." Greta stepped away, shaking her hands free. She lifted a palm to Julie's cheek, as if to make sure she was real. It made Julie flinch—she didn't usually like to be touched, but Greta's hand brought a small ripple of comfort.

Greta blinked away tears, looking at Julie hard enough to see right through her. "Oh Julie," she said again. "I'm doing just wonderful."

Chapter 40

While Greta had been searching for Carly's phone, Eli tried to process the last ten minutes. What Julie did was unthinkable, and he kept replaying it in his mind, seeing Nancy's head snap to the side, hearing the crack of thunder coming off her cheek.

Even good people make mistakes on bad days. He told himself that even though he struggled to believe it. He wasn't a good person. Not after today. Everyone was turning into monsters. The bullies were trying to physically hurt him, his elderly neighbor had murdered three people already, and now Julie, the young woman who pretended to be old, the library's last guardian in his stories, had succumbed to the poison. Eli wondered if Darling had suffered a chemical attack, and the very air was turning everyone into violent animals. Including himself.

Chase and Tyler were in the computer room, clearly waiting for him. Not outside the library this time, not out in the lonely streets, but *here*. Where he would read and sit at the wooden desk and live inside worlds other people had created.

Tyler wore a drawstring backpack Eli had never seen before, and Tyler wasn't the type to carry a backpack unless the contents inside served a distinct purpose.

The guys eventually stood up, but Eli couldn't imagine they'd try anything. Not with the librarians nearby. He quickly walked into Fiction and pretended to scan the shelves. Chase and Tyler followed, maintaining careful distance.

Eli couldn't win. They were stealing the only thing he had left.

In the foyer, Julie and Greta were talking. Eli walked out of Fiction, past the guys, and through the foyer. He made eye contact with Greta, hoping she understood his plight.

I'm not leaving, he tried to convey. *I'm dealing with a problem.*

Greta didn't get his telepathic message. She had a giant grin on her face, which quickly melted, and she shook her head at him, confused.

Eli nodded at the front doors. As he walked by Greta, he said, "I'll be fixing the car by the river, if you need me."

He hoped she understood *that* and walked outside, unbothered by the wind. He imagined it gleefully watching, cheering even, because it needed to be impressed, and Eli wanted to indulge it. He walked past Greta's car, taking a single glance back at Chase and Tyler, who had predictably followed him outside.

He was giving them what they wanted: a chance to hurt him and get away with it. They'd follow him, even if they didn't understand his actions. It made no sense, him leaving the library. Did they wonder, even for a second, that they were being *led* somewhere? Of course not.

They didn't know Eli was having the worst day of his life. They didn't know that every one of his heroes had let him down. All he wanted was to get his library back and save it from forever becoming a place of death. If he had to do it himself, and do it alone, then so be it. The Darling Library had seen enough bloodshed.

Chapter 41

Greta remembered the little girl, how she stared at them from her bedroom doorway, and how they saw her, she slammed the door. They'd always had a rule: no kids. But rules had exceptions. Greta remembered the pretty woman's head in her lap. Julie's mother. A crackhead keeping her daughter locked away in squalor while she sucked down tequila shots at the local dive bar.

Clive had broken into the girl's bedroom, but she had already slipped through a window. He would've strangled her with her own dirty nightshirt, and he wasted thirty minutes searching the woods with no success. The little girl had fled and called the police, and Clive and Greta went into hiding because the sketches were good. The girl's memory didn't fail her.

Julie, made uncomfortable by Greta's silence, crossed her arms and looked around. "Is Eli with you?"

Eli doesn't matter, Greta wanted to say. *Clive and I came here to kill you. We came here to finish what we started twenty years ago.*

Somehow, Clive had found her. Greta knew he'd never truly given up. All those miserable years spent on their farm festered like an infected wound. It ruined their lives. Clive's only solace was finding her. He worked on the computer—yes, it came back so clearly in her mind—Clive spending hours online, not sharing his intentions. Greta knew, deep down, that he'd grown obsessed with something. She never directly asked him. She liked the simplicity of their life. Despite what that little girl had done, Greta never wished her dead.

Clive found the relative who had raised Julie. A single woman with a good job, an adequate caregiver. But by the time he discovered her, Julie had left the house and changed her name. Did he consider torturing Julie's aunt for information? It would've been risky, and Clive didn't want Julie to ever suspect someone was looking for her.

Julie stared at Greta. "Have you seen Eli?"

"He's around here somewhere," Greta whispered, picturing Julie's stomach cut open. A red smile. Intestines slipping out like a thick tongue.

"Well, so are those awful boys," Julie replied. She left the foyer and went behind the front counter. Greta followed, debating how to do it. Her arms ached from all the digging earlier. Beating Julie with a heavy object or strangling her would take too much effort, leave too much room for error. She needed to use the knife in her trunk. It worked last night. If she slipped away and came back with it, would her opportunity still be here?

Eli had left the Fiction room, giving Greta a look she didn't understand. Did he need her help? She had watched out of the corner of her eye as he walked through the foyer and said something to her about fixing the car. Then he'd charged through the front doors.

Julie caught sight of Chase and Tyler and turned to see them follow Eli out the front doors. Eli cut through the parking lot, the bullies trailing him. They followed Eli until all three disappeared around the corner.

Fixing the car. And something about the river. If that meant he was going to fix the problem of the bullies, Greta didn't like it. Yes, he was strong, and incredibly resilient, but that didn't mean he could hurt someone. He could've killed her with that hammer in the basement, but he didn't because he was still young and kind and naïve.

Julie rushed to the window, but the boys were gone. Gone down the streets leading away from Main. She slammed her palm against the windowpane, sending fresh splinters through the glass.

"They're just going to hurt him again." Julie moved back behind the counter and typed something on the computer, one hand drifting to the phone. Greta had to act now, while no one was around. A twenty-year-old wrong could be made right. The headlines would be baffling: *55-Year-Old Woman Slays Librarian, Walks Away Covered in Blood.*

The brazen audacity of it made Greta's stomach flutter.

Julie picked up the phone and squinted at the computer screen, perhaps to call Mindy or Patrick and warn them about the bullies.

It would be so easy. Greta just needed something sharp enough. On the wall behind Julie, a pair of scissors waited harmlessly on a shelf. *Good enough.* Greta had the element of surprise—why would Julie suspect anything?

She remembered Eli's face, the courage he was trying to muster. He needed her help, but now was a particularly bad time. Eli had to take care of himself. This was more important. Julie was right in front of her, and she was the answer to everything. Every question, every missing piece, it all came back to her.

Greta shifted to the end of the counter. Three strides, maybe four, and she'd have the scissors. She checked the parking lot again, wondering if the bullies would throw more rocks, breaking bones instead of glass. She pictured them coming back to the library triumphant, with blood on their clothes.

Eli needs me, she thought. *But I can't help him.*

Julie pressed the phone to her ear, biting her lower lip. The little girl was all grown up, safely hiding in obscurity for twenty years. Julie knew the couple who killed her mother were never caught, but did she ever imagine they'd come back for her and finish the job?

The end felt so close, Greta could taste it. She stepped behind the counter, drawing a side-eye glance from Julie. Greta moved quickly, before Julie had time to react.

In the corner of her eye, she saw the desolate parking lot, and thought, *This is no town for a child. I'm sorry, Eli.*

Chapter 42

Eli walked behind the library and cut over, street after street, to Darling's small roads on the edge of town. Chase and Tyler pursued at a steady pace—no running, no yelling, no need to hurry.

Violence isn't the answer, Dad had told him on the phone. Sometimes Dad was wrong.

Up ahead, the old bridge forded the Little Miami River and was one of the few links between Darling's ugly backside and the woods and country roads beyond. After they built the Main Street bridge, they shut this one down and made it pedestrian-only.

The Little Miami thundered beneath it, lapping over the riverbank, almost touching the road. On each side of the bridge, piles of heavy stones lined the road and riverbed. Eli, Lucas, and Dad would often ride their bikes to the bridge and toss stones in the water. It was another childhood landmark, soon to be marred by bad memories.

Eli left the road, skipped over the guardrail, and landed on the stones. His shoes splashed in a shallow pool of muddy river water. After checking that his jumpsuit was zipped to the collar, he grabbed two baseball-sized stones and turned around as Chase and Tyler caught up to him. They knew this bridge. They knew how quiet it was, and they knew they weren't the only ones throwing rocks this time.

"Go on." Eli lifted his right arm, rock in hand. "I dare you." He wanted to say more; he wanted to scream at them, tell them every feeling, every thought he'd ever had about their attacks on him all summer. He wanted to tell them about his nightmares, about his friends who claimed to have seen a video of Eli running away. A whole summer of running. Eli didn't want to injure them, not really, but what choice did he have?

He didn't want to hear their phones vibrate with frantic calls and texts. He didn't want to hear the wailing of family members, but this had to stop. He was done running.

The guys stood in the road, unmoved by the pushback. Tyler slipped his backpack off, knelt, and opened it. Eli launched his first rock, purposefully sending it down just beyond Tyler's head. If he could scare them, maybe they'd see he wasn't afraid anymore and they'd leave him alone.

Tyler glanced at Eli, then resumed his task. He withdrew a container of peanut butter from the bag. The creamy kind. Creamy fucking peanut butter.

They'll kill me, Eli thought, reaching for his EpiPen. *They don't know what they're doing.*

Tyler held the peanut butter up, brushing greasy hair from his eyes. "This is bad for you, right?"

Eli threw the second rock. Chase and Tyler moved, letting the rock fall between them.

Tyler uncapped the peanut butter, peeled off the protective covering, and flicked it onto the road. The wind carried it away.

Eli grabbed a larger rock. "Don't bring that near me."

Tyler cackled, waving the peanut butter. "Scaredy cat!"

"Go away!" Eli tossed the rock, but they easily dodged it. He needed smaller stones—they'd fly faster. He tried to grab another one, but Tyler was already there, reaching for him. Eli jumped back and tripped on the rocks.

Tyler grabbed Eli's jumpsuit and yanked him up, dragging him over the guardrail. Eli's knees and shins smacked against the metal. He swung at them, but Chase shoved him down, sending Eli face-first into the asphalt. So much for intimidating them. At least they didn't know about his EpiPen, right?

Holding his arms, they rotated him onto his back. He tried to free himself by kicking his legs and arching his back, but it didn't work. Chase and Tyler pinned his arms with their knees, their faces grim, hair rippling in the breeze.

"Stop it!" Eli screeched.

Chase covered Eli's mouth, but Eli whipped his head to the side. "Help!"

"Can you do it already?!" Chase flashed Tyler an angry look. "Make it fast."

Tyler scooped a glob of peanut butter with two fingers. Eli strained—every muscle fighting against them—but it wasn't enough.

Tyler smeared peanut butter over Eli's lips, and the reaction was instantaneous. His airways clogged. His throat swelled. He stopped fighting as his body entered panic mode. His vision blurred, either from fear or because his body wanted to shut down. He hadn't had an allergic reaction in years.

Tyler set the peanut butter down and patted Eli's pockets. "Where do you keep it?"

"No, no, please stop." Eli felt his throat closing, his face on fire. He couldn't stop shaking.

Tyler smiled, feeling Eli's jumpsuit. His fingers closed on the EpiPen still safely in its pocket. "Bingo."

Down the road, tires screeched. The guys didn't look at first, not until the screeching increased. It sounded like a crazy person was peeling down the roads, drifting around the bends.

"Oh shit," Chase said, glancing over his shoulder.

Through his swelling eyes, Eli saw it—a car with a cracked windshield racing toward them. Tyler and Chase tried to move out of the way, but they were too slow. Tyler backed up, holding his hand in the air, not sure what to do with the peanut butter still on his fingers.

Eli thought the tires would crush his skull, but the car flew past him and ran into Tyler. He flopped against the hood and bounced off, flying like a broken toy. He landed in the middle of the bridge.

Greta threw her car door open and marched into the street, clenching the kitchen knife in her right hand. Her back was to Eli, but he pictured her face, alive with rage, spit flying from her lips as she screamed at Tyler.

Tyler wasn't dead. He stared at Greta, blood streaming down his face, and tried to move his shattered jaw. He made a watery cawing sound, like a drowning bird. Tyler tried to drag himself in the opposite direction, but that wasn't how things worked, not with two broken legs.

Greta hovered over Tyler before stooping down, locking her arms under his armpits, and hoisting him up. She shuffled slowly, dragging Tyler to the edge of the bridge. With a grunt she flipped him over the side.

Eli didn't see the body land, but he heard the splash. He imagined Tyler's shocked face, trying to kick his useless legs as the river swallowed him. Somewhere behind Eli, footsteps slapped on the road. Eli unzipped his pocket and clutched his EpiPen.

In a burst of pure adrenaline, Greta ran after Chase because he hadn't moved far. He'd stayed to watch Greta dump Tyler in the river. By the time his brain fired up, he tried running, but Greta was there already.

Eli held the EpiPen against his thigh and pushed the orange button.

Greta caught up to Chase. He turned to fight her, saw the knife, and went to run again, tripping and stumbling into the river. He tried to stand but Greta shoved him farther into the river. Chase was thigh-deep now, struggling to evade the river's pull. Greta stabbed him twice in the chest. He stayed upright and threw aimless punches. But Greta was livid. Despite his size—his boxer-like build—she tackled him. They fell into the water, disappearing under it. Greta emerged seconds later, still holding the knife, her fingers bleeding. Eli couldn't see well—he didn't know what happened, but he could use his imagination. He wondered if Greta stuck her hand between Chase's teeth and pried his mouth open. How fast did the river water surge down his throat?

She strained against the current, latching onto a log stuck in the riverbank. She clung to it, her fingers slipping. She still held the knife and seemed determined to keep it, even if it meant losing her grip. The river stole Chase. His hands briefly broke the surface, but the rest of him stayed under. Greta crawled toward shore, the log the only thing keeping her from following Chase downriver.

She sloshed through the water and ran to Eli, dropping her knife in the grass. Grabbing his wrists, she dragged him to the riverbank. She kicked through ankle-deep water before collapsing to her knees and dunking him in. He panicked when his face slid beneath the surface, but Greta quickly scrubbed the peanut butter from his lips and jerked him above the water line. He coughed and gagged and rolled away from the water. Greta helped him, using her shirt to finish wiping his face off.

Eli landed in the grass, pressing his warm face downward, his head spinning. He could taste the river in his mouth. Greta patted his back, looking small and deflated. Her clothes clung to her wet bones, and for the first time that day, she looked old and haggard. The adrenaline-fueled energy was burning out, leaving her empty.

She fell to the grass beside him, her chest heaving. Together, they watched the clouds above them and let the river and the birds and their beating, ticking hearts fill the silence.

Chapter 43

Julie had never seen anything like it. As she went to call Mindy, Greta Shaw, of all people, came behind the counter, grabbed the phone from Julie's hand, and set it back in the receiver. Then Greta just said, "I'll go get him." And walked out of the library, into the parking lot, and *drove away*. Where did she go? Apparently, to Eli, to go *get him*.

What?

Julie should have been unmoved by bizarre happenings at this point—the shadows, Tori's accident, Mindy threatening teenagers, and Julie herself, slapping Nancy across the face, losing every facet of self-control she'd carefully built for twenty years. *Nothing* should be surprising so late in the day, but Greta Shaw came out of nowhere, with perhaps her oddest, most anti-Greta thing yet. It was almost thrilling, watching Greta walk out of the library like an absolute gangster. Imagine having that level of confidence.

Too shocked to do much else, Julie waited for Greta and Eli to return, only they never did. She shelved the serial killer book, thinking back to her conversation with Greta. She needed to reiterate it to someone, like Tori. But Tori was in the hospital, hopefully in recovery. And the library was empty aside for Julie and Nancy.

The sky outside darkened as night approached. No one came to the library. People were huddled in their homes, warming their stomachs with hot meals, stocking their supplies of flashlights and candles and oil. Whenever Julie glanced out the window, no cars were on Main Street. It was already well past Julie's quitting time, but there was no one to take over, and she couldn't leave Nancy alone.

The wind never left. It only grew, filling the library like a thick, nauseating liquid. As if the library were a womb on the verge of giving birth.

Giving birth to what? Julie thought, staring at the broken window. The shadows were still moving, but much slower than before. They drifted down the walls and into the corners, almost like they were swimming. The lights were dimmer than usual. How was that possible? The library was drenched in pale, weak color, like how everything had looked during last April's eclipse.

Apparently, Nancy *did* notice something amiss. And like everyone else that day, the shadows must've addled her brain, because she walked over to the book tree and turned on the Christmas lights, something Julie would've sworn Nancy would never do.

Nancy rolled a chair out of the computer room and set it beside the tree. Then she sat down and rubbed her forehead. Her bracelets slid down her arm, and for the first time, Julie wondered if each bracelet meant something different. She'd never thought about it before.

Julie rolled another chair over to the book tree and sat down beside Nancy. Minutes passed. They waited for each other to speak.

"What did Chris say?"

Nancy cleared her throat. "I told him about Tori's accident. And about Carly's no-call, no-show. He wanted to see if you could close with me tonight, since there's no one else to do it, and he's still at that conference."

Julie nodded. "Of course. What else did he say?"

"That's it."

"Is it?"

"I didn't tell him," Nancy said, her skin glowing red and green. "I thought you should try and explain yourself first, and we'd go from there."

Nancy knew she could end Julie's career with a phone call. All that power, and she still wanted to listen.

"There's no excuse," Julie said. "I'm not going to justify it. I was out of control, and I'm sorry."

Nancy sighed. "What's going on with you? I've *never* seen you like that."

"My aunt died last night." Julie heard her own voice, in her head and in her mouth, but she couldn't believe how freely the words came.

"Julie, why on earth are you here then?"

Julie wanted to tell the truth: *Nancy, I'm terrified that I blacked out and killed her. I can't go home. I can't face what I've done.*

"Julie, talk to me. *Really* talk to me."

"I'm sorry I hurt you," Julie said. "I don't know what's wrong with me. But I'm not okay. I'm not. There's something broken. All day, I planned on leaving Darling. I just wanted to leave and never come back, because I have a *lot* of problems—"

"Yeah, so?"

"No, I'm talking real, scary problems, and—"

"What about Tori?" Nancy demanded. "Are you going to abandon her? She's hurt, Julie."

"I know."

"You're her friend. You can help her in a way no one else can."

Julie's chest tightened at the thought of Tori waking up in the hospital, her friend and coworker miles away. Not texting, not calling, not caring.

"I need you to be honest with me," Nancy said. "Because that's what we're being right now, right? Honest? I was scared to death back there, when you and Tori were *pointing* at things I couldn't see. I didn't know what to do, and I froze up. I regret that. You don't know how much I regret that. But please, no more BS. I want the truth."

Julie held her breath. She knew the question before Nancy said it.

"Is there something in this library with us?"

Julie nodded.

"It is here now?"

"Yes."

"Watching us?"

"Yes," Julie said. As she spoke, the shadows paused. She held her breath, lifting a finger to her lips.

Nancy looked around, whispering. "What are they?"

"Shadows."

"But *what* are they?"

The shadows moved again, slithering across the ceiling, and perching above Julie and Nancy, an explosion of shimmering black ink.

Nancy followed Julie's gaze, but again, saw nothing.

Julie leaned forward and whispered in Nancy's ear. "I think they're people. They *were* people."

"What do they want?"

Julie hated that question because she knew the shadows wouldn't leave until they got what they came for. Whatever that was. "I don't know."

"Should we leave?" Nancy's voice wavered. She was starting to believe.

Julie didn't expect this question, but she loved Nancy for it.

"Yes. We should leave."

Nancy held Julie's hand, a gesture so warm and unexcepted it sent shockwaves through Julie's body. "We need you, Julie. I need you, Tori needs you, Eli needs you. Promise me you'll stay? If there's something evil here, in this library or in this town, what makes you think you can run away and leave us to fight it alone?"

Julie nodded, squeezing Nancy's hand. "I promise."

Chapter 44

Eli was still a little jittery. He sat in the passenger seat of Greta's car, resting his head against her shoulder. With the windows down, he couldn't hear her heart, but he felt its faint ticking against his skull, like a human metronome, and he breathed to it. Inhale, *tick tick tick*, exhale, *tick tick tick*.

His body had mostly recovered from the allergic reaction. They still should've called 911, but Greta murdered two teenage boys half an hour ago, so calling anyone was a bad idea.

Greta was driving with both eyes open, her shirt bloody again. She shifted in her seat to look through the clean parts of the windshield. Even now, it was a game for her. As if there was nothing inconvenient about a shattered windshield, as if nothing could stop her from having the best day of her life.

"Are they dead?" he asked.

"Who?"

"The guys." He almost said their names. Almost. His heart teetered on the verge of guilt. Maybe they were alive, and he could feel less guilty.

"Oh, I sure hope they're dead. It would really complicate things for me if they weren't."

"I mean, things are already complicated, right?"

"Oh yeah," Greta chuckled. "Big time. I've been really lazy at covering my tracks. But that's fine. I don't expect to be in Darling past midnight."

"I thought you wanted to find out why you and Clive moved to Darling?" Eli pointed at Clive's button-up in the backseat. "That's why we dressed up. To help you remember."

Greta shook her head. "It's a lost cause. I doubt I'll ever remember everything."

Eli sat up, thinking back to Greta's interaction with Julie in the library. "That's bullshit, you remembered, didn't you? Why aren't you telling me?"

"Watch your mouth, bucko. Why do you need to know? I'll be gone tonight, and we won't see each other again."

"If you're leaving, then it doesn't matter, right? Who cares if some little kid knows your secret? I know all your secrets."

Greta smiled. "Not all of them, Eli."

So she wasn't going to tell him. Whatever. It didn't make sense why, after all this hype about her remembering, she refused to tell him why she came to Darling. What was she trying to protect him from?

Greta parked by the flooded baseball fields, facing the river.

"What are we doing?"

She shrugged. "Waiting a minute. Making sure you're back to normal before I drop you off."

His house was on the other side of the river. Alex was probably back from work and glued to his phone. Mom would be cooking while Dad and Lucas played a game. And they had no idea. Their day was normal. Their lives were normal. No one had found the bodies yet or declared Carly and Owen missing. Everyone lived like normal, blind to the precipice of national media coverage and pain on the horizon.

"I'm sorry for everything," Greta cleared her throat. "I know I've put you through things today that you shouldn't have gone through." She stumbled through it, clearing her throat again, eyes forward. "I want you to know I'm sorry. And I'm sorry you hated coming over this last year. I didn't know you felt that way."

"I should've given you the photo album a long time ago," he said, certain that was the only thing he needed to apologize for.

"No, it's all right," Greta said. "I haven't been fair to you, and I need to admit that. What I put you through all year wasn't fair. Everything today wasn't fair. So if you're angry and upset, I really do understand. I'm sorry."

The river churned, creating whirlpools of foam mixed with twigs and leaves. Eli's chest ached. He didn't have the right words. He wasn't smart enough or old enough to give a mature response. He wanted to cry. He wanted Greta to hold him. He wanted to sink into the river, find Chase and Tyler, and drag them to the surface.

"Oh, I almost forgot." Greta pulled Carly's cell phone from her pocket, the one she'd filched from the library before Julie returned from the bathroom. She held the phone in her left hand, leaned out the window, and tossed it into the river. "Not that it matters much. I'll be long gone by morning."

Eli thought about all the pictures, notes, and conversations in that phone. How much was saved on a computer somewhere, or in the cloud? Carly spent years etching her life into that handheld device, just for it to sink like a stone in a river you couldn't outrun. It probably sank into the baseball field and kids would find it when the river crawled back down the bank.

"Do you know about the baseball fields?" he asked.

"What about them?"

"How they're haunted?"

Greta rolled her eyes. "Everything's 'haunted' around here."

Eli shook his head and pointed at the field in front of them. "This used to be the Darling Cemetery. A long time ago."

"Really?"

"But it kept flooding," he continued, gesturing to the high-water levels. "Several times a year, the river would flood over and drown all the headstones."

Greta listened, transfixed.

"So you know what they did? They moved the headstones and started that cemetery up on the hill. But they left the bodies. Whenever we play over here, we're always told we can't dig. Ever. Because the field is full of caskets."

Greta shook her head in amazement. "Are you serious?"

"Yeah, it's crazy. With how bad the flooding is, they think the top layer of dirt will keep shrinking, and eventually, one big rainstorm will expose the coffins."

Greta slapped the wheel, grinning like a child. "I take it back, these fields are haunted. Goodness gracious, I can't believe you never told me that!"

Eli shrugged. "I didn't think you liked those kinds of stories." And that was true. Until yesterday, Greta was his fragile, elderly neighbor. She was someone completely different now. Despite who she was, he couldn't hate her. A stubborn part of him refused to hate her.

Beside him, Greta whistled like the wind—a low howl, rising like a boiling teakettle. She broke off, laughing. "I'm still not very good, am I? Could you tell it was me and not the wind?"

Eli put his lips together and blew. It wasn't nearly as lifelike as hers. He mostly just blew air through his lips, but he gave it his best shot.

"That's not bad," Greta said, whistling. Somewhere, far away, the wind replied.

"What's going on with the wind?" Eli asked, his skin crawling. He hadn't formulated the question until now, but he'd been inwardly asking it all day.

Greta frowned. "What do you mean?"

"It's weird, right?" Eli said. "The wind. It's not . . . normal."

"It's strong."

"Not like that. It feels like it's touching me."

"*It is.*"

"Not like that! Forget it. I don't even know what I'm talking about."

"You going to be all right?" Greta chuckled. "Careful darling, you'll turn out crazy like me." With that, she whistled to the wind, and the wind responded. "There's nothing wrong with the wind, Eli."

Sure, there was nothing wrong with the *wind*, but maybe something hiding in the wind, pretending to be it.

"Come on, let's get you home," Greta said. She backed out and started driving down Main Street.

Chapter 45

Greta parked in Eli's driveway and brushed the hair from her eyes. The sky was darkening, turning the world an eerie gray. She knew something was different, and it had to do with those shadows in the library. Nightfall would come early.

Eli unbuckled his seat belt and placed one hand on the door handle. He stared at his home like he'd never seen it before.

Inside the house, his family rotated in and out of view through the living room windows. Little Lucas skipped back and forth, chanting. Mindy talked quickly, shifting her hands to help explain the point she was making. Patrick moved slowly, hands in his pockets, head tilted down, as if listening but also examining the carpet. Alex's car sat in the driveway, and so he was likely sitting down somewhere. Greta had only met him once. Not a personable fellow.

Eli watched his family, his hand still on the door handle.

"You okay?" Greta asked.

Eli nodded, obviously lying to her. He was far from all right.

"I'm sorry again," Greta said.

Eli shrugged. "What are you going to do now?" He really wanted to know what she had remembered, but she wasn't going to tell him. She had to lie, even if he'd see through it.

"I'm going home," Greta said. "I'm going to clean myself up. Again. Then I'll pack, and I'll leave."

Of course, he didn't believe her. He finally cracked the door open and stepped outside. "Thanks for dropping me off."

"Don't forget this." She handed him his cell phone. "It's been going off all day."

"Oh, thanks."

"Hey Eli." She'd never see him again, and she hadn't pictured herself choking on a goodbye, but emotion overwhelmed her.

"Yep?"

"You're a great kid," she said. "I'm serious. You saved my life this last year. I would be dead without you."

He blinked, caught off guard. They both were.

"I never had kids," she said, swallowing a burning pain in her throat. "I couldn't have any. But after today, I think I know what it feels like. If I could go back, in another life, I'd want my kid to be just like you." She waved and mumbled *goodbye*.

Eli shut the car door, slipping his hands inside his jumpsuit pockets as she backed out and took off down Main Street. She checked her rearview mirror. His eyes followed her car as she drove over the Little Miami River. Eli had always been hard to read, but he was visibly shocked by her sentiment.

Clearly, she had allowed herself to get too close. It was a good thing, leaving him behind. When she lost sight of him, she focused on the road ahead. Driving a few blocks down Main Street, she turned into the Darling Library's parking lot, which was abandoned aside from two other vehicles. Both empty. Both potentially belonged to the librarians inside. Only two? *Must be short staffed*, Greta thought. She checked the time. The library closed in less than two hours. But nobody else was there. Just two librarians.

Greta decided to wait a little longer in case someone showed up. Almost killing Julie earlier had been reckless thinking. It was a public library. Anyone could walk inside. Once it closed, that was a different story. Different rules. Greta thought about the knife in her trunk, stained with mixed blood. She would need it tonight, to finish what she started with Clive all those years ago.

Greta leaned her head back, her thoughts drifting to Eli and how she'd shielded him from the truth. He loved Julie. He loved the library. It was better for him to find out later, after Greta was on the road and wouldn't have to look him in the eyes.

Her memory faded in and out. The memory of *that* night, all those years ago. Why were they careless? If they had killed that little girl, everything would have been different. If Clive were with her, he wouldn't wait. His anger always blinded him. He'd charge in and butcher that woman with his pocketknife. Never mind the police. Never mind the library's patrons. Only rage, pure rage.

Greta wasn't going to make that mistake. For Clive, for herself, she would do it right this time. Search the house. Find the little girl. Make her heart stop. Rip it out and look at it if she must. Just make it stop beating.

Chapter 46

Eli stared at his mashed potatoes, wondering if they resembled anything inside the human body. Too smooth to be brains. Maybe fat? His mom left the potato skins, leaving behind little dark patches. He poked one with his fork. Did dead human skin turn that color after enough time in the sun?

Eli normally disliked family dinners. The questions, the forced conversations, the expectation that he was going to care and participate. This one wasn't bad. His parents asked questions. They wanted to know all about his day. He told them pieces. Dropped little clues they'd remember when the news broke and the bodies were found and Greta had disappeared. They'd look back and ask themselves how they didn't see it. Why he didn't tell them.

He thought about it. He thought about taking everyone to that park and showing them the shallow grave. Secretly, he hadn't shaken the fear of blame. Someone in his family was going to view him as a monster. If he could delay that for another night, so be it. Let Greta run. She could only run so far and so long before it all caught up to her.

After dinner, Eli did the dishes. The windows gave him a clear view of the river and the Main Street bridge. The running water from the sink lulled him, morphing into the foaming, relentless river he couldn't stop staring at. His hands turned the plates and forks and knives. He didn't look down. He felt their surfaces for dried food, holding them under the water, drowning them in the city tap.

The river slithered on by, moving fast, making him dizzy. He reached into the sink, running his fingers along the stainless-steel base. Out of dishes. They were all in the dishwasher, placed at random. He didn't turn the sink off. He let the water splash on his hands and wrists.

In the river, a fallen tree was lodged into the riverbank, too stubborn to break away and float downstream. Branches and sticks had run into it, building a dam. On the edge of the dam, a human head bobbed in the water, stuck between two intersecting logs. The head was once a boy. A shattered jaw made the boy's mouth open wider than normal. The river flowed through his mouth, never dragging him under, never filling him up.

"Eli?"

Eli blinked and turned off the sink water.

Lucas stood in the kitchen, both arms above his head, holding a yellow kite. "Before it gets too dark?"

"Okay."

"Yippie!" Lucas slipped on his knee-high rain boots and jacket. "Let's go, let's go, let's go!"

"Be careful," Dad said from the couch, TV remote in hand. "Stay by the playground, and don't go anywhere near the river."

Eli didn't argue. He never wanted to see that river again. He pulled his shoes on and opened the front door. Lucas ran past him and into the front yard.

"Keep an eye on your kite," Mom said. "The wind's getting stronger."

Eli nodded and shut the door. She was right. He forced himself through the driveway as the wind pushed back. It felt like walking underwater. Up ahead, Lucas was nearly at the park, head down, clutching the kite to his chest. Lucas turned around, nearly falling, and gave Eli a thumbs up. They had the park to themselves.

Eli took his kite from Lucas.

"Think it'll still work?" Lucas asked, squinting at the sky.

Dark clouds soared above them, mostly blocking out a beautiful sunset in the distance. The sky was a mix of gray and dark red. Yes, the kite would work.

Eli smiled at Lucas. "Ready?"

"Yeah! Whoo!"

Eli took the kite in one hand and the spool in the other. He ran through the playground, clearing the swing set before letting the kite go. The kite bobbed a few feet above him. As he ran, he gave it more string, helping the wind take it higher. Before hitting the tree line, Eli backpedaled, ensuring his kite flew above the branches. He gave it extra slack, slowly walking back to where Lucas stood, face pointed skyward.

"What do you think?" Eli asked.

Lucas shook his head. "After a day like this, flying kites will never be the same."

Eli wanted to say, *Nothing will be the same*. The day's events swirled together in his mind, mixing, creating discolored, dreamy memories. Even if he forgot, he wouldn't be the same. Nothing would ever be as it was.

His phone was in his pocket, the battery nearly dead. He had almost a hundred unopened messages from the group chat with his friends. If he opened the chat and read all those texts, it would feel normal. Life would roll backward. Nothing was in place. Nothing looked or felt like it was supposed to—including his friends. How could he face them? How could he look in their eyes and not see the sad, sick expression of Chase's face before the river filled his throat and lungs? The only normal thing Eli recognized was his little brother and the kite in the sky. Not even the clouds were—

Eli gripped his kite string and focused on the clouds.

"What?" Lucas asked. "What are you looking at?"

"The clouds."

"So what?"

Eli pointed. "Do you see that?"

Lucas searched the skies. "I see clouds!"

"Oh my God," Eli laughed. "Holy shit, dude. Look!"

Lucas gripped his hair. "I don't know what we're looking at!"

"Hey, Lucas, can you do something? Go get paper. Not from the printer. Grab the extra-large sheets."

"Yes, sir!" With that, Lucas ran toward home. "How many papers?" he screeched above the wind, arms pumping at his sides.

"A stack!" Eli let his kite fly a little higher. "Hurry!"

Lucas returned two minutes later, holding a hefty stack of paper.

"You're the man," Eli said. "You ready to try something?"

"Does it have to do with the clouds?"

"Yes."

Lucas nodded. "Tell me! Tell me!"

"Okay." Eli pointed at the paper, then at the playground. "Take the papers up there, to the tallest spot by the big slide. You'll need to be high up."

Lucas ran through the playground, jumping up on the platform and running to the tallest tower next to the twisty tube slide. "Now what?"

Eli glanced over his shoulder. "Make paper airplanes."

Lucas grinned. He peeled off the top piece of paper and knelt on the stack. Using the tower's floor, he quickly produced a paper airplane in mere seconds. He played with the wings, carefully bending them to perfection.

"All done?" Eli shouted.

"Yeah!" Lucas held it up. "Now what?"

"Look at the clouds." Eli pointed. "See that tunnel?"

Lucas examined the sky, his eyes reflecting the distorted sunset on the horizon. "Why is it doing that?"

"I don't know!" Eli took another hard look at the clouds. Above them, a channel tore through the sky. It was the same current Eli noticed earlier that day, except at the time, he didn't realize how bizarre it was. The wind was pushing against his back, forcing its way toward downtown Darling. It wasn't explainable, but Eli wondered if the wind was *going somewhere*. If it had been going somewhere all day. If the current in the sky had a destination and was funneling all things, good or evil, toward it.

"It's a wind tunnel," Eli yelled. "Let's find out where it goes."

Chapter 47

Tick, tick, tick.

Greta heard her heart above the wind. That slow timebomb; a ticking clock, always moving. Pumping blood in ways her natural heart couldn't.

Greta touched the scar on her chest. Two and a half years ago, when surgeons attached a mechanical valve to her heart. They left wires dangling from it in case of future surgeries. That made her a cyborg. Eli didn't know that, but he would love it. Greta would write to him soon and tell him about the wires. How after the surgery, when they pulled the drainage tubes out of her chest, she'd never felt a more agonizing pain. How when she went home, Clive had to build a chair for her to sleep in because she couldn't lay down flat. Not with a fragile heart so close to *death*.

Tick, tick, tick.

Eli would love those details. He'd write back and want to know more, his creative brain at work. Greta hoped he would be all right. Perhaps it was the guilt talking, all that stuff about letters. Guilt or not. He was a good kid. He deserved better than what she had given him.

The wind rose. It played with Greta's hair. It kissed her cheek. She listened to its whispers and checked the time. Less than an hour until the library closed, but she didn't want to wait. The wind pushed her. It begged for *death*. Besides, no one else had come to the library.

Greta retrieved the knife from the trunk, thinking once more:

Search the house.

Find the girl.
Make her heart stop.
She strode through the parking lot, the wind at her back.

Chapter 48

They spent an hour cleaning up and shutting down. The shadows paid attention. They followed Julie as if they knew she could see them, but they stuck to the corners and ceiling, always melting into the darkest spot in the room. Despite their human likeness, she had a hard time picturing them as intelligent and resourceful people. In her mind, they were animals who preyed on some but left others alone. Julie knew she was underestimating them, especially after what they did to Tori. She knew what they were capable of, but she didn't fear them. For their own personal reasons, the shadows didn't communicate with Julie or Nancy, and that allowed them to complete their chores in peace.

This is their library. They had dutifully guarded it from Darling's worst offenders and weren't about to leave it unlocked and vulnerable.

The broken window was a problem. Nancy used a stepladder to reach the hole and tried once again to tape cardboard over it. Even duct tape wouldn't work. The cardboard fell off the window and blew through the foyer.

Nancy said she would call Chris and tell him about the broken window and how they closed early. He would understand. After all, they hadn't seen a patron in hours. It felt like the library had a virus no one wanted to catch. Even Chase and Tyler didn't come back. Neither did Greta and Eli. There was nothing. Not even a phone call.

"Ready?" Nancy said. She stood behind the front counter, her face measured. She couldn't wait to leave, despite never seeing the shadows herself.

Julie checked the counter for anything left behind. She tapped her phone to see notifications, but nothing appeared. No missed calls or texts. She'd need to run by the hospital and check on Tori if they'd let her.

"I guess Carly really did quit," Julie said. "She didn't show up at all today. Not even for her phone."

She opened their lost and found drawer, but Carly's phone wasn't there.

"That's weird." She rummaged through the sunglasses, keys, and toys. Still no phone.

"I swear it was here. Did you move it?"

Nancy shook her head. "Maybe she came in and grabbed it when we were all busy?"

"I guess." It made sense for Carly to avoid them. But how would she know to immediately check the lost and found? Either she got extremely lucky or spent five minutes searching the office and counter, and no one saw her. Both were unlikely, but not impossible.

Or someone else took it, Julie thought. *But if someone took it, then what happened to Carly?*

A door slammed. The windows shuttered. Another jagged crack split though the broken window like a lightning bolt frozen in time.

"What was that?"

Nancy crossed the foyer, turning in circles. "The Children's Room?"

They hadn't locked the doors yet. Someone came in the back.

"I'll see what they want." Nancy walked down the hallway.

Julie stared at the drawer, convinced someone had moved the phone. But why? Because they didn't want Carly to find it? Because they didn't want *anyone* to find it?

Carly would've come back for her phone, no matter what. She would've called or stopped by, just to see if it was there. She *lived* on her phone.

Nancy's voice echoed through the hallway. "There's no one here."

Julie froze, all of it, all at once, coming back. She'd spent twenty years paranoid that a pair of serial killers would find her again, and that pattern of thought had never left her, but she'd been suppressing it all day, or simply just distracted by the wind, the strife, the shadows. Too distracted to really think about Carly, about her phone and the note on Julie's calendar. And Greta, showing up early, and the rich smell of bleach, even though Gary never left a strong smell after cleaning. Then Greta again, returning a book she never checked out. Greta, going behind the counter to grab the phone from Julie's hand.

Greta, standing beside the counter after Julie returned from the bathroom. *Beside* the counter, not in front of it.

Julie rushed down the hallway, running into Nancy, who stood by the basement door, hugging herself. "We heard a door, right? Even the windows shook."

Julie shook her head, thinking too fast. "What if something happened to Carly?"

"What?"

"Carly! Her phone's missing. What if she never came back for it? What if someone took it?"

"I don't understand."

"The bleach this morning, remember?" God, the morning felt like years ago. "The bathroom was cleaned by someone other than Gary—that's why it smelled!"

"But if Carly is missing, why hasn't someone come by? Wouldn't people be looking for her?"

"Maybe, but maybe not. She was going out with Owen last night for his birthday. What if they've been missing all day, and everyone assumed they were together?"

Nancy nodded but wasn't convinced. "But what do you *think* happened?"

"I don't know, I feel completely insane right now, maybe it's nothing, maybe it's all in my head, but something weird happened in the bathroom. Why else would there be a smell? Why else would Carly leave a note on my calendar and leave her phone behind? She was quitting, not . . . killing herself." Then it hit her. The basement, the shadows in the corner.

"Oh my God," Julie whispered. "I'm so stupid. Tori nearly figured it out."

"Figured *what* out?"

"Give me one minute, then we'll leave." Julie approached the basement door, already removing her keys, finding the one she needed.

"What are you doing?"

"I'll explain in a minute." Julie unlocked the door. "You have your phone?"

"My phone?"

"Yes! I need the light."

Nancy handed her an old iPhone, but the flashlight still worked fine. "I need to check something. One minute, then we're leaving. And maybe calling the police."

Then Julie ran down the stairs and into the basement.

Chapter 49

Lucas understood what Eli wanted. He had to throw the paper airplanes into the sky and hope the wind took them somewhere. It was like tossing a paper boat in the river and watching it float downstream. But way cooler.

Eli had never been more impressed with his brother—the way he stood in the playground tower, one hand clenching the railing, the other holding a paper airplane above his head.

Lucas leaned against the railing and launched the airplane. They watched, positive it would fly to hell and back if they asked it to. It flew six or seven feet before the wind forced a nose-dive. Crash-landing, the paper airplane skidded across the playground and through the street.

Lucas didn't even look discouraged. He sank to the floor and made another plane. Eli looked back at his kite. It was stuck in the wind tunnel, trying to fly into town, a little yellow ship in a black sea.

"Three . . . two . . . one!" Another airplane took off, flying farther this time. Sailing over Eli's head, it made a sharp curve and landed on Main Street—skipping off the pavement and barrel-rolling through the neighbor's yard.

"Rats," Lucas said, making another plane.

Eli stared at the wind tunnel. *Paper airplanes won't be enough*, he thought. They needed another way. With the sun going down, they were about to lose their light.

When Eli turned back around, Lucas wasn't in the tower. He was *climbing* the tower. It had a plastic, pointed roof, and Lucas was already halfway up it. Eli wanted to scream at him to get down. A fall could break bones or worse. But Lucas wouldn't have listened. He was nearly at the top, a paper airplane pinched between his teeth.

Lucas crouched on the roof, holding the tower's pointed top with one hand, lifting the paper airplane. Eli couldn't take his eyes off him.

The stack of paper, now unattended, became the wind's latest victim. The top pieces peeled off and scattered around the playground, bouncing from railing to railing. Eventually, the rest followed. Paper poured from the tower like a waterfall, cascading around Eli. Lucas, standing above the flying paper, gave Eli a savage grin, threw his arm back, and launched his airplane. It *soared* through the air, catching invisible waves. Dive-bombing then pulling up at the last second. It flew past Eli, toward their house.

"Go, go, GO!" Lucas cheered.

The airplane flew over their house, crashed into a tree, and fell out of sight—probably in the river. In the last rays of sunlight it turned gold, as if on fire and burning as it fell.

"That was nuts!" Lucas screamed. He sank to his hands and knees to avoid falling off, and slid down the roof's side, connecting with the tower railing. His boots snagged on the railing, and he fell forward, landing inside the tower, right on top of what remained of the stack of papers. Lucas struggled to his feet, laughing.

Eli shook his head. "You're stupid!"

Lucas shrugged, gathering a few pieces of paper. "More! More! More!"

"Don't go back on the roof, dummy. Paper airplanes won't work!"

Lucas leaned against the railing. "Then what?"

Eli stared at his kite. It was almost full dark. The yellow glider in the sky dimmed with every passing minute. Near the swing set, a metal bench was bolted into the ground. Eli ran over and felt the metal beneath it. The support bars formed ridges. Not sharp enough to cut his skin, but good enough for string.

Eli double checked his kite's position. It was still in the wind tunnel, still straining toward downtown. He glanced back at Lucas, who watched Eli with puzzlement, turning into surprise.

Holding the string against the metal ridge, Eli scraped it back and forth, between both hands. After several tugs, it snapped, and he let go. The string slipped through his fingers, and the yellow kite spun wildly, flying away from them.

Eli bolted through the park.

"Are you going for it?"

"Yes! Tell mom and dad I left something at Greta's."

Lucas frowned, not wanting to be left behind. But he understood.

"Thank you!" Eli shouted. "I'll be right back."

Lucas pointed at the flying kite and jumped up and down. "Go! Hurry!"

Eli took off down the sidewalk, the kite flying over the river, leading him into downtown Darling.

Chapter 50

Julie sprinted down the basement stairs and jogged through the narrow aisles, her clothes catching on the sharp corners. She didn't slow down to avoid scrapes—this was more important. This was life or death. Changing aisles, she headed straight for the far corner. The empty space beneath the bathrooms.

No light touched this end of the basement, giving the corner a cave-like depth. No shadows either. They'd migrated upstairs. But *something* was there. Why else would the shadows swarm that spot?

Julie held the phone high, casting pale white light over walls lined with pipes of various sizes, all glistening like metal worms.

Blood. So much dried blood. It had run down the walls in messy trails, dripped on the pipes, puddled on the concrete.

Far away, Nancy's voice echoed from the stairs. Calling Julie's name.

Someone had died in the bathroom. And not an accidental death, no.

A murder, cleaned up with bleach.

Why else would Carly never pick her phone up, or call in, or at least tell Nancy that she wanted to quit?

Julie turned to run, her ankle clipping a bookshelf, knocking her to the floor. Her palms slid on the concrete. Nancy's phone *crunched* in her hand.

They had to get out. They had to call the police and show them the blood.

Struggling to her feet, Julie limped through the aisle, her leg collapsing with pain.

"Julie, are you okay?"

Julie neared the stairs and looked up. Nancy stood on the top step, the hallway light glowing behind her, turning her into a silhouette. Julie was about to reply when something moved. Behind Nancy, a figure quietly advanced. Nancy sensed the movement and tried to turn around, but the newcomer was faster. They filled the doorway, hands outstretched, and seized a fistful of Nancy's hair.

The figure yanked Nancy's head sideways, thumping it against the wall. Julie's ankle gave out and her knees hit the floor. She crawled away from the stairs. Something thumped again, and Nancy's body rolled down the stairs and landed on the concrete floor, her head bent at an odd angle. An eye was partly dislodged, and her eyelid twitched, fluttering like a dark moth.

The figure's shadow fell over Nancy's body. The person halted on the steps—waiting for Nancy to move. Nancy would never move again, but the person didn't know that. A step creaked. They were coming downstairs.

Julie pulled herself into a corner, trying to regulate her breathing. When she looked back, the person had gone back up the stairs. A door slammed above her. Footsteps thundered down the hallway.

"Hello?" Gary's booming voice echoed through the building. "Anyone home?"

She should've called Gary. She looked at Nancy's phone still in her hand. It turned on, but the cracked screen wouldn't respond to her touch.

Julie struggled to her feet, favoring her bad ankle. She limped to the bottom of the stairs and looked up. The killer was gone. Julie looked at Nancy and felt a tremor in her heart. Something brushed the hairs on her arm. Her skin darkened. Shadows swam over her and latched onto Nancy.

"Hello?!" Gary shouted, louder.

Julie forced her brain to slow down and consider the possibilities. It was herself, Gary, and the killer still in the library. If she could reach Gary, they could fight back. But where was the killer?

A sharp noise cut through the silence, making Julie jump. Whistling. Gary's strong, vibrant whistling. Julie often joked about wearing earmuffs when Gary cleaned because when Gary whistled, you could hear it from the parking lot. Now, the tune of "Be Thou My Vision" filled the library with angelic clarity.

Julie ignored the pain shooting through her leg. She took the steps one at a time. Halfway up, the hallway dimmed. Julie paused. Waited. The hallway light had gone out. Then another light vanished as well. The Children's Room went dark. The rooms branching off the hallway received the same treatment.

Julie climbed the rest of the steps, creeping into the dark hallway. She wanted to scream Gary's name, but her voice didn't work. Her brain kept freezing. She staggered forward, too stupid and slow. Easy prey. If she ran out of the Children's Room door, she'd be free. But that left Gary with the killer. And Gary had no clue what he'd walked into.

Up ahead, Non-Fiction went dark. Then the foyer lights disappeared. Same with Fiction, leaving only the office lights. Gary's whistling continued. He was in the office, unaware.

Julie sank to one knee, straining to see through the dark. "Gary! There's someone in here!"

Gary immediately called back. "I know! She said she's leaving!"

She?

The office lights went out, and Julie stood in darkness. After a day of waiting, the shadows were now perfectly invisible. The wind whispered down the hallway, snaking between her ankles.

Julie couldn't move. No sound same from the office, and the library fell quiet, disrupted only with the howling wind. And the clocks, ticking.

Tick, tick, tick.

Chapter 51

The yellow kite flashed in the dark sky.

Eli followed it, sprinting over the river, tripping on the uneven sidewalk, but never falling. His body didn't grow weary or out of breath. He'd spent his entire summer running, preparing him for *this*.

Main Street stretched out before him. No cars, no signs of life. Everyone was sheltered inside, some with the lights back on, and some without. Stores were closed and barred, same for the apartments and ramshackle houses with their broken blinds and dull TV-glow.

Streetlamps created pockets of orange light on the street. Up ahead, his kite crash-landed on the road and skipped, catching on signs and benches before cartwheeling away.

It had fallen out of the tunnel, but the wind was still taking it somewhere, and the wind *wanted* him to follow, so Eli ran after it. He raced down Main Street, pushing himself faster, watching the kite zip out of view.

When he stopped by the library, he heard fluttering, like a flag in the wind. In the library parking lot, his kite was plastered against the iron fence lining the walkway to the entrance.

Eli felt the wind pushing him toward the library like it had also pushed him down Main Street. He walked to the other end of the library parking lot. Maybe it was his imagination, but the wind was at his back again. Impossible. The wind couldn't move in every direction at once.

He went behind the Children's Room, feeling the wind shift with him, attempting to pin him against the library. Or maybe he had nothing to do with it. The wind wasn't following him or leading him anywhere. It was circling the library. Pressing down on it. *Not* the wind. Something *in* the wind. Trying to get inside the building.

Eli ran back around to the front entrance and sure enough, the wind pushed against his back. All the wind, from all the directions, leading to the Darling Library. It had done that all day. He saw the wind tunnel earlier that morning, flowing into downtown like a river in the sky, and again at Darling Cemetery, the same thing.

Eli surveyed the parking lot. Why the library? What was important about it? And did it have anything to do with the strange shadows he saw earlier? A few cars were parked nearby, including Greta's in the back corner—right where he'd walked by moments ago, distracted by the wind.

He had known earlier she wasn't telling the truth about going home and leaving town. Greta had unfinished business, and it had something to do with the library, or she wouldn't be parked here. The car was empty. Was she inside the building?

What did the library have to do with why she came to Darling?

Eli turned to walk inside the building as the first light went off. The hallway went dark, followed by the Children's Room. One by one, every light vanished. Eli looked at the cars again, then back at the library. His kite made small whipping noises. Then it ripped, split in two, and smacked against the library's brick wall.

Inside the library, the final light disappeared.

Chapter 52

Julie was frozen in the hallway, considering her options. Not that she had the time. Every wasted second kept her in danger. She needed to act and fight or run and get help. *Something.*

"Hello?" Gary called. The office lights turned on. "What are you doing?"

Julie had to move. She sprinted into the foyer, straining to see. "Gary, run!"

"Hey—" Gary started before his words turned to grunts, and the office went silent again. The wind fell against Julie's face, making her eyes water. The office lights turned off once more.

"Gary?" she whispered, not loud enough for anyone to hear.

Orange streetlight seeped through the windows, giving her enough light to see Gary emerge between display cases, crawling on his hands and knees.

A trail of blood poured from his dangling cross necklace. He slid to his stomach, his open throat wheezing. The angry black gash oozed darkness, staining his clothes, soaking into the carpet.

He stopped breathing, and although she had trouble seeing, Julie knew the shadows were on him already, filling their bellies.

Behind Gary, a small figure stood by the library's front doors. A child cloaked in shadow, his hair glowing red from the exit sign above him.

A woman followed Gary's bloody trail. The same woman who'd spent the last year reading encyclopedias in the Reference Room; the woman

Julie would help sit down in a big comfy chair; the woman Julie often sat with, listening to the dull timebomb *tick* of her heart, just to give her company. To prove she wasn't alone.

Greta Shaw hunched over Gary and poked him with a shiny red knife, like you'd do to a dangerous animal you wanted to stay dead. The shadows were undisturbed by her. She held her fingers just above Gary's back, as if hoping to feel the shadows as one feels a pool of water. She smiled, then looked at Julie.

"Julie, Julie, Julie," Greta whispered. "What's your real name?"

What was she talking about? How did Greta know she used to have a different name?

"I can't remember." Greta laughed, stepping over Gary's body, over the shadows. "Funny, right? After everything I've remembered today, I can't remember your name."

Greta moved toward Julie, lifting the knife. "You knew it would happen, didn't you? That one day we'd come for you. Clive figured it out. He used to keep a picture of you in his wallet. In case he saw you in the grocery store or on the street."

Everything shifted. Julie's childhood raced back to her. The Kentucky Duo, the police, her mom's dying eyes. Julie, as a kid, racing through the woods, tears running down her cheeks. And yes, she *knew*. She knew someone would eventually find her. And yet she told herself every night for years that it wasn't true.

But Greta? Sweet, forgetful Greta? She looked nothing like the monster from Julie's nightmares.

Greta stood in the orange light and admired the dark wet blood trailing down her arms. Sensing someone behind her, she turned around and addressed the kid by the front doors. "Eli? *What* are you doing here?"

Eli didn't reply. Hands inside his jumpsuit pockets, he looked unbothered by the murder scene before him: Gary, bleeding out, and Greta, holding the knife. Julie tried to understand his reaction—was it shock? Or something worse?

"You knew I wasn't finished," Greta told him. "That's why you're here. You knew I was lying! All this time I was afraid you didn't understand me. She's *the one*, Eli." Greta shook her head, pointing at Julie. "She's the one Clive and I missed. Remember how we said no kids? We would've broken our rule with her. If we'd just broken it, everything would've been better."

Eli stepped into the light, his face impossible to read.

"I know why you're here," Greta said. She lifted the knife, offering it to him.

Eli moved forward, reaching out, gently taking the handle.

What? Julie wanted to scream. *What's going on?*

"Help me." Greta licked her lips. "Help me do this. I didn't tell you because I wanted to protect you. I didn't think you'd want to see this, but I was wrong, I was so wrong, you need to see this. You can help me, one last time. We can make this right."

"Eli," Julie said. "What are you doing?"

"For years, we had dreams about you." Greta looked at Julie and then closed her eyes. "We used to stay up late talking. We wondered if the police moved you somewhere safe. We thought a relative might have taken you, but they were so secretive about it. By the time we started looking, you were long gone. How could I have forgotten? All this time, with you helping me read every night, in this library. And I never knew your face."

Julie tried to think of something to say, but all she saw was the poster the sketch artist drew. The poster Julie never forgot.

Greta's age. Her face, her size, her curly hair—gray now, but dark brown before. It all matched. She was skinnier, with wrinkled skin, but still the same woman. The same woman in her living room all those years ago.

"We waited for so long." Greta moved closer. Her warm breath kissed Julie's lips. Her eyes swam with big wet tears. "We wanted it to be special, finding you. I think Clive knew the moment he saw you behind that counter. I think he knew exactly who you were."

Words came and went, like passing clouds. All Julie could do was stand there and wait for what came next. Any plan she conjured fell to pieces. Any retorts or arguments she could use to save herself disappeared inside Greta's swimming pool eyes.

"I could go on." Greta touched Julie's face for the second time that day. "Clive wanted a ceremony. But we don't have time for that. I just want you to know who you're looking at. You ruined our lives. We spent the last *twenty years* hiding, all because of a little girl."

The broken window made a sharp cracking sound. The wind pushed harder, forcing the glass to bend inward. Julie stared at the broken window, then at the knife, still in Eli's limp hand. This was their chance. Greta had made a mistake by trusting Eli to help her. She didn't know Eli like Julie did—he was just a gentle kid.

Julie bolted for Eli, to get him out, to get the knife, and to end this nightmare. But Greta seized Julie's neck and dropped her weight. Julie tried to stay upright, but her ankle gave out. Her knees hit the carpet, followed by her head. Greta wormed her fingers through Julie's hair, took hold, and tried to drag her through the foyer. Greta, not strong enough to keep pulling, rammed Julie's head against the floor. Everything dimmed and slowed down.

Greta peered at Julie, her teeth shining. Greta then stretched out her other hand, offering it to the boy in the camo jumpsuit. The jumpsuit with the scar on the right shoulder; the boy with the knife in his hand.

Eli zipped his jumpsuit to the collar. Then he stepped forward and took Greta's hand.

Chapter 53

Greta patted the top of Eli's hand. "Are you hearing it too?" Her fingers were slick with Gary's blood—the man who had tried to teach Eli to whistle once, a year ago, back when whistling was just whistling, and not the voice of the wind.

"Hearing what?" He couldn't look away from Gary's parted lips, painted red and black, or suppress the desire to touch Gary's cooling body. To feel his chest and empty heart. To touch that drippy red smile in his throat.

Greta squeezed his hand. "The wind. Can you hear it?"

Julie stirred on the floor, shifting her arms and legs as if in a dream.

Eli gripped the knife. He could end this right now. Greta wouldn't see it coming, would she? She trusted him. He imagined the desperate loneliness in her eyes when he forced the knife between her ribs. She'd die heartbroken and confused, wondering why, after everything she'd done for Eli, he'd turned on her so callously.

He raised the knife ever so slightly, his fingers sweaty. He couldn't do it. He didn't want to kill her. He didn't want to see her frail body on the carpet beside Gary. At the start of the day, he had believed her to be sick and suffering from a head injury. Part of him believed that again. She saved his life earlier. She told him she wished her kids could've been like him. Now she waited for him—she'd somehow gone back to being the forgetful old lady who needed his help.

He could still save her, right? Or was he too late?

"You hear it, don't you?" Greta dropped his hand. She stared at the broken window, brushing strands of hair from her face. "It wants this. It wants me to kill her. They all do."

The shadows.

"Julie hasn't done anything wrong," he said. The shadows weren't visible in the darkness, but they were there. Still waiting.

Greta half-smiled. "You're not listening, Eli. *Listen*."

Julie rolled on her back, trying and failing to sit up straight. The wind picked up. The broken window vibrated, lengthening the cracks. Tiny shards spilled onto the floor.

"Listen," Greta said. "Really listen. It's calling you, Eli. It wants you to help. They're all watching. They've been waiting for you!"

That didn't make sense, what would the shadows want with him? He was just a kid.

"Twenty years," Julie whispered, getting up on her hands and knees. "It's been twenty years."

"Are you ready, Eli? Are you *listening*?"

He nodded, wondering if this could be the only way to save her.

Greta grinned and closed her eyes and spoke to no one. "He's ready."

One final crack and the window exploded. Eli flinched, glass raining on him. Greta clapped, lifting her arms in the silver-orange shower. The hurricane wind roared through the library, and Eli lost his footing. He dropped the knife and sank to his knees.

Books slid off the displays. Pages whipped between covers. The library itself shifted, and a great rumbling filled the air, evolving into something so deep and terrible, Eli's bones shuddered beneath his skin, like they were trying to *get out*.

Greta screamed and danced with delight. The wind didn't knock her over. It broke around her like a stone in the river. She lifted a hardcover from the floor and threw it through the other window, shattering the lower half.

Eli crawled to Julie and tried to help her stand. Her feet moved sluggishly beneath her, but she finally stood straight up, eyelids fluttering. "Twenty years," she whispered.

"Run, now." Eli pushed her gently, but she resisted, trembling.

"Please, Julie, you have to go."

Greta hurled another book. Then another. Until there was nothing left to break. She stood before the open windows like an offering, stretching her mouth open, eating the wind.

"Go!" Eli shoved Julie. "Please, go!" Julie needed to run while he dealt with Greta. He didn't trust the wind and what it was doing to Greta's mind. If he could make the wind believe he wanted to help Greta, would that let him in? Could he trick the wind into giving itself away?

Eli left Julie's side and walked into the wind, one foot after another, until he stood beside Greta in the orange streetlight. Transfixed by the wind, she didn't move or acknowledge him. Her curly gray hair had thinned, exposing a shiny scalp underneath, running with sweat.

Eli kept his head down. He wanted to attempt something. It was ridiculous, of course, but he had to try. It was the only way.

"You want me to believe?" he whispered, letting a soft whistle escape his lips. "Then make me believe."

He looked up and opened his mouth, and the wind poured down his throat and filled his stomach. It burned in his chest and behind his eyes. Shadows gathered around them. Shadows shaped like humans. Dozens of them watched and waited. Waited for what? For *him*?

He was about to find out.

He grabbed Greta's hand and closed his eyes.

And he wasn't in the library anymore.

He was *there*. In her haunted house. Her Memory Mansion, where the air pulsed with the rhythmic *ticking* of her heart.

He ran through her haunted house, through the great halls filled with memories—memories she'd told him about and memories from the photo album. Some he knew, others he didn't. He ran to the deepest corners. He saw the lifeless bodies left in living rooms and messy beds. He saw Greta as a child, swinging on a playground as high as the swing allowed. Greta in a white dress, kissing Clive. Greta kayaking, beaming despite the obvious sunburn on her cheeks and nose. And of course, Clive was there, shirtless beneath his lifejacket, smiling at Greta like a shark.

It was all there. All *ticking*.

The walls hummed with life. Why did the air feel strange? He lifted his arm, feeling something slither over and under it simultaneously.

Of course. The wind. He turned in circles, feeling it now. The wind was inside her haunted house. It was everywhere.

He walked farther in, following the wind's gentle current. Was the wind going somewhere? After all, it had been going somewhere in Darling all day, why not have a destination in Greta's mind as well?

He entered a circular room with three doors. Two were perfectly still. One rattled—the door labeled *Death*.

The wind pushed against it, straining the hinges. The doorknob twisted and shook as if it were locked, and something wanted in from the other side.

"Death is a door," Eli said, approaching it.

The door was old-fashioned. It had a keyhole shaped like a skeleton key. He knelt and peered through it, seeing nothing but darkness. Only shadows.

"Death is a door," Eli said again. "It goes both ways."

And all at once, he understood. Death wasn't on the other side of the door. It *was* the door. Death was a door that opened both ways. A person dies, and the door opens. Giving just enough time for something to slip through before it swings shut again. Something from the other side. Something long dead and possibly angry. Hunting for a second chance at life.

The wind wanted Death. All day he'd assumed the wind was helping Greta. It gave her memories. It made her invincible. But he'd been wrong. The wind didn't want her to remember. It wanted Death. It was trying to get her killed. Because *Death* was a door, and the shadows were in the library, waiting for Death. Waiting for the door to open, as it had when Gary died. No wonder the shadows were drawn to violence and to the prospect of death. It was their way in, their chance to slip through the door. Eli wondered if any had got through already and imagined that they had. If so, did they feel the need to stay and watch the fight for the library? Or were they already out there, roaming Darling's streets, ghosts in search of a new home?

Then Greta screamed a high-pitched wail and the house disappeared and left Eli in darkness. He opened his eyes and was back in the library with Greta hunched beside him, dropping his hand.

The knife protruded from Greta's shoulder. Julie gripped the handle, her eyes wide and frightened, and with a grimace, she pushed the knife deeper.

No, Eli thought. *If she dies, we'll let them through.*

Chapter 54

Greta's shoulder burned with a hot, searing pain. It paralyzed her and she fell to her knees, scattering fallen library books and shards of glass.

Julie looked dumbfounded, clearly shocked at her own ability to stab someone. *The first time is the hardest*, Greta thought. Like everything else, it required practice. Clive did the killing the first time he and Greta seduced someone. After the light had left the man's eyes, Greta used the knife on the man's body for practice. Practice makes perfect, after all. Greta used the knife in their later years because it really was quite easy once you got the hang of it. Human skin was so soft.

Greta pushed on the knife's handle with her fingertips, dislodging it. She tried catching the knife, but it slipped to the floor between her and Julie. Blood ran down her shoulder and back, but the pain had lessened, and it wasn't very deep. She could already feel the wind smothering her cut like a warm salve.

The shadows closed in, intently watching. Greta had an idea why they were there. She heard their muffled voices through the wind. They wanted inside. Not inside the library. They wanted to be on this side of the veil.

Greta staggered to her feet, the shadows urging her as the wind had all day.

Kill, kill, kill.

She needed no encouragement. Killing the long-lost little girl would be a pleasure.

Eli stood off to the side, clearly confused. He'd seen inside her mind. He finally understood her, but he loved Julie and this library, and Greta wished he didn't have to see what came next. She had hurt him so much already. He clearly wasn't ready to help her do what needed to be done. He didn't have it in him. Not yet.

"Twenty years," Julie said, shaking.

"What?"

"I waited twenty years for them to catch you. I spent my *life* afraid you'd come back for me."

Julie, the cozy young librarian, had spit dripping from her lips. Her fists were clenched, and she faced Greta without a shred of fear. Greta liked Julie, truly. But she had to end this before the girl riled up some real courage.

"Your mother was also scared of me," Greta said, glancing at the knife on the floor. "I'm the one who cut her. She wouldn't stop shaking in my arms, and for a good reason. She wasn't worried about herself, no, in the end, despite all evidence, she died a good mother. She was scared of what I would do when I found you. And now she's not here to find out."

Greta dove for the knife, but Julie shoved her back. Julie spiraled to the floor, the knife just out of her reach.

A burst of wind exploded through the windows, hard enough to knock Julie over. Greta went for the knife, but Julie had already recovered.

Julie stayed low and lunged for the handle. Their hands fell on the knife at the same time.

Chapter 55

As Julie reached for the knife, she remembered what had happened last night after blacking out. The memory hit her: falling asleep reading and then waking when she dropped *David Copperfield*.

Aunt Susan was startled at the noise and bolted upright. She climbed out of the bed and reached for Julie. *Are you all right? Don't be scared, child, you don't have to be scared.*

Then Julie threw her aunt back on the bed and grabbed a pillow. With the wind in her face in that dark, shadow-filled room, Julie held her aunt down. She eventually pulled the pillow off Aunt Susan's face, stumbled away, and ran through her house, opening every window and forcing aside every curtain because the wind told her it loved her. It promised her the world and spoke with her mother's voice.

Julie clutched the knife, coming back to the present. Greta tried to pry Julie's fingers from the handle, but Julie moved without thinking. A different woman had taken control. A woman she hadn't known existed, quietly growing beneath the surface. A woman capable of even the worst things.

A *killer*.

Julie jerked the knife away and scrambled to her feet. Greta lurched for Julie's hand, but Julie backpedaled and swung the knife down, nearly slicing Greta's hands. Greta paused, clearly unsure of how to fight without a weapon. Julie felt a primal satisfaction deep inside her. That was all she needed.

Julie rushed forward, slashing the knife, aiming for Greta's throat. Now Greta was on the defensive. She fell back, almost tripping on her feet. Julie could see the arrogance melting from Greta's face. For the first time, she looked afraid.

Julie pursued Greta into the Reference Room, moving through pockets of orange light—wildly swinging, Greta dodging. Greta ran around the reading chairs, keeping them between her and Julie.

"Greta."

Until he said something, they'd both forgotten him. Greta searched for Eli's voice, but he was already beside her. "Don't trust the wind," was all he said, but his eyes focused on Julie. He was giving her a shot. Greta let her guard down and glanced at Eli with confusion, maybe disappointment.

Julie jumped onto the reading chair and skirted over the back, barely landing on her feet. Greta turned too late. Julie put one hand against Greta's chest and shoved her, pinning her against the bookshelf.

Whispers flowed urgently through Julie's ears: *kill her*.

Maybe it was her mother, who never got to see her little girl grow up.

Kill her.

Julie raised the knife and stabbed just as Greta shifted her head. Instead of going through her right eye, the blade raked along Greta's scalp. Greta shuddered, but she said nothing. She didn't even beg for her life. Julie pulled the knife back, brought the point to Greta's mouth, and pushed. The knife slid between Greta's teeth.

"Don't," Eli said, reaching out, too scared to touch Julie's arm. "Please don't. They want her to die. They're waiting for the door to open." He looked behind him, in the direction of Gary's body. "We're letting them through."

Despite the shadows around her, Julie *wanted* to kill Greta. It would take nothing. A little push. Barely any force. And the knife would exit the back of Greta's throat. But Eli was right. Killing Greta would give the shadows exactly what they wanted. They were watching, begging her to do it. She felt them swim around her, powerless now that she recognized their whispers.

Julie thought back to the resurfaced memory from last night, and already the details were slipping away because it wasn't real. The whole thing was fabricated, whispered to her, twisting her reality.

Julie withdrew the blade and pressed the tip against Greta's stomach. "Don't move," she warned. Not that it mattered. Greta blinked uncontrollably. Her breaths came in sporadic huffs. Blood spilled from the back of her head.

Then Julie realized why: the back of Greta's head had slammed against the bookcase, creating, or reopening a wound. Julie stepped back, afraid the shelf had sunk into Greta's head, and the woman was dying. Blood ran down the shelves; small streams trickling down, dripping, painting the books with red speckles.

Greta sank against the bookshelf, her eyes glazing over.

Julie clutched the knife hard enough to turn her whole hand bone white. She tossed it on the floor behind her, her chest constricting. What did she do? After another look at Greta's glassy eyes and bloody head, Julie turned away. What did she just do?

Eli sat beside Greta. "Can we call the police?" He spoke too calmly. He was far too relaxed for what had just happened.

Julie couldn't respond. She rushed from the quiet room. She found her phone on the counter and dialed 911. Her fingers trembled. She had blood on her hand. But whose blood?

She spoke to the dispatcher, her voice barely functioning, her throat burning with relief and shame and terror. It was hard to talk. Hard to even think over the sound of thick, heavy silence.

Because the wind was gone. The endless howling dissipated until the air returned to normal. Even the trees outside turned into statues. Julie flipped on the lights until every corner was lit, but it didn't matter. The shadows had left. She paused to look at Gary and Nancy, and the last of her anger melted away, turning to shame and regret.

Julie returned to the Reference Room. Greta was slumped against the books, passed out. Eli still held her hand. Every few moments, he pressed his palm against Greta's chest, just to feel the *ticking*.

When the sirens came down Main Street, Eli glanced back. He looked at Julie as if he didn't recognize her anymore.

As if he were sitting in a room with a stranger.

Chapter 56

Three weeks gone and Darling had yet to see another storm. Eli thought Greta killing five adults and two teenagers was bad enough, but the windiest day of the year had devastated the whole town in many cruel and horrible ways.

Houses burned down from candle fires. Rural families went ten to fifteen days without power. Darling saw its worst flooding in years. Four people died, not including the Greta Shaw murders. *Another* murder occurred that night (it was personal—cheating spouse or stolen money or something like that), one death from a house fire, a drowning, and a suicide.

As for Eli, that was the hardest night of his life. Later, his parents told him they were proud of him. They said things like, *Everyone is proud of you*, and *We can't imagine what you went through.*

Eli answered the police honestly. He never lied, not once. Not about what Greta did or what he did for her. He worked with detectives and federal agents for days, his parents hovering nearby, nervous but understanding. But *did* they understand? Of course not.

He led the detectives to the park where the hiker, Owen, and Carly were crudely buried. It felt like giving a tour of his worst nightmare (and over here, we have a young woman, nice looking, who just showed up out of the blue, and Greta had to kill her, and yes I helped bury her). It was too clinical, too documented, measured, and scientific. He recounted the events leading up to Chase and Tyler disappearing—his story solidified by the body they recovered miles downstream. They found Chase's bloated corpse, but Tyler was still missing. He told them the things Greta said about her past, and they eagerly recorded it, hoping to solve not just the murders at hand, but dozens of murders potentially linked to the Kentucky Duo. The police thanked him for staying strong. So did his parents.

In the following days, Darling mourned the loss of so many people. Kids didn't play outside. Sidewalks were unused and overgrown. Main Street traffic never stopped. Cars rolled through, carrying tourists or unsuspecting travelers who eyed the riverside town and wondered why Darling looked so sad and empty. People sat on their porches. When they discussed the murders, they spoke in whispers, and when all was said that could be said, they retreated to their televisions and tried to forget. Half the town attended candlelight vigils. The other half stayed home and watched the gathering of small fires through dirt-smeared windows.

Eli couldn't distance himself from the town's grief. He was a celebrity—the victim, abused and tortured by a deranged serial killer. His parents constantly fought reporters, true crime experts, and every podcaster, blogger, and writer in the state. They wanted his story. They hungered for it—that horrific addition to Ohio's infamous murders.

The only people who didn't need the gory details, oddly enough, were his friends. All the attention Eli received made them uncomfortable. At first, they joked about the whole thing. He didn't blame them. How could they empathize? The whole story sounded like a horror movie they'd seen before. Nothing new. Just crazy shit. And crazy shit happens. They didn't treat him differently at first. He was the one who pulled away.

It started a week after everything happened. They all met up at his friend's house to play video games (Eli's parents thought a little normalcy would help). After two hours of playing shooters, arguing about what gun performed best, Eli realized he felt nothing. No interest, no curiosity. A hollow emptiness. His friends were aliens. Their spats centered around things that didn't matter. He couldn't stop staring at their faces and picturing their skulls. All those bones hidden under wet meat. He wanted to touch their foreheads, feel the hard bone behind their skin, and ask them if they ever thought about death. Ask them if they realized their skulls never stopped grinning, even when they were asleep.

Now, three weeks after that night, Eli was tucked in bed, his sleeping bag pulled to his chin. He stared at the crack in his ceiling and thought about shadows. Then Lucas asked him a question. A question Eli had waited three weeks for Lucas to ask. He was surprised it took his little brother this long to get around to it.

"Eli?"

"Yeah?"

They breathed in the quiet darkness. Lucas was afraid to ask but did anyway. "What'd you do with the photo album?"

The photo album: Greta's lifelong memories stored in old plastic pages, reduced to three by five windows with brief, chicken scratch handwriting. On that night in the library, when Eli first heard the sirens, he pulled his phone from his pocket. He called Mom. Told her to hurry over. Bring Dad. Bring Lucas. He truly wanted them there, but in the corners of his mind, he knew the reason.

The police were waiting when his family showed up. Julie was already talking fast, explaining a jumbled version of events. The bodies, Greta's behavior, why Julie's prints were on the knife (Eli *saw* what happened, he'll verify, ask him). Eli hadn't said much yet. He wanted his parents close. He needed them to know he never wanted any of it to happen.

When they arrived, Eli made eye contact with Lucas. Eli opened his arms for a hug, and when Lucas ran to hug him, Eli whispered instructions. A secret between brothers.

Once Mom and Dad swooped in and bombarded him with questions, bouncing between him and the police and projecting their general confusion and shock, Lucas asked if he could grab something from the car.

Mom said *yes* without thinking, and Lucas jogged to the edge of the parking lot where they'd parked. No one watched him go. No one cared. Only Eli saw.

Lucas opened the car door and glanced at the library, the crime scene. Convinced no one was looking his way, he walked behind the car, into the grass, and ran to the end of the lot. Only Eli saw him reach through the open window and remove Greta's photo album from her car. Only Eli saw Lucas bring the photo album back to his parents' car and hide it in the backseat.

They never mentioned it after that. Lucas patiently waited, confident his big brother had a good reason for keeping secrets.

Eli debated what to tell Lucas. Not the truth. No one needed to know the truth. At the time, Eli hadn't fully known himself. But the police were about to take over. Lock everything down. The photo album was the most valuable thing Greta owned and he felt responsible for it. The police would pick it apart, analyze it, and give photos to the press.

"I gave it to the police," Eli lied. "It was stupid to take it. I figured Greta didn't want it rotting away in a storage box. But it was evidence, so . . ."

"Why did Greta kill those people?"

Eli struggled through the same question. He had an answer for Lucas, and whether it was true or not, Eli didn't know for sure. But he believed it.

"Because the wind told her to," Eli said. "There was something wrong with it. Something evil that told her she needed to hurt people." Eli watched the corner of his room, waiting for a shadow to move.

"Why would the wind want that?"

Eli didn't blink. Didn't take his eyes off the corner. "Not the wind. Something hiding in the wind. But don't worry about it, okay? It's gone now. It went somewhere far away."

This seemed to reassure Lucas because he didn't ask any more questions. Evil up close was monstrous. Evil far away was manageable. And big brothers were supposed to protect little brothers. But who protected big brothers?

Eli rolled over and touched the photo album hiding beneath his pillow. By now, he knew what to do with it. A little secret—not between brothers this time—a secret for himself. A special project he would start soon.

And one day, he'd give it to Greta.

Chapter 57

NEXT SUMMER

Julie leaned back in the metal chair and perched her feet on the stone wall surrounding the fire pit in front of her. The flames warmed her ankles and warded off the chilly summer evening. The sun had just set, allowing only the brightest stars to make it through the smear of violet sky.

Riverside Bar had a large outdoor patio with live music and a packed house on the weekends. Two inside bars. One outside. Fire pits and heaters scattered among the metal tables and chairs. Umbrellas closed and tied. Julie had waited thirty minutes at the bar until a spot by the fire pit opened, then she quickly abandoned a one-sided conversation with a guy ten years younger than her, because . . . no thanks. Relationships were almost impossible. So, Julie staked her claim at the small fire pit and set her beer down in front of the chair beside her. She didn't usually have conversation-strikers (like the preppy college kid at the bar), but it was best to be prepared.

Her spot overlooked the Little Miami River, which reflected dark trees and a pale, watery moon. The bustling patio echoed with humor and drunk laughter and chatty banter, but she focused on the river and wondered, not for the first time, what drowning felt like.

"What's cookin', good lookin'?"

Julie snapped back to the present. "Geez, lady. It's about time."

Tori threw her hands up. "I told you I was running late."

"Didn't check my phone. I'm trying to live in the moment."

Tori smiled. "Good for you." She hugged Julie tightly before sitting down.

"Ever been here before?"

Tori shook her head. "Drive by it all the time though. I realize now I've been missing out, I mean come on! A fire right next to the river. Stringed lights? It's very romantic."

"If not for all the drunk people, it would be."

The waitress came over, and Tori ordered a beer. "I'm not usually a fan of beer, as you know, but I didn't bring my own wine bottle, and I can smell your cup from here, and it's making my mouth water."

Another waitress swung by and handed Tori a plastic beer-filled cup. Foam spilling over the edge, Tori took a long sip. "So, what's this for? Are we celebrating? Please tell me you did the interview."

"I did the interview."

"So you're famous now?"

"I hope not."

"You will be." Tori snapped her fingers. "Just like that. The true crime community won't stop talking about you. I'd bet money Netflix makes a documentary about you. Not another Kentucky Duo one, but one about *you*. Just wait. This is only the beginning."

"I'm taking it slow," Julie said. "My therapist recommends I take it slow. And I agree. One podcast interview was enough for now. I hate hearing my voice. I won't listen to it. But a camera would've been worse. I'm not ready for that."

Tori shrugged, also propping her feet up on the stone wall. "I think that's smart. We had a fan of yours at the library a few days ago, when you were off. I didn't tell her when you'd be working, but I'm sure she'll be back."

"What does she want?"

"Hell if I know." Tori laughed. "You were national news, Jules, the big leagues. People want to meet you. Shake your hand. Some of them, maybe this girl, wish they were you."

"I don't get it."

"People are curious," Tori said. "They don't get to witness messed up shit. So they live vicariously through the people who do. I don't know. There's an attraction to that stuff. Obviously, I used to love all that. Used to. I can't seem to get into it as much anymore." Her voice cracked and she took a long sip to smooth it out. "Sorry. I'm bad at talking about that day. I know, it's been a year, but those final minutes, driving away, and how close I got to leaving my daughter without a mom. Or some other mom without a child. That shit keeps me up."

"That wasn't your fault."

Tori shook her head. "I don't believe that. Yes, things were influencing me, but I'm still responsible, and there's nothing else to blame. I can't explain what happened in the library. Can you?"

Julie shook her head. She couldn't explain any of it. Not even close. It felt like a drug-induced dream. Another world with another version of herself.

During that impossibly long night, when the police, paramedics, and coroner came to her house to record Aunt Susan's death, Julie looked for the shadow, but it was gone. The wind and the shadows had flown to other towns, where they looked for death and whispered to those who listened.

Julie gave the police the medical records Aunt Susan had brought with her. The coroner went through the process of confirming her diagnosis. Although in the end, cancer didn't kill her—she died from a stroke. Tired and ready to sleep, the coroner signed for her body to be released to a funeral home.

Julie waited for something to happen. For a paramedic or police officer to take a closer look at Aunt Susan with suspicion in their eyes. That never happened. No one blamed Julie because she wasn't to blame. The wind made her open the windows, and the shadow that came inside her house and scared Aunt Susan was likely the cause of her stroke. If the shadows were good at anything, it was sniffing out death and altering mental states. That memory in the library was exactly what Julie suspected: a forgery. Julie never would've harmed her aunt, even though, as she discovered throughout that impossible day, she was more than capable of hurting someone.

As days passed, and as Julie woke up every morning, she told herself it was time to change. Really change. She started therapy. She met Tori's family and came over for wine dates. And eventually, she went back to work at the library, determined not to let the painful memories define her. Greta Shaw was the cause of so much grief in her life. She wasn't going to leave the only place that gave her purpose. She was safe at the library. The shadows were long gone.

However, since that night, the Darling Library's reputation as 'haunted' skyrocketed. While Julie had yet to see anything she'd claim was supernatural, the influx of fresh stories bothered her. Both Nancy and Gary died while the shadows were there, and if Eli's words had any truth to them, the door between this world and theirs opened twice, and something might've slipped through.

"No. No one can explain it," Tori said. "So unless I can pinpoint why and how it wasn't my fault for breaking down like that, I'm going to carry the blame."

"How have you been recently?"

"Despite the mess you're seeing right now, I've actually been okay. A little bit better."

"I'm proud of you." Julie kicked Tori's shoe. "You look like you're doing good."

"I don't even know why I'm complaining." Tori finished her beer, smacking her lips with a satisfied sigh and burp. "I'm not the one who really saw shit. I would've been messed up for good if I saw what you saw."

Julie half-smiled. "I'm doing my best, right? Just like you."

"Yeah. Just like me. Hey, speaking of traumatized-but-recovering people ... you seen Eli lately?"

"Yeah, some. You?"

Tori shook her head. "He's quiet now. Even more than before."

"I asked him how he was doing," Julie said. "About two months ago. I knew the one-year mark was coming up."

"And?"

"Normal stuff. He told me he has nightmares, but they're going away. He looked really good, actually. I was surprised. He suffered more than any of us."

"That's the truth. Poor kid, at least he's holding up." Tori twisted in her seat. "Damn waitress disappeared on us. No worries. I'll swing by the bar and grab another round."

"My hero."

Tori winked and stood up. She limped through the crowded patio. Her walk had improved a lot. Apparently, her physical therapist seemed optimistic about her recovery. Tori didn't say so, but she was afraid of limping forever. The way she talked about physical therapy. The hopeless comments passed off as dark, comedic quips. The longing in her eyes when she spoke of Sophie playing soccer, and how she couldn't practice kicking the ball with her daughter without pain shooting up her leg.

Tori glanced back at Julie through the crowd. She waved her thumb at the bartender as if to say, *We're in business, baby*. Tori leaned against the bar, taking pressure off her left leg. She wore short sleeves, showing off her tattoos. They never joked about her wearing long sleeves at the library anymore. Not with Nancy gone.

Some things could not be fixed, which was why Julie didn't go into detail about her conversation with Eli. Tori didn't need to hear about any more broken things.

Eli had pretended everything was normal. He responded to Julie's questions with his classic shy answers. Elusive as always. Always brewing something smart in that brain. Except his mischievous look was gone. That innocence in his eyes. When he looked at her, she thought they shared a bond. They had one, after all. Only they knew what happened in the library that night. The way Eli held Greta's hand, breathing in the wind beside her. The way Julie slid the knife between Greta's teeth, about to sever her mouth from her head if Eli hadn't said something.

After their stifled conversation, Julie couldn't shake the feeling that Eli was hiding something. Or he was just lonely. What other kids could he relate to, after going through all that?

Julie felt a change happening in her. A turning key. An unlocked door. She had a responsibility now. She knew that. And running away, or convincing herself otherwise, would be wrong. She had to tell Eli what he needed to hear. She'd forever regret it if she didn't.

Tori returned with matching plastic cups. She handed one to Julie and sat back in her own chair. "Miss me?"

"I always miss you."

Tori raised her cup. "Here's to us."

Julie smiled. "Here's to us." They tapped their plastic cups together and drank.

****

Julie hoped Eli would come by. School hadn't started yet, but he came to the library often, carrying his school backpack, and would set up shop in Fiction at the small wooden desk in the window. Alone and far away from everyone else. He would work there for hours, and Julie could never figure out what he was doing. He'd leave without checking out a library book, his backpack full of secrets he didn't want to share.

Three days after meeting with Tori, Eli came to the library. Julie was checking out a long line of patrons and saw him enter Fiction and vanish behind the shelves. After finishing the line, she made her way to the wooden desk in the corner.

Eli heard her coming. He flipped his notebook shut and stared at her. She wouldn't waste time with pleasantries because he didn't need bullshit. His face was leaner and more defined. He didn't look like a kid; he looked like someone who'd seen too much.

"I don't know what you went through," Julie said. She'd prepared a speech in her head but hadn't expected to struggle with the words. She paused, trying to remember the things stuck in her heart.

"I don't know what you went through," she repeated. "But you know what happened to me, when I was young. It took me twenty years before I could talk about it. I can't get that time back. And I really, desperately wish I hadn't wasted it by hiding who I was."

Eli didn't flinch. His emotions were locked away.

Julie wasn't about to drag this out. Eli didn't need a lecture, but he needed the truth.

"What I'm trying to say is, I know a little bit about trauma and what it does to people. It's not good, Eli. If you ever need someone to talk to, please come talk to me. Tell me about that day. About what Greta did to you. Because I promise you, you're not alone. Okay?"

He nodded, something stirring in his eyes. Still, he said nothing, and his hand stayed firmly on his closed notebook.

"Talk to me, whenever you want. You know where to find me."

With that, Julie walked out of Fiction, through the foyer, and got back to work.

Chapter 58

AUTUMN

Eli rode in the passenger seat of his mom's car. A pack of cigarettes waited in the cupholder, shifting in slow circles as the car bounced from pothole to pothole. They'd just taken an exit for Cincinnati. This was part of their new weekly routine. Mom would find a spot to smoke while she waited for him. Then they'd stop somewhere and pick up chocolate ice cream or a cookies n' cream milkshake from United Dairy Farmers. Eli's backpack rested in his lap, and he hugged it against his chest.

After running a few yellow lights and dodging a few more potholes, they pulled into the hospital roundabout, where cars unloaded their passengers before moving to the parking garage.

"Need me to go in?" Mom asked, slowing the car down. Asking the same question she always asked, even though they both knew the answer.

"No, you can drop me off."

"Text me when you're done. Be safe, please."

"I will." Eli stepped outside and swung his backpack over his shoulder.

"What's it going to be today?" Mom asked.

Eli patted his backpack. "Agatha Christie."

If Mom found his choice of fiction disturbing or inappropriate, she didn't say so. She squinted in the late afternoon sun. "Please be careful and text me if you need anything."

He nodded. "I'll be back soon." Shutting the car door, he waved to her as she drove around the circle and into the parking garage.

The hospital doors retracted with a screech. The receptionist waved to him. Giving him that sad, knowing smile, like they all did.

"Eli." The receptionist, Alice, beckoned him over. "Want a sucker while I sign you in? I got strawberry and watermelon."

He took one from a plastic container and dropped it in his pocket. "Thanks."

"How's your mom?"

"I think she gets bored waiting for me," he said, trying to think of clever things to say. Things that made him sound normal. Did they believe him? Even Alice had that look. Like she was dealing with a fragile, unstable kid. A kid who could lose control at any moment.

"I doubt that." Alice typed on her keyboard, causing the printer to power on. "She's proud of you."

Yeah, yeah, he thought. *Everyone's so proud.*

"Here you go." Alice handed him a sticker with his name on it.

He stuck it to his shirt, right over his heart, then waved to Alice and made for the elevator, taking it to the second floor. When the doors opened, he turned right and followed the curving hallway. When he came to a set of locked doors, he stood in front of the camera mounted on the wall and pressed the intercom button.

"Name, and who are you here for?"

"Elijah Wright, here for Greta Shaw."

"C'mon in, Eli."

The doors unlocked with a click. Eli pushed through, letting them swing shut behind him. Two women sat at the nurse's station, wearing matching blue scrubs. The one sipping coffee was Hailey, also known as his babysitter. Eli didn't recognize the other one. She looked new.

"Hey buddy." Hailey set her coffee down. "How ya doing?"

He stopped at the desk. "I'm okay. Just here for a reading."

"Sure thing."

He slipped his backpack off his shoulders and slid it across the counter. Hailey unzipped the pockets and rifled through, finding nothing but three things. The same three things he'd brought with him for the last month.

"You're all set." She re-zipped the bag and handed it to him. Her security check was autopilot for her. She had no reason to suspect Eli of anything. "Agatha Christie. Love those mysteries. They're classic."

Eli shrugged. "Greta loves classics." The new nurse watched him with narrow eyes and a false smile. She glanced between him and Hailey, unable to conceal the thought stuck in her brain: *This isn't normal*. Eli didn't care what she, or anyone else thought.

Hailey gave a warm, nonjudgmental smile. Much better at hiding her pity than her co-workers. She maneuvered around the counter and beckoned for Eli to follow.

Together, they continued down the hallway, skipping the first few doors on the right. They stopped at Room 2247. Those numbers appeared in his dreams. Not his nightmares. His good dreams. Harmless, memorable numbers.

It took them months to approve this. It took even longer for Mom to be okay with it. She still wasn't. She only agreed to it under two conditions: it was a limited amount of time (eight weeks), and Eli's therapist had to be on board.

Convincing the therapist was easier than Eli anticipated. After all, Eli Wright was quickly finding himself in the spotlight. People loved tragedy, just like the shadows. Once Eli learned how everyone would treat him differently, he taught himself how to cater to their expectations. They expected a grieving, recovering child, and even now, at almost fourteen years old, they believed he'd fall apart at the slightest trigger.

Mom didn't want him to see Greta. She couldn't fathom why it would help him. Eli convinced his therapist, and he didn't have to fully lie. He simply said he didn't know who he was anymore, and seeing Greta would humanize her. The therapist liked that. It felt like an experiment, and he wanted to see how it would pan out. He was probably writing a book on Eli and needed a redemption arc to enrich the narrative. Eli was a high-profile case, otherwise he never would've gotten approval to visit a serial killer.

Once the therapist approved, and Eli and Mom settled on eight visits over eight weeks, she did most of the work to make it happen. Eli wondered why she toiled away to get him visitation. He wondered if she blamed herself for what happened. That if she'd been more present, things would've been different.

Mom didn't realize what he was doing at the hospital every week. None of them did. They thought he was reading to Greta like he had done before. But he wasn't just reading to her.

If any of them knew—*actually* knew the truth of his visits—they'd have more fear in their eyes. He knew, deep down, his actions weren't normal. But that didn't stop him.

Hailey opened the door and that familiar smell hit him: sawdust and rain. It had transferred to this room, almost supernaturally, from Greta's house.

Greta lay in the hospital bed, arms extended over the covers, hands open, almost reaching. Her eyes were closed—quiet and unmoving. Her chest rose and fell with the same steady rhythm Eli had grown accustomed to. He'd tap his finger to the *ticking* while he read, using its tempo as a metric for the tone and fluctuation of his voice.

Beside her bed, a small chair, thinly padded, waited for him. Another chair was pushed to the far corner of the room. Hailey sat there. They didn't want to leave him alone with a serial killer, coma patient or not. Fair enough.

Hailey sat down in her chair and brought her phone out. She put Air Pods in and watched something on her phone.

Eli sat, placed his backpack at his feet, and removed a pen and notebook. Spiral-bound, hundreds of pages, and only partly used. Its maroon cover was cracked and weathered from constant use. Today marked Visit No. 4. And he had planned something special for this week. Hailey, lost in her TV show, didn't look up at him.

Eli moved to the edge of the bed and took Greta's hand. He cradled it, smoothing out her wrinkles with his thumb. He swept her curly gray hair from her forehead. So peaceful. So sleepy. The room had no noise aside from the beeping machines, and her *ticking* heart.

It was time to move on. Time for a new chapter. Eli scooted forward and touched the soft metal band wrapped around Greta's ring finger. Gold, faded, a little dirty. The authorities didn't take it off her. Why would they? She was as good as dead. Eli pulled Greta's wedding band off her finger and dropped her hand. He slipped the ring in his pocket as Hailey looked up. She smiled at him awkwardly. On the first visit, he'd explained several practices his therapist told him to try. Things like holding Greta's hand, writing her letters, and talking to her, not just reading her stories. His therapist didn't say those things at all, but Hailey had no reason to think Eli was lying to her.

He was just a kid.

Hailey went back to her phone as Eli sat in his chair and opened his notebook. Words and pictures decorated the thick, cardstock pages. His own handwriting stood out as crooked and scratchy, done in the late night with an irreversible pen. The pictures were his handiwork as well. Sort of.

He flipped through the notebook, passing chapter after chapter—a scrapbook with a story. The only story he cared about anymore. Not even Lucas knew this one.

This one belonged to Greta.

Eli had created this notebook, this story, using a few things he took from Greta. Namely, her photo album. He'd removed all the photos and kept the stack shoved in the corner of his pillowcase. Using a pair of scissors, he cut them up, physically editing the pictures he didn't like. And there were a lot.

The photo album served as a timeline, which made his job easier. Even still, he had trouble piecing it all together. Many pictures were taken out west. Grassy plains, sandy backdrops, mountains, rocky hills, and hiking. Sweeping canyon views, gorgeous rivers, buffalo, and elk. There weren't many pictures of their farm. If he had to guess, the last twenty years were a dark period for them. They didn't need to take pictures of their chickens, vegetable garden, or the rocking chairs on their porch. Apparently, they used to travel a lot. That all stopped when they went into hiding. And the goofy, smiling photos stopped too. It made him sad. Greta deserved a better story.

This new scrapbook he'd made was a collection of cut-up photos, starting with Greta's birth. Not much there. Just a rough drawing of a swaddled baby. Not quite a baby picture, but it had to do. Greta didn't have baby pictures of herself. After that, he flipped through more pages that told the story of Greta's young life. Drawings of her playing soccer, on a swing, and playing the piano. Since he didn't know much about Young Greta, he had to improvise. He wasn't sure he would like her true story anyway.

According to his version, she grew up with wealthy parents, both doctors. They raised her with refined humility. They adored her. And she ventured into her teen years with all the ambition of a naïve explorer. The world at her feet, she excelled in school, volleyball, and debate club. Her fling with the school quarterback didn't go anywhere, and after that, Greta moved on. Became picky. Didn't date much until college, where she dated here and there until she graduated. Nothing serious. Nothing personal. Her dreams just didn't include them.

Eli turned page after page, rereading those fascinating college years. He reached the new chapter—the one he wrote yesterday. He'd spent hours on it. Cutting, gluing, writing. He glanced at Greta. Her chest rose and fell, as steady as the rising and falling sun, as gentle as the swell of the ocean.

"Can you hear me?" he asked, not expecting an answer. She never answered. "It's me again. Eli." He cleared his throat. Starting the conversation was always the hardest. "I don't know if you remember anything. About what happened. About this . . . sleep you're in. I hope you don't remember. It was awful." Deep breaths. Deep, shaky breaths. "If you don't remember, that's why I'm here. Because when you wake up, they're going to say terrible things about you. Things you did. To me, and others, and yourself. And it's all a lie."

He clutched the notebook. He hated this part, this necessary ramble. But if she was listening, she needed to be told. None of it was her fault. She wasn't herself and shouldn't bear the blame for all those bodies.

"Don't believe what they say," he carried on. "Don't believe any of it. No matter what they tell you. That's why I'm here. In case you don't remember, I'm here to tell you the truth. Your life story."

In her own way, Greta had loved him. Her actions that day were the result of head trauma and a poisonous wind. He kept this opinion to himself—everyone wanted her to be the famous Darling Killer, but he was *there*, in the library. He felt the wind inside her haunted house. She didn't crave Death like they did. She wouldn't have hurt anyone if not for that wind.

He glanced at the pages, smiling at no one. "Chapter Four: The Roaring Twenties." Greta would've loved that title. She would've made quite the flapper. "You graduated college, making your parents proud," he read his own words, his heart warming from their confidence. *What a story, Eli*, he imagined her saying.

What a story.

"You started work as a teacher," he read. "Teaching math, of course." On the page about teaching, the picture he'd used came from a photo of Greta and Clive, dressed smartly, standing in front of some city's music hall. Captured moments before some opera or symphony. Except Clive was cut out, then cut up and flushed down the toilet. Greta was left there, young and bright, beautiful and unique. Standing in a black dress and heels.

Eli made the decision early on to leave Clive out of this story. He pictured himself inside her mind, her haunted house, laying bricks in front of the door called *Clive*. Greta would wake up and *know* something was there but wouldn't be able to place it. The doorway, now covered by bricks, would be only a scar, a distant memory of pain. Erasing Clive had to happen. Without Clive, Greta never killed anyone. Never left a mutilated body behind, rotting on a living room floor. Without Clive, she never helped create the Kentucky Duo. Without Clive, Greta achieved her dreams and married a clever lawyer in her early thirties. But he was skipping ahead. That part of her life hadn't been written yet.

Eli continued reading, going into vivid detail about her classrooms, her students, and the creepy principle. He wondered what was going on inside her mind. What was rebuilding in place of the haunted house? He hoped it was museum, brimming with life—the life he knew she should have lived, painting over the old broken memories with something new. Something better. When she woke up, this story of his would be all she knew. Along with this scrapbook.

Eli read. Greta slept. Her wedding ring shifted in his pocket, reminding him of Clive's existence. After he finished reading, Mom would take him home (after ice cream or shakes, of course). Later that night, he would walk on the Main Street bridge and throw the ring into the river. And then later, while everyone slept, he would write the next chapter of *Greta's Story*.

Acknowledgements

God made me creative. Without His gifts, I wouldn't be here and this book wouldn't exist. There's a reason He built me this way, and this book feels like a small baby step toward whatever future He has in store. It feels like burning the ships; the ones that take you safely back home.

This novel is really the product of my childhood, my imagination, and my greatest fears. I write a monthly email called *The Ghost Story Newsletter*. If you want to know more about me, and why I write these types of stories, then I encourage you to sign up on my website. If you want updates on the next book, or insights on what it's like to be an author, or even pieces of short fiction, you might find it interesting. I hope to see you there.

I'd like to thank Erin Healy for her terrific editing and influence on the narrative. Tiffany Avery, for her invaluable editorial work on the intricate details. My early readers, Martha and Katie Jones, Anna Nwa, Aaron Bogan, Norma Athearn, and Rachael Boucker. Every one of you made this novel better. Thank you to Annie Hoober, Brandon McCauley, and numerous teachers who pushed me to keep writing.

Although this my first published book, I've spent years sending many people earlier novels, short stories, and flash fiction. For everyone who helped push me forward, who kept me writing and encouraged and focused, thank you! From telling my brothers I was taking writing seriously, to sitting with Gage, Dustin, Chandler, and Matt at Thortons, to my coworkers in Maine, who shared in my early victories and defeats, who encouraged me to keep going, to all of you, I remember those conversations, they meant the world to me. What I'm trying to say is, my gratitude extends far beyond helping me with this book. You all set me on a path that may last a lifetime. So thank you again, for now, and forever.

Special thanks to Libby and Steve, who truly are the *heart* behind this story. This book would be lesser without you. To my parents, for their continual support, even if they don't prefer "scary stuff."

Thank you to my wife, Caitlin, for every time she watched the kids so I could write. For those endless conversations, doubts, long nights, bottles of wine, and lazy bookstore strolls. It's been a wild ride, and I hope it never stops. Here's to a lifetime of adventure.

And lastly, to you, reader, for taking a chance with this story. I hope you can forgive any of my mistakes and inaccuracies, but most of all I hope some parts of this tale will stay with you forever, as they do with me. Because then if we cross paths at a bookstore or an author event, we'll have something in common.

em jones

Made in the USA
Monee, IL
25 April 2025